BURNT OFFERINGS

ROBERT MARASCO was born in the Bronx in 1936 and educated at Regis High School in Manhattan and Fordham University. A classical scholar, Marasco taught at Regis before turning to writing, with *Child's Play*, an eerie melodrama about incidents of evil at a Catholic boys' school. The play was a surprise success in 1970, running for 343 performances on Broadway and earning a Tony Award nomination for best play of the year, and was adapted for a 1972 film.

Marasco also wrote two novels: *Burnt Offerings* (1973) and *Parlor Games* (1979). *Burnt Offerings* was a bestseller and spawned a 1976 film adaptation directed by Dan Curtis and starring Oliver Reed, Karen Black, and Bette Davis.

Marasco died of lung cancer in 1998.

STEPHEN GRAHAM JONES is the author of fifteen and a half novels, six story collections, and more than two hundred stories, many of them selected for best of year annuals. He has been a finalist for the Bram Stoker Award, the Shirley Jackson Award, and the Colorado Book Award, and he has won the Texas Institute of Letters Jesse Jones Award for Fiction, the Independent Publishers Award for Multicultural Fiction, and an NEA Fellowship in Fiction. Stephen earned his PhD from Florida State University and now teaches in the MFA programs at CU Boulder and UCR–Palm Desert.

Burnt Offerings
ROBERT MARASCO

With a new introduction by
STEPHEN GRAHAM JONES

VALANCOURT BOOKS

Dedication: For My Parents

Burnt Offerings by Robert Marasco
Originally published by Delacorte Press in 1973
First Valancourt Books edition 2015

Published by Valancourt Books, Richmond, Virginia
http://www.valancourtbooks.com

ISBN 978-1-941147-70-2
Also available as an electronic book.

All Valancourt Books publications are printed on acid free paper
that meets all ANSI standards for archival quality paper.

Set in Dante MT 10.5/12.6
Cover by Pye Parr

INTRODUCTION

You don't just live through a haunted house novel. You learn from it. *The Haunting of Hill House, The Shining, The House, Lunar Park*, all of them whisper to you in the best and the worst possible way.

Robert Marasco's *Burnt Offerings* is part of that evil chorus. It keeps me safe.

Every time I move, every time I'm checking out the next new place, I'm taking a lot more into consideration than the wiring and the paint, or which direction the morning sun comes in.

Drive by the house you're interested in at night, I say. Watch the windows. See if anybody's waiting for you there. And then drive home with the dome light on, and check that back seat as often as you can.

It won't be often enough.

And that's healthy, that's good, that's right.

We want to stay alive, after all, we want to stay sane. So we tell ourselves these stories, and we've been telling them for a long while now, since . . . *The Castle of Otranto*? Some certain castle in Denmark, that had dead fathers creeping through its halls? A cursed mead hall you didn't want to fall asleep in, as that's when the monster comes?

The central dilemma for us, for people, it's that as much as we might spook when our dog won't set foot in a certain room, we *need* that room. Without shelter, we're out in the elements, prey to all the things that want to eat us.

Not everything that wants to eat us fits neatly in a biology book, though.

As near as I can tell from walking the halls and stairways of this genre, there's two kinds of haunted houses. There's the Stay Away kind, like we get with *The Amityville Horror* or *Poltergeist*, where you're punished for your trespass, and then there's the Hungry House. Whereas Stay Away houses just want to be left alone, Hungry Houses aren't complete without people to digest for seasons or decades or centuries. A Hungry House has to seduce you into its long embrace. A Hungry House knows the injuries you've been nursing in secret, and it uses them against you.

Hill House was Hungry. The Overlook Hotel was hungry. So is this pretty house Marasco gives us in *Burnt Offerings*. And, if only it hadn't been published in 1973, right?

Not that *Burnt Offerings* was by any means neglected—its film adaptation would come in 1976, and is pretty faithful to the novel—but 1973 was right before Stephen King was about to create something in the bookstore that had never really existed before: the horror shelf. Before King there were horror readers, definitely, scrounging all the Lovecraft and Machen and Blackwood they could up from the old boxes, and devouring everything Richard Matheson published, and reading their uncle's old *EC* and *Creepys* by flashlight, but with the advent of color at the drive-in, horror had been parked there for a while. Hammer Films and Herschell Gordon Lewis had the horror crowd transfixed, at least until a little novel with the innocuous title *"Carrie."*

I was two years old the year *Carrie* hit, so can't vouch for this, but I have it on good authority that, before King, horror didn't have its own hallowed ground in the bookstore. That means in 1973 *Burnt Offerings* would have been shelved alphabetically between, say—and here I'm dreaming, but who knows—L'Amour's *The Quick and the Dead* and Pynchon's *Gravity's Rainbow*. Which is no problem; *Burnt Offerings* stands side by side with any novel, from 1973 (*Jaws, Princess Bride, Breakfast of Champions* . . .) or whenever. But, look ahead just a decade, to 1983, when the horror shelves were spilling over, when the fan base had gone locust, was chewing through the pages as fast as the publishing houses could print them.

In that kind of frenzy, a novel as finely written and precisely imagined as *Burnt Offerings* could have delivered Marasco to the top of the shelf with Robert McCammon and

Clive Barker and Peter Straub, and then, *then*, what else might he have written for us, right? What else would we now have?

You see one standout oddball of a beautiful novel like *Burnt Offerings*, and you want to find a stash of all this guy's horror, burn through it the same way you did Vonnegut when you first found him, or Shirley Jackson, like this is a secret only you know about. Like this book, it was written for *you*, man.

And maybe it was.

As far as Robert Marasco and the horror novel, though, it starts and ends here. He does have another horror movie, the pre-Chucky *Child's Play*, adapted from his successful play in 1972, and there's also the dark and twisted 1979 novel *Parlor Games*, but it draws more from Hitchcock than from Poe.

So, while Marasco didn't build a career on *Burnt Offerings*, still, I think we should count ourselves lucky to have been gifted this singular haunted house novel. Yes, the blueprint was laid down by Shirley Jackson and then built up by Matheson and King, but Robert Marasco was there as well, making sure the hinge on this door is dry enough to creak, making sure that pillar's shadow can look like something else, if seen from the staircase.

And there's nothing saying you can't read *Burnt Offerings* every year or two.

That's what I've been doing for a while now.

With this new edition, now you can too.

The best haunted house novels, they leave you walking those long dark hallways alone. They leave you pretty sure you just heard a chair scrape in the other room, the room you know is empty.

The best haunted house novels, they grow their walls up around you, they give you a place to live, if you dare.

Open this book, step in.

We haven't left the light on for you.

Stephen Graham Jones
December 2014

"Not so fast, sweetheart. *Back.*"

David, eight, stopped halfway across the living room, drew his shoulders up as though something sharp was about to hit him, and then turned slowly. Marian was standing in the small foyer in the rear of the apartment, between the two bedrooms. Her arm went up like a semaphore, pointing toward his room.

"That room was spotless when you came in," she said. "Remember?"

He dragged his feet over the rug and the wood floor she had just finished polishing. His sneakers made small rubbery sounds.

"Feet, please," Marian said as he walked past her. She followed him in. "See what I mean?"

David pulled his schoolshirt off the doorknob, opened the closet, and reached up for a hanger. "I forgot," he said lamely.

"For a smart kid you forget an awful lot." She watched him stab at the shirt with the hanger. "If you put the pants on first, you'd save a hanger, no?"

"The pants *too?*"

"Of course the pants too. And the shoes."

His pants were on the floor, next to a chair. He scooped them up and started to stuff one leg through the hanger.

"Honey . . . ?" Marian said patiently.

He lowered the hanger, emphatically. "I can't do it when you're watching me. I get nervous."

"Then I won't watch you." She turned her back to him, facing the windows. "Say when."

She could hear him muttering above the sounds rising from the courtyard three stories below. She moved toward the windows and adjusted the rings on the red cafe curtains which had been drawn against the glare of the apartment house directly opposite—a wall of glass and smooth white brick. Marian

heard a loud female voice scream "Dar*lene!*" in the courtyard.
She leaned closer to the window and looked down.

It was a fairly large concrete area with vague grass borders;
primarily a passageway, lined with benches, to the entrances
of the multi-winged building ten yards away. From three to
five especially, the benches were filled with women, young
mothers mostly, each of them with a baby carriage within
reach. She heard the cry, "Dar*lene!*" again, louder, and saw a
young woman in shorts and a sleeveless blouse spring up. She
was pointing at someone out of range. "Now you're *really*
gonna get it!" Two carriages parted to let her pass. She ran out
of sight, and from the shriek that followed, Darlene had really
gotten it.

The week had been unseasonably warm—seventy-six
today and only mid-May—and the courtyard, as it did each
spring, had blossomed into a swirling, echoing playground.
With summer, the hours would lengthen and the din become
impossible.

Summer. Apartment. Queens. The overtones were ominous. Again.

She sneaked a look at David. He replaced the hanger,
which now listed heavily, and slipped his schoolshoes into the
shoebag. As he did, a piano started in the apartment below.

Three-thirty. She could set her watch by it. Scales first,
struggling for traction for five minutes or so; then a leap into
Bach, or Beethoven, or whatever 2-D was working on this
month, three-thirty to five, five days a week. The clinkers
would still be there at the end of the month, but faster, louder,
more practiced. Like that one. She winced. And that. On a
scale, for God's sake. Well, there was no point in complaining
again because the lease says very clearly, nine to nine . . . So
just smile and walk heavy.

David slammed the closet door shut and challenged her
with an arms-akimbo "*Okay?*"

"Okay," she said. She moved across the red shag rug in the
middle of the room and crouched in front of him. "Looks
better, doesn't it? Admit it."

He wouldn't. It looked fine before.

She tucked his tee shirt in, then pulled him toward her and kissed his face loudly. "I'm a problem, I know," she said sympathetically, "but you're not so easy yourself."

He tried to pull away. "I'm gonna be late."

"Late for what?"

"*Things.*"

"So be late. The only time I get to see you is when I'm yelling at you. That's why I yell so much."

Impatiently, he let her smooth down his hair which was thick and dark, like Ben's; hers was long and dark blonde, and once, just after she had turned thirty last year, there had been a single strand of gray which she had yanked out.

"No bike on the boulevard, remember, and home by six. That's S-I-X, six, got it? Now kiss, please."

He barely kissed her on the cheek and, reanimated now, bolted from the room.

Marian sat back on her heels and waited for the door to slam shut and rattle the windows. The room was back in order, temporarily; a magazine view of what a boy's room should be, with Peanuts pillows arranged neatly on the bedspread, a small desk-bookcase unit, highly polished, football posters and antique gun prints. Daffy Duck and Alfred E. Neuman hung evenly over the bed. A model frigate was on the bureau, and scattered around the room were a model Mustang and Dracula and Mummy, and a mechanical Frankenstein who dropped his pants and blushed (from Aunt Elizabeth who had one like it). They had all been dusted, and the room smelled fresh and oiled, like the whole apartment.

The door slammed and the curtains billowed slightly. Marian was playing idly with the pile of the rug. She could feel the floor vibrating with the sound of the piano below. Her impulse was to hammer, but it was embarrassing enough already to run into the woman in the hall or at the mailbox. She found a white thread and picked at it; then a bit of soot which smeared her fingers; and then, leaning forward on her knees now and digging under the pile, a small patch of blue fiber, the color of her bedroom rug. Empty the vacuum, she reminded herself. She spread her hand over the rug, straightening the pile, then stood up, went to the closet and rehung David's clothes. For a minute or so she just stared into the closet. The scales below had finally become Bach, and maybe she liked 2-D's Bach after all, because something in the melody moved her to touch David's suit jacket, and his raincoat, and the ratty blue bathrobe which she'd have to force herself to replace someday. The feel of it and the melody below, clinkers and all, sent her to the window where she waited for him to cross the courtyard. He didn't, but if he had, she would have called "David!" and thrown him a package of Yankee Doodles.

The apartment consisted of four good-sized rooms with flaking plaster walls, spackled regularly by Ben, and parquet floors that rose, slightly and annoyingly, beside two of the doorsills. Once a month Marian really took the place apart, and waxed and buffed the floors, and at least once a month Ben, in stocking feet, would slip, grab onto the back of a crushed velvet wingchair, and say *"Jesus Christ!"*

The building itself was old, situated on a wide and busy boulevard in Queens, lined with supermarkets, bars, hamburger chains, and several Chinese and Italian restaurants specializing in take-out orders. A popular firehouse was two blocks away and the LaGuardia landing pattern directly overhead. The neighborhood was young marrieds primarily and singles, in the newer buildings; older people and chiropractors in the others. And the Rolfes—Ben, Marian, and David—who had been living there four years, at one hundred sixty a month. A bargain, and thirty dollars less than their previous and first apartment, a crammed three farther out in Queens. In the great tradition, they left seeking space, just as many of the young couples would eventually leave this neighborhood and resettle in small houses out in Nassau or Suffolk. The Rolfes as well, Marian was sure; they were just a few years behind.

Four years ago they discovered that a small three could no longer contain what five years of marriage had accumulated. Especially marriage to Marian who was, by her own admission, somewhat acquisitive—or as Ben once put it, in an infrequent rage, "a goddamn packrat." And so, rather than walk sideways, with an occasional crouch, to get from room to room, they moved. To space and economy and convenience. The building was large and, God knows, lively; filled with pregnant women, small children who yelled in hallways, and big children who scrawled obscenities in the elevator when the elevator was running; with cooking odors and an old man who peed under the mailboxes; hammering radiators, dubious plumbing; with a roach problem and, on one unspeakable occasion, a mouse problem. It was minimally superintended by a polygynous black, Mr. Ives, who was usually referred to as "The Phantom."

Each year 3-D seemed less of a bargain, at least to Marian who spent most of her time in the apartment. (Three or four times a year she would sign up with Office Temporaries to help pay for some new and irresistible buy—a French Provincial buffet or, her proudest possession, a mahogany and bronze doré desk.) Along around May, faced with the prospect of the summer, she would become moody, testy; she'd spend a good part of her time cleaning the apartment and then cleaning it again. ("Christ," Ben said, "it's Dunsinane all over." When he explained the reference she hit him.) Instead of listening therapeutically to Ben's pre-dinner complaints about Mr. Byron, the high school principal, or the dumb kids, or Miss MacKenzie, the cretin who headed Tilden's English Department, Marian would counter with a litany of her own, ticking off the heat, the noise and the soot, the sameness, the landlocked and godawful boredom of the city in summer. City, hell. *Queens.* Space, economy, convenience—they became irrelevant from June to September when the apartment, as far as she was concerned, became uninhabitable, completely. Why not do it, just once? Spread the dustcovers, leave the key with Aunt Elizabeth, and head for someplace cool and quiet, or anything and quiet. There was always Office Temporaries in September.

She had dusted just a couple of hours ago and already there was a layer of soot on the windowsill in their bedroom. She lifted the curtains, blew along the length of the double sill until she felt an ache under her ears, and slid the windows down. The wall of windows and white brick faced their bedroom as well as the other rooms. And The Supervisor, Marian noticed, was at her post, overlooking the scene in the courtyard. A huge woman filling a fourth floor window, she was always there, it seemed, like some bulbous gargoyle, leaning on a pillow and staring impassively. Ben insisted she was a household god and naked from the waist down.

Marian added *private* to the someplace cool and quiet. Just a little bit of privacy. To be able to make love maybe once without closing the windows and lowering the shades, or worrying about the beds on the other side of the wall, the floor, the ceiling. (*She* did, anyway; Ben couldn't care less.) They made love with the light on, and once something in the apartment above, hitting the floor with a plaster-splintering thud, had sent the shade rattling up while they were at it, exposing them to a wall of lighted windows.

"I feel like a dirty joke," she had told Ben when he climbed back into bed. He laughed like hell; she turned over and went to sleep, which shut him up.

All right, maybe she was exaggerating—for emphasis, like an overdone room in a department store. Maybe it wasn't so bad after all, though probably it was. Just a month, two months away and she was sure she'd come back refreshed, the galloping paranoia checked for the next nine months.

She had looked over the real estate section of *The Times* yesterday, reading the more likely prospects aloud to Ben who grunted non-committally at each. She hadn't pressed it; Sunday the summer seemed less threatening. Today it was real, within earshot, and was *that* on the button. And the possibility of spending it in Queens, with—maybe—two weeks upstate, and occasional trips to Jones Beach or Bear Mountain, more unsupportable. Ben was free, all summer; no courses, no summer teaching. David was free; she was nothing if not free. And they weren't exactly broke.

She nodded to herself, convinced, and went into the living

room. The piano's hammering was directly below. She bent over the magazine rack and pulled out *The Times* which was opened at Vacation and Leisure Homes. Once again she ran her eyes down the columns, concentrating on the vague prospects she had circled yesterday ("jerking off," Ben called it). Soon she didn't even hear the clinkers.

Bus Stop, hydrant, driveway. The goddamn area was getting worse than Manhattan. There had been two spaces on the Boulevard, both of them with meters, and one on Thirty-ninth, too small for the Camaro. He had gone around the block twice, had tried some of the sidestreets whose One Way signs took him farther away from the apartment. Ten minutes ago he had passed his building which was now buried somewhere beyond the range of Carleton Towers and Gibson Arms and Mayberry Heights. Who the hell was Carleton or Gibson, where were the lousy Heights? And why, four days out of five, did parking a dinky yellow compact assume such Wagnerian proportions? The light in front of him turned red. Ben banged his attaché case beside him, said "Shit," and reached for a cigarette.

A jet roared above the spindly trees which were already in full leaf. Coming toward him were four or five boys, David's age, on bikes. They stopped pedalling at the intersection, one of them gliding into the cross street and swerving suddenly to avoid a car which fortunately had been travelling slowly. Ben grimaced and then shook his head. Bike lecture. Tonight.

The teacher in him would have shouted something at the boys, the runty one especially, but fifty feet ahead, on his side of the road, someone was getting into a parked car. He looked at the light nervously, at the menacing cars coming toward him, and the sneaky bastard cruising down the sidestreet, toward the green light. Come on, light, *change*. The woman got into her car, her backup lights glowed. There was movement, and in a clumsy, bumping moment there were the beginnings of space. Ben inched the Camaro forward, the light changed, and as far as he was concerned, there was a God after all.

By the time he reached the luncheonette across the street from his building, Ben had forgotten where he'd parked the car ten minutes before. The realization had come into his mind unbidden: a sudden twinge like a nudge in the ribs, and a small, mischievous voice saying, All right, wise guy, now where'd you put it? He picked up a *Post* and a pack of cigarettes, paid the old lady who never smiled, and left the luncheonette, glancing at the headline. He waited at the corner for the light to change, and while he knew exactly where the car was, he mentally retraced his route, just to fix it in his mind. Straight two blocks, a right to the light, left to the next light, and bingo. He looked at the lead story—New York was on the brink again, read a boring paragraph about budget cuts—and stopped. There were *three* lights actually: two he'd made, one he'd stopped at. The kid on the bike, Davey's age . . . Christ, this was stupid. He *knew* where he'd parked the damn thing. He folded the paper and slipped it under his arm.

A bus lumbered by, close to the curb. He turned away from the exhaust fumes, shifted his attaché case to his left hand, and pulled his tie looser. The thought persisted—grating, trivial. He tried to dismiss it, to think about something more important—the fiscal crisis, noise, corruption in high places, traffic, pollution; the looming, ugly heap of stone across the street. What kind of place was this to raise a kid? Nassau, Suffolk— there were alternatives, weren't there? Maybe even Rockland, or farther upstate. Marian was right: the city became less appealing every day, more abrasive. Maybe they should start thinking about it seriously. That was important, much more important than the fact that, yes, he'd lost the goddamn car.

Well, should he look for it now or wait until morning; leave the house fifteen minutes earlier and wander the streets like the absent-minded idiot he obviously was? He shifted his attaché case to his right hand. His jacket was sticking to him, a transistor was blaring nearby, and someone was going horn-happy behind a car making an illegal turn. A part of his mind was turned off, asleep, and the sounds were working on him like a piece of undigested food. Tension, it's called. Hell, the things in his day—the frustrating, petty, stupid annoyances he could *really* get worked up over.

How long before it snaps, he wondered, before the sensible piece of his mind says, "I've had it, sonny, you're on your own?" Breaks off and flies up, up, like a balloon? Going, going. . . . He drew a deep breath, tracing its flight over his building, puffed out his cheeks and made a small popping sound. The little girl he just noticed waiting next to him on the curb looked up at him. *Smile, honey.* He repeated the sound effect for her, more elaborately, and this time she brought her hand up to her mouth and giggled.

"Hi," he said. "What've you got in the bag?"

"Ring-Dings," she said after a moment, and giggled again.

"What're Ring-Dings?"

"Cake," she said, and Ben heard "idiot" in the subtext.

The light changed and the little girl ran across the street on long skinny legs.

On the opposite corner he stopped just briefly, drew one final blank which he decided was absurd and wasn't going to bother him at all right now, and walked toward the building entrance. He nodded a bright "Ladies" to the cluster of old women on camp chairs beside the entrance, gossiping and watching traffic. In the vestibule, which smelled of cabbage, he met Mr. Girolamo who had had a heart attack last year and now spent most of his time waiting for the mailman. Mr. Girolamo asked whether it was hot enough for him, and Ben said, Sure was, and how was he feeling these days? Just fine. The elevator, he added, had been repaired that morning. Well, let's see what goes next, Ben said, and Mr. Girolamo, who was sixty and looked eighty, laughed, tentatively.

Marian had changed from jeans and her faded work shirt to a light blue blouse, the color of her eyes, and a red denim skirt. She was in front of the bathroom mirror, pulling a comb through her hair. Somewhere in the D line a toilet was being flushed, and behind the flowered shower curtain was a slow, steady drip, staining the porcelain blue. The sounds had long ago become part of the ambiance; she was scarcely aware of them. The comb whispered through her hair, long, downward strokes. She stopped, leaned closer to the mirror, and turned her face to the right a bit. She brushed her temple with one finger, separating the strands. Four cylindrical lamps had been fixed over the mirror (Ben's "Operation Sow's Ear"); she adjusted one of them—a white, not a pink—and aimed it at the side of her head. False alarm. She readjusted the lamp. Thirty-plus, she said to the mirror; face it. She washed off her comb and wiped the pink marble counter (theirs, not the building's), playing some quick chess with the colored bottles and tubes and the jar of "display" soap. When she heard the key in the lock, she brushed a few strands of hair from her shoulders and turned off the lights. The room smelled of lilacs.

"Me," Ben called.

When she came into the living room, he was checking the mail and tossing it aside. She put her arms on his shoulders, said, "Hi, baby," and kissed him. She could see the newspaper with her markings beside the phone on the desk. He hadn't noticed.

"It is hot!" Ben said, moving away from her. He stopped in the middle of the room and sniffed. "The place smells of lemon oil."

"I've been a real busy girl," she said. "How about a beer?"

He said, "Fine," and growled, very expertly, at the sound of the piano under his feet. When she left the room he was snapping and growling louder.

She went into the kitchen which had a small dining area in front of a window hung with bright summery curtains. The vinyl floor, a rose pebbled pattern, gleamed. Marian took two beers from the refrigerator and then reached into the old-fashioned glass-paned cabinet (she had painted the panes bright green for glasses). Any minute now he'd see the news-paper with all those suspicious-looking phone numbers and checked and crossed-out ads. Should she have made the calls or waited? Too late now. She poured the beers in front of a large pegboard hung with shining copper pots.

"I can't take it," Ben called suddenly from the living room. His voice rose to a parody of a yell: "I can't take it!"

She looked toward the sound and before she could say anything, the copper pots began to tremble and ring. The whole apartment was shaking, the floor in the kitchen throbbing. There was a muffled thud, thud, thud coming from the living room, a tinkle of glass.

"My God!" she cried out, "*Ben!*"

She rushed into the living room and saw Ben bouncing up and down on the rug, right above the sound of the piano. The lamps were shaking, a porcelain figure was sliding close to the edge of an end-table. She grabbed it, looked fearfully around the room, and shouted, "You're crazy, stop it, Ben, stop it!"

He gave one last heels-together jump and stopped as the piano began to limp under him. "Listen," he whispered, "I think it worked."

"You're absolutely mad. Nuts." She moved around the room, straightening the pictures and sconces, checking the lamps and bowls and figurines and vases that filled all the polished surfaces.

"I whupped it good," he said. The piano had stopped.

"Very funny, very funny." Surprisingly there was no damage. Her panicky look softened into a helpless reluctant smile. She shook her head. "Idiot."

"Where's that beer?" he said, dropping onto the couch.

When she came back with the beers, the piano started up again, as resonant as before. Ben threw up his hands. "It's got to be a conspiracy. The whole bloody city is after my ass." He patted the cushion beside him. Marian handed him his glass, took out two coasters, and settled beside him.

"*You* face her now," she said, nodding at the floor.

"Let the old bitch worry about facing *me*." He took a sip. "She'll think you did it. That's what I'll tell her anyway."

"You would, wouldn't you?"

"It's every man for himself, sister."

"Hey," she said after a pause. "I've got a great idea."

"Yeah?"

"Let's move."

He smiled, staring into space, and pulled her closer to him. He had unbuttoned his shirt. She played with the seam and then slipped her hand inside, rubbing his chest which was hard and damp.

"There's no one down there, you know," she said confidentially, "just a piano playing itself. And feet above us that run back and forth. No real people, just resident sounds." She walked with her fingers up his chest. He settled deeper into the couch, touching the wall with the back of his head. "Unwinding?" she asked.

"Getting there." He gave a long sigh, then lifted his feet onto the coffee table. Marian leaned forward and moved the cut-glass cigarette box.

"I ever tell you about my last breakdown?" he asked.

"No."

"Remind me sometime."

She nodded. "Always something new to find out, even after nine years. Is that what they mean by the adventure of marriage?"

His hand moved to her knee which he stroked lightly. He was staring, expressionless, at a small crack in the ceiling. She could see, beyond his profile, the windows of the neighboring building. A figure in striped drawers was moving in one of the apartments.

"So how'd it go today?" she asked finally. "Or shouldn't I ask?"

"You shouldn't but you did," he said lazily. "How's it always go? The kids were bright, responsive; on fire, all of them. Then to top it all, a faculty meeting that for sheer heart-pounding excitement ..."

He belched and she said, "Pig." He turned to face her, and the smile was innocent and vulnerable, and whether he was over the hill, as he claimed, or not, she still found it irresistible.

"You know something?" he said. "I don't like what I'm doing very much." He said it as though it had come as a revelation to him.

"You always say that this time of year."

"And I always mean it."

"A month to go, right? You'll survive."

"Not this time, baby. I'm cracking." He sat up, and looking at her sideways, announced: "I lost the car."

"How'd you manage that?"

He told her. She laughed and he failed to see what she found so funny. "It's a sign, you know." He made the sound of something large collapsing—he was great with sound effects.

"You mean—?" She pointed to the side of her head and twirled her forefinger. His mood seemed to have changed suddenly, and instead of a reply in kind—like a vigorous nod of his head—he reached for a cigarette quietly. "About time you caught up with the rest of us," she said, but Ben only half heard her, distracted by something—the piano, the children playing under the windows. Or the beer. Beer worked on him, quicker than wine; he seldom drank anything stronger. "Hey!" she said, nudging him, and whatever part of him had left the room came back. He said, "Hi."

"I've got the answer to all our problems," she announced brightly. "*Flight.*" She sprang up on the word, saying as she crossed the room, "Now don't yell. Just listen."

She looked back; he was lighting his cigarette. She lifted the paper and a green beanbag ashtray from the desk, and carried them back to the couch. When he saw the newspaper, he let his chin drop to his chest wearily; he exhaled a balloon of smoke and Marian could see stars, spirals and exclamation points in the motes. "Shut up," she said.

She placed the ashtray in front of him even though there was another one, delicately frilled Belleek, on the endtable beside him. Ben waited for her to settle on the floor in front of him.

"Her position became suppliant," he said, stentorian.

"Listen." She poked him, cleared her throat and read: "'Unique summer home. Restful, secluded. Perfect for large family. Pool, private beach, dock—'"

He laughed.

"*Listen.*" She read on: " 'Long season. *Very reasonable* for the right people.' " The italics were hers.

"Racist pigs," he said.

"That's not what they mean." She held the paper out to him, like a particularly ripe tomato. "Two and a half hours from the city. What could be more perfect?"

"What city?" he asked. "Warsaw?"

"New York, dummy."

"And very reasonable, hunh?"

"That's what it says."

Ben put his cigarette down, brushed the paper aside, and grabbed both her hands, pressing them into an even more suppliant position. "Honey," he said, "that desk was reasonable, remember?" He nodded at the antique desk where his papers were, and some of his books; the kitchen table was where he actually worked.

"What has that got to do with it?"

"A lesson in semantics, the decline and fall of meaning."

"Oh, stop; we're not in your crummy classroom."

"Lucky us." He went on, careful to keep it light and without any note of reproach: "The breakfront was reasonable, or so they told me, and the fancy chairs—"

"*Bergères.*"

"—the endtables, the lamps, the chotzkies, and Christ knows what you've got stashed away in the closets. 'Reasonable,' or some parody of the word, has left us with roughly two thousand in the bank, after nine years."

"That's probably two thousand more than a lot of people have," she said. "Why are you foaming at the mouth, for God's sake?"

"Because a house with a beach and a pool and a dock is not going to be reasonable, nohow. Now that's what we call nipping it in the bud."

"Ben J. Negative. All the time negative."

"We can't swing a summer place." He brought her hands up and down, keeping time with the words. The newspaper fell between them, scrawled with telephone numbers and doodles. "What's wrong with two weeks upstate, three weeks if you want?"

She said, *"Yech!"* and pulled her hands away. For a long between-rounds moment they looked at each other, Marian with an exaggerated pout that would make him feel hopelessly cruel and unreasonable.

"Benjie," she whimpered, moving closer to him. "Why be such a shit?" She crept between his legs and pressed her face against his chest. Her hair brushed his arms.

He let her maneuver herself into position. Then, "I get it," he said.

"Get what?" He could feel the words against his chest.

"Your tit 'n' ass getup. You're trying to seduce me into it."

"Would I do anything so cheap and transparent?" She hugged him tighter. "We could at least look, couldn't we? Just to prove how right you are, and smart, and level-headed." She looked up at his chin; her expression, if he could see it, was one of helpless guilt. "I did, after all . . . call them."

"You called them," he repeated calmly.

"These sweet little gingerbread people who're so reasonable. They're expecting us."

"When?"

"Saturday?" she asked. His silence encouraged her. "Just think, Benjie—a lovely ride over the grasslands, a picnic lunch with all your favorite yummies. Don't make me a liar. Say yes."

"No."

But of course he'd go along with her, just as he had for the past several years. He'd mouthed the words, offered the obligatory protest, and she'd reacted antiphonally. They'd start with the reasonable thousand-dollar-a-month beach cottages and work their way down to the jerry-built lakefront cabins, or the bungalow colonies with their tribes of screaming kids and five-day widows. Queens transplanted. Cots, rickety furniture, dimestore landscapes on the walls, and bare wooden floors that were always damp and gritty with sand. He could just see Marian in a setting like that. But the fantasy persisted.

She was silent, waiting for him to relent, and he could feel a sly, sneaky touch inside the leg of his trousers.

"I suppose," he said finally, "there are worse ways to spend a Saturday."

She smiled, but with no hint of triumph. The voice was vaguely repentant. "You're not mad are you—about the calls? I should've waited, I know, but you can be—and I *love* this in you, I really, truly love it—you can be so impossibly negative at times." She brought her face level with his. "It could be so good for us if it worked out. No worrying about Davey and that damn bike. Or me, for that matter; wondering whether you'll find me here or splattered on the pavement below, if I have to spend another summer in this bin."

"I'm not mad."

"That's my Benjie."

He shifted position, a little uncomfortably. "What I am, however, is something close to horny, and unless you want to give all the folks yonder a really hot show—" He was sliding back up on the couch, freeing himself from Marian who looked quickly in the direction of the open window. The Supervisor was still at her perch, fat breasts pillowed on the sill. Below her the courtyard continued to roar. "Besides," he said with a small chuckle, "we don't have a car anymore, remember?" And as he said it, the piano below thundered to an off-key climax, and the name Mayberry Heights came into his mind. And the building half a block away from it on Wood Avenue where he'd parked the Camaro—absolutely, no question—in front of its large lobby window. He remembered very clearly the plastic fern, the lamp, and the chairs inside, all of them chained to the wall.

(2)

The next morning Marian called Aunt Elizabeth and told her they would be away all day Saturday; could Ben take her to the supermarket Friday night instead? Aunt Elizabeth, who was seventy-four, said that Friday was her poker night. Then what about Thursday? Art class, and Wednesday was out—she was going to the theatre. Aunt Elizabeth told Marian not to worry, she could easily wheel her shopping cart the three blocks to the A & P, but Marian, who like Ben assumed that a seventy-four-year-old woman living alone must be helpless, insisted, and so they settled on Friday afternoon when Ben usually got home earlier. Aunt Elizabeth, although she didn't mention it, would have to cancel her three o'clock appointment at the beauty parlor.

Much of Ben's reluctance to leave the city for any length of time was based, Marian knew, on Aunt Elizabeth's supposed dependence on him. She was Ben's only living relative, his father's sister; bright, witty and good-natured, he was devoted to her. Although she lived fairly nearby, they saw her infrequently; her schedule always seemed to be booked solid. But at least he was there if she needed him, which, surprisingly, she did that morning—her air conditioner had broken down. But no rush, Friday would be fine. She wished them success with the summer house and said that her bikini and her water-wings were all ready.

"Are you serious, Aunt Elizabeth?" Marian asked her.

"About the bikini? Of course I'm serious."

"Besides that. I mean, if we were to find something, would you consider spending the summer with us?"

"In the country?"

"As our guest. I'm sure Ben would feel a lot easier about leaving if you came along."

"Well," Aunt Elizabeth said, "it's certainly an idea, isn't it?"

"Please think about it."

"I will, Marian. Kiss Davey for me, will you?"

Marian hung up. That, she thought, was inspired.

The temperature climbed all week and the nightly weather reports started adding THIs and discomfort glosses to the evening banter. Wednesday, the children below the windows were playing in shorts and sun dresses, their mothers exposing white arms and thighs. Ben came home sweating and one night, when the building opposite hummed with the sound of air conditioners, suggested they start thinking of one themselves, even though neither of them could stand them. Marian spent an afternoon rearranging drawers and closets, pulling out summer clothes and burying the spring and winter. The heat and noise had suddenly become invigorating.

The prospect of going away for the summer delighted David who asked Ben, Thursday, when he should start packing his snorkeling equipment.

"I'd hold off a while," Ben said. "And I wouldn't get my hopes up either. Chances are we won't find anything, not this year."

"That's not what Mommie says," David replied.

"Well, Mommie can be a little premature sometimes," Ben said, glaring across the table at Marian who insisted she hadn't said a thing at all.

Ben, if not exactly sanguine, said little more to temper Marian's enthusiasm. There was even something encouraging in his insistence that they set up several houses to visit in addition to the very reasonable one—plainly beyond them—she seemed so inordinately excited about. Which Marian did promptly, happily and displaying an incredible catholicity of taste.

They were to take the Long Island Expressway out to Riverhead, the woman on the phone had said, get onto Route 25 and keep going, beyond Mattituck and Cutchogue and the Little Peconic Bay; get off 25 at Orient Road (tricky, she was told, so watch out for it), and then follow a series of secondary roads, which Marian had copied down carefully, crossing the island until they reached Shore Road, and look for number Seventeen.

"Which is a hoot," the woman had said. "There's no Fifteen or Eighteen or anything; just Seventeen."

Her name was Roz Allardyce and she had sounded jovial and friendly and very interested.

When Marian showed the directions to Ben, he said, "My God! Are you sure you've got this right?"

She said, "I copied down exactly what she told me."

Ben studied a map of the island and was able to follow the route up to the Little Peconic Bay. "The rest we'll have to take as it comes," he said, adding, "Maybe we ought to try some of the other places first."

"Oh, Ben, no," Marian pleaded. "We'll find it, I know we will."

Marian had told Miss Allardyce to expect them around eleven. To allow for Saturday traffic and the probability that they would get lost somewhere at the end of the island, Ben suggested they leave the apartment before eight.

"Cautious, as always," Marian said.

"Hell, someone here's got to be."

She sat next to him with the map open on her lap and the scrawled directions tucked into her tote bag. Apartment buildings, terraced most of them, rose above the Expressway like palisades. Nothing like a little distance to see it clearly—the sprawling dreariness of the city, the bricked-in anonymity. Was he looking?

"Awake?" she asked.

"Uh-huh."

"Excited?"

He made a whoopee sign, and she hammered the side of his arm. Whether he'd admit it or not, he had accepted the idea, he was more than merely humoring her. And maybe it was the bright shirt, or the weekend, or just the three of them riding together, but already he seemed less tense, less distracted.

In a while the buildings were a gray mass behind them, like something glacial, and there were rows of small houses with trees and neat, billowy shrubs; and then houses with saplings and newly sodded lawns. The sun had come out and the air, heavy with unseasonable humidity when they left the apartment, had become clear. Marian rolled down her window and the air washed over David who was burrowing in the picnic hamper behind them.

"Look at all that beautiful space," she said, "and the air— just smell it, Davey!"

David pulled out a package of Yankee Doodles. "Are we in the country yet?" he asked.

"Soon."

"Riverhead," Ben said. "Where are those directions?"

The directions, surprisingly enough, were accurate. They found Orient Road and then turned off onto a narrower blacktop which soon passed through a neat and quiet cluster of small wooden buildings. A tavern, a general store, a post office, flagless, with the name "Mohonkson" in peeling gilt on the window, W. G. Ross, M.D. Fat trees lined the road.

"Bustling," Ben said.

Marian said, "It's heaven!"

Ten minutes later Ben slowed the car. "This has got to be it—Shore Road."

"Is there a sign?"

"Nope. There's also nowhere else to go. What do the directions say?"

"Seventeen Shore Road."

"Thanks."

They were on a narrow dirt lane, obviously little used. Deep, rich foliage pressed the road on both sides; the trees overhead seemed to lock together. It was all shimmering green, and still, and somewhere beyond there was a sense of space and water.

"Lovely," Marian said quietly, and Ben stopped the car for a moment and said, "God, yes." And David, who was peering over the front seat and really smelling the air for the first time, asked, "Is this the country?"

The car bumped slowly over the road for a quarter of a mile or so; still no sign, no break on either side of the road. Marian was leaning forward, trying to see beyond the foliage. And finally she said, "Look," and pointed to an old stone wall half hidden under thick vines and bushes. The wall disappeared and, about fifty feet away, broke through the shrubbery once again. It was huge, ancient, solid. They followed it, and soon there were two massive pillars flanking a gravel drive perpendicular to the road. Marian leaned over Ben. Barely visible on one of the pillars was a bronze plate with the number 17.

"Magic number," Marian said. "Turn in."

Ben inched the car forward a bit and then stepped on the brakes. He was looking down the shaded drive which dipped out of sight a little beyond the pillars.

"Why are you stopping?" Marian asked.

"A little intimidating, don't you think? For something so reasonable." Before she could say it, he added, "I know, I know, negative, as usual."

"Drive," she said, adding a small-voiced "Please?"

The ad, she admitted to herself, had hardly prepared her for something so formidable; it was the entrance to an estate. She was about to say something about a gatekeeper's house or a guest cottage, or possibly an apartment above a garage, but Ben had turned slowly into the drive, and she moved closer to the windshield, silent and fascinated, as the car dipped and turned and tunnelled deeper through the woods. Sunlight flashed through the tall trees, and when she closed her eyes for a second she could feel it and almost hear it hitting the car like rain. The drive narrowed even more now, and the foliage was brushing the sides of the car. Ahead, vines buried themselves under the gravel.

David was kneeling in the back seat, watching the road disappear behind them. He had seen a rabbit, and something larger, he insisted, swinging through the trees. Ben saw it too, he said.

"Like a gorilla?" David asked, excited.

"More like a wild goose," he said, looking pointedly at Marian who heard neither of them.

There was another turn, and the growth was even thicker, the shade deeper. A dead branch had fallen halfway across the gravel; Ben steered left, pushing into the low shrubbery. There was a rustling sound, and then a small, quick slap. Ben cried out, "Jesus!" and pulled his arm off the windowsill. The car swerved right, back onto the gravel.

Marian threw her arm against the dashboard. "What happened?"

"Goddamn twig hit me." He was rubbing his elbow against his thigh, steering with one hand. "Roll up your window." He looked at David through the rearview mirror. "You all right, Dave?"

"Saw another one," David said, "real close this time." He shot at it through the rear window.

The drive widened at that point, and brightened. The bushes drew back from the road, and the trees grew thinner, some of them leafless and dead. Straight ahead, abruptly, the woods ended.

"All clear," Marian said. She looked at his elbow which he was holding close to his side. "We'd have to do something about those bushes," she said, and waited for the look. It came.

The woods rose in back of them, solidly, rimming the great stretch of open field they were now driving through. Coarse high grass, with some thickets and isolated, dead trees; it was hot and silent and heavy with the smell of weeds baking. The road, more dirt than gravel now, turned to the right, and the house that suddenly burst on them, way in the distance, with the huge shimmering bay beyond it, made Marian gasp and cry, *"My God!"* And when David leaned forward and said, incredulously, "That our house?" she said, "Ssshhh!" so emphatically that Ben looked at her and said, "No, Dave. That is not our house. Nohow."

A great, rambling mass of gables and dormers and rounded bays, the house was set on the highest point of land, between the water and the rising sweep of open land bleached yellow-green by the sun. It covered the hill, climbing from a broad paved drive shaded by elms and maples. Wide steps led to the central part of the house which was fronted by a long portico and flanked by two great wings, their gables peaking above the trees. Gray and massive, with the look of generations about it, it made Marian think of buttresses and spires. And like a cathedral there was something that ordered its complexity, a spine running the vast length of the house. Where was it?

The car had stopped and Ben was saying something to her. She felt his hand on her arm with a slight start, and when she finally pulled herself away from the house, she saw that he was nodding at something outside the car.

"There it is," he said.

She looked to her right. Set back from the road was a small cottage, shuttered and overgrown with vines. Weeds grew high, buzzing with insects and covering the path to the small rickety porch.

The house had stunned her and it was a moment before she could ask, "There's what?"

"Our unique summer place," she heard Ben say, "the reasonable one." She was looking back at the house. One of the wings was rounded, with French doors—she could count five —opening out onto a terrace. And somewhere in the rear, in partial view, was a solarium or greenhouse. "Incredible," she said, "just incredible. Isn't it—?"

But he had opened the door and was climbing out of the car, saying, "Well, we've come this far. . . ."

David pushed the front seat forward and followed him.

"Where are you going?" she called out the window.

"Snoop." He passed in front of the car. David was fighting his way through the weeds, slashing the air and making machete sounds. Ben opened the door for her and swept his hand toward the cottage. "Just what we've always wanted, right? A little vine-choked cottage. Care to look?"

She did, quickly, without leaving the car. "This can't be it," she said, looking at him for confirmation.

"Who says? It's a cinch that isn't." He looked at the main house.

"Have you ever seen anything like it?" she said. Her voice was low and reverent.

"Not on dry land, I haven't." He pushed the door shut, leaned in and tried to kiss her cheek. "Hey, baby . . ." He turned her face away from the house, toward him. "Let's not think too big, hunh? Not this year anyway."

She smiled, a little guiltily. He moved away from her and stepped into the weeds, calling, "Dave? Where'd you go?"

"Ben?" she called out. "Maybe you shouldn't."

"Why not?" He slapped something on his wrist. "It'll save them a pitch."

He climbed up to the porch, bounced a few times for her benefit, and then grabbed for support. The door, when he was through clowning, was locked, and so were the shutters, tight. Marian watched him disappear around the side of the house.

He was probably right, she realized: it was the cottage. And yet, hadn't the ad said something about a large family? She pulled the torn page out of her tote bag, and, yes, that was exactly what it said—"Suitable for large family." The cottage was small, three or four rooms at most. Besides, who'd attempt to rent a wreck like that? She folded the paper and slipped it back into her bag. "It's the house," she said aloud. "That incredible house." She settled back in the seat and stared ahead, reassured. Her eyes rode along the curves and angles of the house—there was a small shaded porch outside one of the upper rooms—and rested on a huge rounded bay under the west gable. It rose a floor above the rest of the house, isolated, jutting above the water and the opposite shore which was a thin pastel line. And that was it, wasn't it?—the spine, the focal point. The whole thrust of the house was toward that gable and those blank windows. The closer she looked at those windows, the lovelier and more irresistible the house became. "It's the house," she repeated.

"What's the house?"

He startled her; he was standing beside her, outside the car. "Just thinking out loud. See anything?"

"Nothing," he said, "sealed tight. I *can* see all sorts of possibilities though. Malaria. Encephalitis. We're wasting our time, babe."

"Maybe it's not the cottage," Marian said. "Could be the house, couldn't it?"

"In that case, we're really wasting our time." He raised his hands to his mouth. "Let's go, Dave!" he called.

David came running through the weeds. Ben crouched, ready to cut him off; he grabbed him as he leaped out into the drive, swinging the boy over his shoulder and carrying him squealing with pleasure back to the car.

Marian tensed; that kind of rough stuff made her nervous. "When you two are through horsing around . . ." she said.

They climbed in and Ben started the car, saying, "Here goes nothing."

David leaned forward between them. "I saw a bike in the weeds," he said. "A three-wheeler."

"Must be kids around," Ben said over his shoulder.

"I don't think so. It was all busted up." He waited and then added, "There was blood all over it."

"No kidding?" Ben said.

He used his scariest voice. "Dried up blood."

Ben shuddered. "Wowee!" he cried. "Think it was some kind of gorilla blood?"

"Gorillas don't ride three-wheelers," David said.

"Then what's that coming up behind us?" Ben asked.

David turned and looked out the rear window. "A two-wheeler," he said, "with training wheels."

Marian, staring intently at the upper windows, said to herself, *Let it be the house, please let it be the house.*

For some distance the drive skirted the field which must have once been a vast and manicured lawn, terraced as it rose toward the house; there were traces of thin, low retaining walls. To the right, before the woods began, was a narrower piece of open land; formally planted at one time, there was a vague pattern of shrubs and hedges, gone to ruin, surrounding the remains of a delicate summer pavilion. What a shame, Marian thought. And the house, as they drew closer —that was more than a shame: a crime, a genuine old fashioned mortal sin.

It was still overwhelming, more so as it loomed larger and its details became more distinct—carved modillions and mullioned windows and the shape of the columns in the upper porch. But the roof-tiles rippled, and the shingles, once white, were dirty gray and broken, with ancient rust stains; some of the windows had been patched with cardboard; and the balusters running up the central steps were tilting, many of them, or missing (one lay buried in the scrawny shrubbery beside the steps). And for every tree that billowed so impressively from a distance, there were two that were bony and long dead.

"God, what a waste!" Marian said as Ben drove past a five-car garage with an upper storey. There was a huge old Packard parked in front of one of the garages whose doors hung open very loosely. The car seemed packed tight with boxes and lampshades and bits of furniture; a wooden headboard was tied to the top, and the trunk was open.

"What time were they expecting us?" Ben asked.

"Eleven."

"We've got half an hour."

"They won't mind."

He stopped the car in front of the house; the drive was paved very thinly with gravel. When they got out the house stretched and towered above them, and on the other side the wide field rolled back to the woods which were a solid wall of green.

The steps squeaked, all of them; sixteen, according to David who bounced on one until Marian grabbed him and whispered, "David!" She stopped Ben near the top. "I'm nervous," she said.

"I don't see why," he replied. He climbed ahead, up to the

portico. The columns were high and round and peeling; the porch broad and shaded.

Almost as soon as Ben knocked, the door was pulled open by a short old man, pink, round and panting. He was wearing a peaked cap, sweat stained, ballooning trousers and a tank-top undershirt; a small nipple peered out beside the worn strap.

"We're the Rolfes," Ben said; "we've come about the summer place." Marian crossed the porch; she was smiling tightly and still holding on to David.

"I know, I know," the man said; he was having trouble catching his breath. "Been expectin' you. I'm Walker. The handyman." He chuckled as though it were some private joke. "Come on in."

He opened the door wider; Ben motioned Marian and David in first.

"You folks can wait in the parlor while I go find their nibses," Walker said. When he turned there was a large and dirty dustcloth trailing from his back pocket.

David pulled loose as Marian stood motionless in the entrance hall. The chandelier caught her eye first: a great cluster of crystal—Waterford, no doubt—hung high above the bare wooden floor. The droplets were cloudy and the floor dull and scraped; there was a large oriental rug rolled up against one wall. Still, the hall was impressive—almost as large as their whole apartment. A magnificent staircase, carved mahogany, curved up to the second floor; near the base and following the curve up and out of sight was a metal band, like a track.

"Marian?" Ben was waiting outside the double doors Walker had just opened.

"Yes, coming." She tried to absorb the details: double doors on either side of the hall which narrowed to a passageway beside the staircase; rooms beyond—dining room, kitchen, library, the greenhouse? She had never been in a house anything like this; the layout she visualized was strictly Hollywood "grand." But gone, or going, to seed. And again, what a pity!

What Walker referred to as "the parlor" was even more impressive—an enormous, sun-filled room, rounded at one end and cut with the French doors she had seen as they approached the house. An Aubusson was in the middle of the room, off-white, with pale rose and blue flowers; the walls were all antique *boiseries*, white and gold; and over the scrolled mantel of the fireplace was a Chippendale mirror that made her gasp. And, God! why was the rug so worn, and the walls peeling, and the drapes so heavy with dust? If someone had had the taste to collect so much exquisite crystal and silver, then why weren't they responsible enough to keep it polished and gleaming?

"Make yourselves at home," Walker was saying. "Just watch where you sit; lot of old stuff in here." He pulled the dust-cloth out of his back pocket and passed it perfunctorily over a gilt console. He was moving toward one of the windows. "Musty," he said, sniffing.

Marian stood next to Ben, her eyes travelling over the room; she took his hand and squeezed it, as if to say, "Help me, please!"

"Cozy," Ben said, and then stage-whispered, "Money. Very *old* money."

David was at the other end of the room, watching Walker struggle with the window. "Hey!" he called out suddenly, "they got a boat." The window opened with a wrench and a breeze flew into the room, knocking a fluted shade off a lamp.

"Look at the view if you want," Walker said. He lifted the shade, pulled the plug, and stuck the lamp under his arm.

David became more excited. "Dad, they got a boat!" he cried.

"Busted," Walker said.

Ben had come to the window. "Where's the pool the ad mentioned?"

"Can't see it from the house," Walker said. He waved vaguely. "It's down there."

Ben looked out beyond the terrace to the lawn sloping

down to the bay where he could see a twisted pier and a small
cabin cruiser jutting up, waterlogged. There had been formal
gardens at one time, with a large stone fountain in the center.
What a waste is right, he thought.

Marian had found a coral lacquer secretary, beautifully
embellished with black and gold figures, against the inside
wall. She touched it, hesitantly at first, absorbed in the detail;
her hand followed the cool, polished curve, very lightly, reaching the small finial. One piece, tucked away in a corner, and
it was worth more than everything they had or ever would
have, as far as she could see. To be able to live with something
so beautiful—not own, merely live with, for a month, two
months. *God.*

David's voice broke in. "How come your plants are all
dead?" he was asking. She looked away from the secretary and
was startled to see Walker, David next to him, watching her
and smiling. She moved away self-consciously. "I couldn't help
admiring it," she apologized. "It's lovely." Walker kept smiling
at her, and David said, "Your front steps're busted too."

"David!" She smiled feebly in Walker's direction. Why was
he watching her like that?

"Everything's busted around here," Walker said, and
finally looked away from her, adjusting the lamp under his
arm.

Ben had stepped out onto the terrace. "Go with Daddy,"
Marian said, calling, "Easy, easy," as he ran across the room.
"It's all right, isn't it?" she asked Walker.

"Sure. Look over the place if you want." He was beginning
to leave the room.

"How old is the house?" Marian asked.

Walker stopped and shrugged. "Who knows?" He noticed
something across the room. "Heck," he said. He came back
to Marian and placed the lamp and shade next to her on the
floor. "Watch this stuff a minute, will you?" There was a
large landscape, elaborately framed, hanging above the sofa.
He walked toward it—small, quick steps, as though he were
used to sudden obstructions—knelt on the sofa and reached

up to straighten the picture, making it even more crooked. "Better," he said, inspecting the picture, and as he came back to her, it crashed to the floor behind the sofa. Before she knew it, Marian cried out, *"Walker!"* Her tone was inexplicably sharp and proprietary, and immediately one hand went up to her mouth.

Walker looked stunned for just a second, and then there were the traces of a smile. "Yes, ma'am?" he said, quietly and evenly.

Her fingers remained over her lips. Why had she said that, why had it burst out so instinctively? Whatever there was of a smile faded and he was standing in front of her now, still and submissive.

"It's not—there's no damage, is there?" she said lamely, but at least the words broke his stare and the uncomfortable silence. He muttered something apologetic, turned and climbed back onto the couch, bringing the picture up with a series of grunts.

"Busted," he said, red-faced with the effort. "A lot of things fall apart around here," he said, dragging the picture behind him. He gestured for the lamp: "Ma'am?" she handed it to him and it went under his arm. He mentioned something again about "their nibses"—still very hangdog—and left the room, closing the double doors behind him.

Marian stared after him, thinking, please, don't let him come with the house. Not a clod like that. She raised her eyes to the ceiling and followed the carved pattern, its detail grimy and vague, down the length of the room. If he does, if Walker is a condition, then this room at least is out of bounds.

There was an alcove at the opposite end of the room which she headed for, cataloguing the furniture and the bric-a-brac (someone collected yellow and blue Meissen) as she passed them. Ben was calling her from the terrace—something about the view. "In a minute," she called back. She looked into the alcove and saw a glass door, clouded and dirty. The greenhouse. She could just about make out the long shelves and tables behind the glass. Should she? Why not?

The heat and the rotting smell hit her as soon as she managed to pull the door open. The glass walls and the roof were grey, crusted with dirt. Warped shelves and sagging tables, extending the length of the greenhouse, were filled with dull orange pots—empty, most of them, or trailing stiff brown vines. There were pots on the dirt floor, shattered, and rusted tools. Despite the smell and the heat, she moved deeper into the room, dipping her fingers into a pot, picking off a petrified flower. It was appalling, and, goddamit, she'd think of some way to tell them that. What's another word for appalling?

The second time Ben called "Marian?" she heard him. The smell kept him just outside the greenhouse door. "For Chrissake, what're you doing?"

"Look at it," she said, poking inside a clay pot. "Every plant dead. Soil's like powder."

"Look, you wouldn't like strangers nosing around your rubber plant. Come out of there."

She looked over the room once more, gave a long sigh, and came toward him. "It kills me, such waste. Kills me!" She gave a low scream and hammered his chest with both fists.

"Stop taking it so personally."

"I can't help it." She tried to block it out. "I thought you were watching David."

"He went down to look at the beach."

She was standing in the doorway, giving the littered shelves one final, frustrated look. "They might not like that."

"They sure as hell won't like this. *Out.*" He pushed the door shut.

She looked out over the terrace and saw David running toward the beach. He stopped, picked up a stone, and scaled it toward the water. "I don't know whether that's a very good idea," she said to Ben, and then noticed that he was not behind her. "Will David be all right?" she asked, louder, and heard him call, "Yeah" from the alcove.

The terrace was paved with flagstone; weeds grew between and through the stones, and wound around the balusters barely supporting the cracked ledge that bordered the terrace.

The garden furniture was, of course, unusable. But that view! And the space!

"Hey, you see these?" Ben called from the alcove.

She hadn't. Opposite the greenhouse door was a wall filled with pictures—photographs, twenty or thirty of them. He was crouching in front of them.

"Weird," he said, "they're all the same."

Marian came beside him and looked at the pictures. They were arranged in neat rows, almost covering the wall. Each of the photographs was the same size, with the same thin silver frame—and, as Ben had indicated, exactly the same view of the house: looking toward the front from halfway across the wide field. Some seemed older, sepia-toned, with black and white shots in the middle of the wall, and color prints hanging to the right.

"Notice anything?" he asked her.

The house, especially in the color prints, gleamed—pure white against the lawn and the bay beyond; the rails and balustrades were whole, the windows unbroken; nothing seemed patched or faded or crumbling. The trees shading the house were full and there were beautifully sculpted hedges. It was exactly the way it should have been, and obviously was —at some time. Overwhelming.

Ben stood up. "Crazy, no?" he said.

Marian was studying the pictures. "Yes," she said. "Pity they've let it fall apart."

Somewhere in the house a door slammed shut, and there were raised voices. "Here they come." He grabbed Marian's arm and lifted her to her feet. "Now remember," he said, "I'll do the talking. Just look pretty and keep your mouth shut."

She took a minute to think about it. Ben was holding her with both hands now. "Marian . . ." he warned. It was his negative voice. "The cottage is out, okay?—Queens or no Queens."

She smiled. "I'm with you, Benjie," she said. "The cottage won't do."

"That's my girl. Just leave the graceful exits to me."

(3)

The voices were in the hall, just outside the closed doors—Walker's and the cracked rasp Marian remembered hearing on the phone Monday.

"Where do you want this stuff?"

"In the car, where else?"

"There's no more room in the car."

"Well, make room! What do we pay you for anyway?"

Ben had gone out onto the terrace to check David who was amusing himself, safely and in plain view, at the foot of the lawn; away from the water, as Ben had told him. When he reentered the room, he said, "He's fine; playing—" but Marian was holding up her hand and nodding in the direction of the voices. The knob was turning and one of the doors moved a bit. Marian cleared her throat.

"And take that mirror out too," the woman said. "It's cracked."

"Not the only thing around here that's cracked," Walker replied.

Ben snickered and Marian was trying hard not to smile. The door was pulled shut suddenly and whatever the woman retorted was muffled to a small paragraph of sibilants. When it finally flew open, a small, energetic woman in her early sixties walked in briskly. She was sharp-faced, with highly lacquered pepper-and-salt hair. Her outfit, dark blue, was tailored and expensive, and she wore a double strand of pearls.

"Sorry to keep you waiting," she said, extending a jewelled hand to Marian and then to Ben, almost as an afterthought, "but I've had a *morning*." She looked toward the hall and then raised her voice. "Some people just don't know which side is *up* anymore." There was no reply, just a distant shuffling in the hall. "Old fool," she muttered, and then turned abruptly to Marian. She smiled sweetly and said, "I'm Roz Allardyce.

Brother will be down soon as he pulls himself together."

Marian let Ben make the introductions. Before he could mention David, Miss Allardyce said, "There's a boy too, isn't there?"

"Our son, David," Ben said. "He's gone down to look at the water."

"Is that all right?" Marian asked.

"Sure, let him romp," Miss Allardyce said. "Kids are good for the place. Anybody else?"

"Just the three of us," Ben said.

She remembered speaking to Marian, remembered the name Rolfe even though she was bad at names and, besides that, had a headful of names at the moment; the phone hadn't stopped ringing since the ad appeared last Sunday. "I keep forgetting how many folks there are who want to get out of that terrible city."

"There've been other people?" Marian couldn't help asking, and if Miss Allardyce hadn't been watching her so closely, she would have pantomimed an apologetic "Sorry, too anxious" to Ben. But she *was* watching her, like Walker.

"*Other people?*" Her voice broke on the laugh. She cut it off and the voice became low and confidential. "The wrong kind, most of them."

Marian tried not to look at Ben who was jerking his thumb in his and then Marian's direction, and nodding.

"We're very particular, Brother and me," Miss Allardyce continued, touching Marian's arm for emphasis. "We don't do this that often to begin with; last time was two, three years ago, I forget. Some years there's nothing but wrongos, and others . . ." She smiled, her makeup flaking in the crevices, and let her hand slip from Marian's arm.

"But it's still available?" Marian asked, and this time she made it sound less anxious.

"It's available," she said after a pause, and to Marian it was clearly an invitation.

Ben moved closer to them. "I suppose we ought to get down to particulars," he said to Marian.

"A practical man," Miss Allardyce said, still looking at Marian. "Just like Brother." She finally turned her attention to him. "Particulars are simple enough, Mr. Rolfe." She waved her hand over the room. "What do you think of it, the old homestead?"

Ben followed her hand. "This?"

"That's right, this."

The question was unexpected. He thought a moment, nodded, impressed, and said, "It's quite a place."

"Indeed it's that. Over two hundred acres, a lot of it prime waterfront property. Where do you see that nowadays? And the old barn itself—well, I'm sure Mrs. Rolfe appreciates something this special. Right?"

Marian let her eyes travel over the room, as though she were seeing it for the first time. "It's extraordinary," she said quietly.

"Your kind of house, am I right?"

"Anybody's, I'd think."

"You'd be wrong. Not anybody's." She flicked her forefinger against a red Sandwich vase, which rang. "Know anything about antiques?"

"A little," Marian said.

"Then you've got some idea what's in here. The house is crammed with them." Her voice became soft and reverent. "Our mother is—was, really—a great collector." She paused and seemed to go within herself. "Our sweet darling."

"It's just lovely," Marian said and her words were full of sympathy.

Miss Allardyce composed herself with a deep breath, more like a sigh. Her face became sharp again—a ferret, Marian thought—and the bark was back in her voice. "Hell to keep up. Too much for two old wrecks like Brother and me, especially since the accident." They were spared the tangent by the quick shuffling sound out in the hall again. "And of course that old fool's no help; been senile for years now." She raised her head slightly and yelled, "*Walker!*" The shuffling stopped, something was muttered, and then he appeared just outside the door, struggling with a large carton; a lamp and shade, dismembered, lay on top.

"What now?" he asked testily.

"Brother's gardenia plant, next to the window."

"What about it?"

"In the car, please. It's dead."

"Right now?"

She closed her eyes; her face reddened under the makeup and her voice shook, just slightly. "Whenever your busy schedule permits." Her eyes opened as Walker shuffled past the open door. She shook her head ruefully. "A crime, just a crime the way things go around here. Brother's greenhouse used to be something miraculous. Now not even a plant. The responsibility of a place like this—too much, too much."

At least she was aware of it, Marian thought, whatever that was worth. And maybe the old lady's words, which seemed to be addressed directly to her, triggered it—the strange proprietary feeling that came over her again; the feeling that this house, which she had never seen before, was somehow reserved for her. It showed obviously; something a little deeper than blank awe, and less objective, had crept into her face, because Miss Allardyce looked straight at her and said, "I know, you're thinking what you could do with it, aren't you?"

Her accuracy made Marian color a bit. Did she look that hungry? "I'm afraid I am," Marian said, and gave Ben a helpless shrug.

"My wife," Ben explained, putting an arm around her, "is the type that clips pictures out of *House and Garden*. Like other ladies cut out paper dolls. She's got albums filled with them."

"Nothing wrong with that, is there?" Miss Allardyce said. "Until the real thing comes along."

"Nope." He gave Marian a warts-and-all squeeze and then released her.

"You were getting down to particulars," Marian reminded him.

He heard the *please?* and said, "About the cottage, Miss Allardyce . . . I'm afraid we had something a little different in mind."

"Cottage?" she replied, "What cottage?"

"The one down the drive."

"The old shanty?"

"That's the one."

She looked at Marian. "What's he talking about?"

It was confirmation, and relief, enough for her to say, very sincerely, "We assumed it was the cottage you were renting."

"Who'd want an old wreck like that?" Miss Allardyce said distastefully. "It's this house we're renting." And then to Marian, with a nudge in her voice: "You knew that, didn't you?"

Marian looked at Ben innocently. "Oh," he said, and the disappointment was to her clearly token. "That solves that."

Miss Allardyce drew her head back and looked at him over imaginary glasses. "There's nothing wrong with it, is there?" she asked, a little affronted.

"Nothing at all," Ben said. "It's just a little more than we were looking for."

"Then that makes it a real nice surprise, doesn't it?"

"It's that, all right." He let her see how impressed he was, giving the room a long, appreciative look. "But not for us, I'm afraid. Right, babe?"

Marian hesitated. "The ad did say 'reasonable.'" She looked at Miss Allardyce for corroboration.

"'Very reasonable,' as I recall," she said. "And so it is, for the right people."

"Who are they?" Ben asked.

Miss Allardyce paused and her small eyes, watery blue, became calipers. "Oh, a nice young couple," she said casually, "with imagination and muscle. Someone who'd love the place the way Brother and I do . . ." She waited, watching Marian.

He was weighing it and in all probability whatever he said would come out suitably thoughtful and cautious and, inevitably, negative. Marian had been through it before; Miss Allardyce hadn't. And so she said, diffidently, "Assuming that was us, what would 'reasonable' be?"

He reacted with a "Marian, honey . . ."

"There's no harm in asking, is there, darling?"

"Something like this is way over our heads," he said. "It's an estate, it's—"

"Four walls and a roof," Miss Allardyce said simply. "You know what they say about nothing ventured, Mr. Rolfe."

"My husband is a *mad*deningly practical man, Miss Allardyce."

"All right," Ben said with resignation. "In the interest of peace. Four walls and a roof—let's talk about them."

"Good," Miss Allardyce said. "Now there are of course a few preliminary questions." Marian nodded and looked at her anxiously. "We're talking about the summer. You'd be willing to take the place all season—whenever to Labor Day?"

"We could," Ben said, as non-committally as possible. "Term's over June twentieth."

"Ben's a teacher," Marian explained with an enthusiasm that surprised them both.

"So let's round it off to July one, how's that? Give Brother and me time to get things in order."

"Fine," said Marian. She added, "Isn't it?" to Ben who shrugged a tentative "yes."

"And there's just the three of you, is that right? You two and the boy out there?" Her voice had assumed an official tone, as though she were reading off a questionnaire.

Marian waited for Ben to reply. When he nodded, she said to both of them, "Four, really. There's Aunt Elizabeth. Think how she'd enjoy this, Ben. We were talking about it this week, the idea of her getting out of the city."

"Who's she?" Miss Allardyce asked.

"Ben's aunt."

"How old?"

The question surprised her. She let Ben say, "Seventy-four."

"An old gal then." She thought and then asked Marian, "You wouldn't mind, having an old gal around?"

Trick question possibly. Despite the energy and the lacquer, there was lots of crepe hanging on Miss Allardyce. "No, not at all," she answered, and honestly.

"Some people would, you know."

"Aunt Elizabeth's a doll."

Miss Allardyce paused; the question was obviously important. "That's very sweet," she said, "very sweet indeed." Her voice had become surprisingly soft. It rose again, inquisitorial. "Just four then? No other family?"

Ben was leaving the preliminaries to her. "Ben's parents are dead," she said.

"Yours?"

"In Florida." Miss Allardyce grimaced at that. "A sister in California."

"Okay, four." She seemed disappointed.

"Is it important?" Marian asked.

"Not necessarily. It's just that there are more than thirty rooms here. It can take a heck of a lot of people to make a house this size come alive."

"There are just four of us," Ben emphasized. A house that size was exactly his point. Absurd. Marian wondered if they'd seen more of the thirty rooms.

"No matter," Miss Allardyce said. "We can close most of them off," and Marian could hear herself saying, The west wing is closed; we'll have to put you in the east. Grandly. "It's quality that counts anyhow," Miss Allardyce said, and smiled. "Not that it's important, but—pets?"

"None," Marian said.

"Good. Brother can't abide them. I'm sure you could provide references?"

"Yes."

"Not necessary. Brother and I make up our own minds." She moved a little closer to Marian. "What's more important, Mrs. Rolfe, is that you'd be willing to stay and tend the place, as far as you could. Maybe even bring some kind of life back into it. Would you?" The voice had suddenly become less impersonal; there was even something of a plea in the last words. She looked at Ben. "All of you?"

She was waiting, it seemed to him, more for a commitment than a reply. "That's a pretty big order," he said. "We're used to an apartment. Small, hot, and noisy," he added, for

Marian's benefit. "We wouldn't know the first thing about running a place like this."

"It takes care of itself, Mr. Rolfe. Believe me. What I meant was—how shall I put it?" She stirred the air with one hand and found the words: "Love it, the way Brother and I love it." She stopped and became meditative. "And our darling, of course." Again, the reverent pause. "That's all. The rest comes naturally."

When he started to say, "Yeah, but this kind of responsibility . . ." Marian said, "Of course we would," very quietly. She reached for his hand and pressed it. He returned the pressure, hard enough to make her wince.

"It seems to me," Miss Allardyce began slowly, working out the figures in her head, "we're talking in the neighborhood of—seven hundred." She looked up, underlined the figure with a firm nod, and waited for them to react.

"A month," Ben said.

"A *month?* Heck, no!" she said, vastly amused. "Seven hundred for the summer."

"For this?" The figure and his surprised reaction (enthusiasm, in Ben) made Marian close her eyes in relief.

"The house and all two hundred plus acres. The pool, the beach, the works. Now is that a *deal?*" Her expression had become almost philanthropic.

"We'll take it!" Marian said. It came out like a great sigh. She squeezed Ben's arm. "Won't we?" she pleaded. "Won't we, *please?*"

It's certainly something to think about, he was going to say, but there was a sudden noise in the hall—a metallic clattering and the low buzz of a motor.

"Brother," Miss Allardyce announced. The motor stopped, then started again. "Told you it was reasonable," she said, listening. "For the right people."

Again, the buzz stopped; the clattering, louder now, was coming from the staircase which, Marian remembered, had a metal track running up its base. *"Walker!"* a phlegmy voice boomed, *"Walker, for Chrissake!"*

"Heck." Miss Allardyce shook her head. "Brother's stuck on that damn inclinator again."

Walker wheezed past the open door, calling, "Hold y'r horses, I'm comin'!"

"Get me offa this goddamn contraption!" Brother yelled. His voice rattled and broke into a fit of coughing. The motor was buzzing on and off. Miss Allardyce rolled her eyes, said, "Excuse me," quickly and sweetly, and started to leave the room.

"It's movin', it's movin'," Walker was saying.

"It's movin' *up*. I want *down*, you horse's ass!"

Miss Allardyce turned in the doorway, raised a hand to her mouth, and whispered, "He's a cripple," defensively. In the hall, Walker said, "You got a filthy mouth." She slammed the door shut behind her, cutting off the sounds.

"Unbelievable!" Marian said immediately. "An absolute *steal*. There's no question, is there, darling? We'll grab it?"

Something had come to a thudding stop in the hall. Ben hunched his shoulders and said, "Jesus!"

Marian shook him insistently. "We'd be crazy not to."

"In that case we'd fit right in with the rest of them."

"Pay attention to *me*," she said, steering him away from the noise outside. "You can't tell me you're not impressed. *Seven hundred* for two months!"

"I'm impressed," he admitted.

"Then it's set. Tell them yes and give them a check."

"Let's hear a little more, hunh?"

"Why, for God's sake? They're handing it to us."

"You don't find that a little suspicious?"

"Not at all. If they're crazy, then it's nice crazy."

"And those qualifications? Taking care of it? It's going to take a little more than love to keep something like this up."

"Let me worry about that. Benjie," she said, whimpering, "I love you too much to divorce you, really I do."

The doors were opened. ". . . himself killed one of these days," Walker was saying.

"I wouldn't talk," Brother said, "the way she bangs around in that sawed-off jalopy."

He rode into the room in a wheelchair, a plaid blanket covering his legs. He was puffy and pallid, with thin red-gray hair covering a freckled pate; his eyes were bulging and red-rimmed. Miss Allardyce followed him, saying, "I confine my driving to the open road." She looked over her shoulder and said, "Scram!" to Walker who disappeared, grumbling.

Brother steered the chair toward Ben and Marian. "Morning," he called, a little breathlessly.

Miss Allardyce introduced them. Her brother's real name was Arnold and he was full of beans today.

"I'm always full of beans," he said. A chuckle rattled around in his throat. "You're the folks going to take the house, are you?" His hands were very white with large liver spots. And extraordinarily cold.

"We've just been getting the details," Ben said.

Like Walker and Miss Allardyce, Brother seemed to be studying Marian especially. "I like 'em, Roz," he announced after a moment, "I like 'em."

"There's only four of them," Miss Allardyce said, lowering her voice. "An aunt and a boy, too. The boy's down at the beach. And the aunt's an old gal."

"Good enough," Brother said. He spun around, skirted a boulle writing desk with some old leather-bound books on it, their spines broken and curling, and came to a stop just inside the open terrace doors. He squinted down at the beach.

Some distance to the left of the wooden pier was a small rock jetty which rose, jagged, about five feet above the strip of beach. David was climbing the rocks. Brother narrowed his eyes and the boy's figure became clearer. He grabbed on to a rock, started to pull himself up, and then drew his hand away suddenly. He fell, and by squinting even more, Brother could see him slide down the surface of the jetty, his arms flying out for support. Brother's face remained impassive. David was in the dark sand, one knee clasped to his chest; he was rocking back and forth, his head thrown back in pain, soundlessly.

Brother watched a few seconds longer, with Ben and Marian silent behind him in the middle of the room.

"Cute little feller," he said. "What is he—six, seven?"

"Eight," Ben said.

"And full of the devil, I expect." Brother chuckled appreciatively, and then aware of Ben approaching the window, he wheeled around quickly to face him.

"He shouldn't be wandering around like that—" Ben started to say, but Brother raised his hand limply and said, "He'll be fine, just fine." He wheeled himself through the narrow passage between the desk and a wingchair, forcing Ben back to the center of the room and blocking his view of David on the beach.

"He's very good, really," Marian said. "All I have to do is tell him what's out of bounds." She caught Ben's eye. "*If,*" she said to him hopefully.

"There've been kids here before," Brother said. "Never any problem with them."

"Part of what I was saying about choosing the right people," Miss Allardyce added. "We've never been wrong yet, have we, Brother?"

"Nope." He reached into the pocket of his robe (heavy flannel over pajamas buttoned to the neck) and pulled out a ragged tissue.

"Do you rent every summer?" Marian asked.

Brother was blowing his nose and turning paler. "It depends," Miss Allardyce said. "Last time was when, Brother?"

Brother held up two fingers weakly, his nose grinding into the tissue.

"Every other year's the way it usually works out," Miss Allardyce said, watching Brother with some annoyance. "Like I said, it depends. Some years it works out better than other years."

Brother lowered his hand. His eyes were wet and redder. "Our Rest-and-Recreation's what Roz here is talking about," he hastened to say. When he smiled, his dentures clicked. "I'm coming apart, as you can see—"

"Oh, Brother!" Miss Allardyce said.

"Oh, brother is right." He shook his head tragically, then summoned the strength to say to Ben, "Roz has given you all the details, I expect."

"Yes," Ben said.

"Including price?"

"Seven hundred for the summer." He said it flatly, without the enthusiasm Marian would have put into it, so she quickly added a spirited "Yes!"

Brother brought his hand down on the arm of the wheel-chair; he glared at Miss Allardyce. "'Scuse us a minute," he said, and pushed the chair against his sister, nudging her away from them.

"I told you to ask for *nine*," he whispered hoarsely.

Miss Allardyce looked uneasily at Ben and Marian who were watching them. She leaned closer to Brother. "It was seven before."

"That was two years ago."

"Brother, we'll lose them."

Brother smiled at Marian. "Her? Not a chance. *Nine.*"

"Why, for God's sake? We don't need the money."

He was looking at Ben now. "Seven's too low. He's a suspicious type, can't you see that, you old fool?"

"All right." She moved away from him and, not at all convinced, said, "If you say nine, then it's nine."

She came back to them smiling guiltily and looking mortified. "Have I messed it up, have I ever messed it up!" She looked back at Brother who had not moved. He shoved her on with a jerk of his head.

"Something's wrong," Marian said, alarmed.

"Well . . ." she began, "Brother here's the businessman of the family, and what with the way everything's gone up these days—I mean, you know yourself—he says it's nine; nine hundred for practically two and a half months."

"Just give the price, Roz," Brother called out pleasantly.

"Nine hundred," she said, firmer, and waited.

"That's a bit of a jump," Ben said. "More than we'd planned on spending."

They hadn't, as far as Marian could remember, decided on any figure. And if seven hundred was a steal—which even Ben would have to admit—then what was another two hundred? Three weeks at Office Temporaries, if it came to that; or behind a counter somewhere, anywhere. Would he really get mad if she said it? He'd get over it, sooner than she would if he turned them down, and so she said, "It's still a bargain. Let's take it."

"Look," Ben said, and there was an edge in his voice under the grin, "why don't you go sit in the car, hunh?"

"Of course it's a bargain," Brother said, wheeling back to them. "Where would you find a place anything like it—with all that land, all that space?" He swept his hand toward the windows, surprisingly energetic.

"Never mind the land; look at the house," Roz said. "When've you ever seen a house like it?"

"It goes on and on," Brother said. They were beside each other; almost imperceptibly, their enthusiasm was moving them toward Ben and Marian. "Rooms and rooms; ones we don't even know are there probably. Basements and sub-basements . . ."

"A marvel of a house," Miss Allardyce exclaimed, "an absolute marvel! Thanks to our mother." Brother nodded. Roz passed her hand over the surface of a table. "Just look at this room, look at the treasures in here."

"Just to live with them, Mrs. Rolfe? Ain't it worth it?"

Marian stared at them silently.

"And, God, Brother!" Miss Allardyce said, "—when it comes alive—tell them that, tell them what it's like in summer."

"They wouldn't believe it." His hands levelled the space in front of him. "It's beyond anything you ever seen. Look at it, for God's sake, look at the character of the place."

Miss Allardyce shook her head ruefully. "And where do you find character nowadays. Nowhere, right?"

Their voices had risen. Miss Allardyce was holding onto Brother's wheelchair. Still they were moving forward.

"Take it, Mr. Rolfe," Brother said, "take it."

"How on earth can they resist it, Brother? Look around, look at what the years have brought to the stone and the wood. There's centuries in these rooms, Mrs. Rolfe. This house—why, it's been on this land longer than anyone can remember. Isn't that right, Brother?"

"Far as we know it's always been here," Brother said. "And believe me, it'll be here when we all kick off."

They were closer. Miss Allardyce's voice lowered and became almost hushed. "It's practically immortal. I sincerely believe that."

"And so," Brother said, "do I."

They stopped, staring at Ben and Marian who remained very still. Marian could still hear their voices in the silence which had become tense and uncomfortable to Ben. He broke it with a small, nervous laugh. "Other things being equal," he said, "I'd be sold."

"We got carried away, didn't we?" Miss Allardyce said apologetically. "It's so easy, I suppose, when you love something as much as Brother and me love this house. We mustn't push it, Brother."

"We never do," Brother said. "The house always sells itself."

To the right people, Ben said to himself. And if it had been yes, possibly, a few minutes ago, it was closer to no, probably, now. They were watching him expectantly, Marian included. He stalled by looking thoughtfully over their heads, at the far corners of the room. He tried to ask himself why—what was behind the vague uneasiness he was feeling? Not the nine hundred necessarily; and if their enthusiasm was a little disconcerting, well, they were eccentric to begin with. Was it the splendor of the house that he found intimidating, the fact that something so clearly beyond their reach seemed to be theirs merely for the asking? It was all happening too fast, and something, he couldn't help feeling, was being left unspoken.

"Mr. Rolfe doesn't seem to be sold," Brother said to Marian.

"But he can be," Marian said, and the threat, Ben was sure, was either playful or imaginary. "Can't he, Mr. Rolfe?"

"I'm waiting for the catch," Ben said, smiling.

Miss Allardyce looked puzzled. "Catch?"

"You mean there's nothing more?" Ben asked. "Nine hundred and it's ours?"

She nodded. "Half now, half at the end of the summer. Or whatever arrangement you and Brother decide on."

"Fine with me," Brother said. "Agreed?"

There had been a look between them, very quick, which Ben caught. "There is a catch, isn't there?" he said, lightening it with a grin and a wave of his finger. Brother was fidgeting and Miss Allardyce colored slightly. Ben pursued it, saying, "Uh-hunh, I thought there had to be something."

"Well," Brother said, red-faced, "there is . . . one other thing."

Here it comes, Ben thought—the graceful exit; just, please, make it impossible enough to satisfy Marian.

Miss Allardyce pulled back her shoulders and dropped the sheepish look. "Hardly a catch," she said.

"Hardly," Brother repeated. He sat absolutely still, his white hands resting on the arms of what might have been a chair of state or an episcopal throne. The rattle was no longer in his voice when he announced it: "It's our mother."

"Your mother?" Ben said, and Marian put out her hand to quiet him.

"Our mother," Miss Allardyce repeated, drawing herself up even more.

"What about her?" Marian asked quietly. From what Miss Allardyce had been saying earlier, Marian assumed their mother was dead.

Brother smiled and shook his head, lost in admiration. "An eighty-five year old gal," he said, "who could pass for sixty."

"Fifty," Miss Allardyce corrected him.

"God bless her, yes! She'll outlive all of us."

"A woman solid as—" She searched for something to express it.

"—this rock of a house!" Brother said, rapping an end-table which wobbled slightly.

"Our darling!" Her voice filled the room.

Miss Allardyce fell into position behind Brother's chair and rested her hands on his shoulders, her face directly above his.

"What Roz and me mean to say," Brother explained, watching their reactions very closely, "is our mother—well, she never leaves the house. Never leaves her room, even, isn't that so, Roz?"

Roz nodded. "This house is just about all the world she knows. It's her life."

"And vice versa," Brother said. "The whole thing would just come down without her."

"And so would we, Brother," Roz said, "so would we." She patted his shoulders, comforting.

That settled it, of course, as far as Ben was concerned; surely even for Marian. There was no surprise though that he could see, no reaction at all; only rapt attention.

"Believe me," Miss Allardyce continued, to Ben especially, "you'll never even know she's around."

"Never even see her probably," Brother added. "That's how quiet she is, that's how much she keeps to herself." He looked toward the ceiling and shook his head again, with wonder and affection. "Our mother . . ."

"Our darling," Miss Allardyce said.

Marian was following their gaze up to the coved ceiling, trying to visualize the room somewhere beyond the plaster rosettes and the fan traceries that were speckled with gilt. And as she stared at the ceiling, the hum of their voices which had become low and soothing, hypnotic almost, brought out the exquisite patterns more clearly. She could see what the ceiling must have been like in its full glory, the room, the house, and everything in it.

"It just kills us," Miss Allardyce was saying, "going off without her like this. But would she have it any other way, Brother?"

"'Course not," Brother said. "And believe me, there's no use arguing with her. Delicate as she is, there's steel under it all."

Miss Allardyce laughed lightly. "Oh, we've learned that all right. Her word is *law*. Always was and always will be, as long as she's with us. Which is always, please God."

"Always," Brother repeated reflectively.

For a moment the ceiling had become almost transparent to Marian, the pattern working on her like a trompe l'oeil. Brother went on, his voice growing softer, more inward, as though he were alone in the room.

"In her room all the time," he said, "way at the end of the house where you'll never see her, never even know she's there."

"All you'd have to do is leave a tray for her," Miss Allardyce said, "three times a day. Just put it on the table in her sitting room—"

"Never the bedroom," Brother cautioned Marian. "It's kept locked all the time."

"Always," Miss Allardyce said, "our poor, gentle darling."

Their voices were blending. Marian could barely hear the difference.

"What could be simpler? A tray in the sitting room three times a day—which she might, and then again, might not, even touch."

"And for that simple—'catch,' as you call it, Mr. Rolfe," Brother said, "everything here's yours, with no strings attached." He repeated the word to Marian: "Yours."

"Her marvelous house," Miss Allardyce said, letting her eyes roam around the room, "that's been here for so many years; that she's watched come alive and grow so many times . . . when we've despaired, Brother and me."

"She's been a pillar of strength to us . . ."

"A tower of hope . . . our darling."

Miss Allardyce's hands were tight on Brother's shoulders. She loosened them in the silence and let them fall to her sides with a long, weary sigh, keeping her eyes, soft and distant, on Marian and Ben who remained motionless. Brother reached for his tissue again, and the sound seemed to call Ben back. He cleared his throat uncomfortably. The voices had worked on him like a moving point of light—a coin or a candle flame. Was it just him; the mind suddenly going blank again, like another car incident? He looked at Marian whose eyes were wide and shining. She faced him slowly.

"I wouldn't mind, Ben," she said. "Really I wouldn't." She was saying it as much to the Allardyces as to him.

It took him a while to collect himself, to wrench the sound of their voices from his mind; he covered it by looking even more thoughtful. When he was sure it would come out normal and even, he said, "That's something we hadn't counted on."

"I suppose not," Miss Allardyce agreed.

Marian kept silent; obviously she had made up her mind.

"And you'd just . . . leave her?" Ben asked them.

"We've done it many times, Mr. Rolfe." There was a note of resentment in her voice.

"That's what keeps her young," Brother said. "Why, if she thought Roz and me would pass up our trip this summer, she'd become an old woman overnight. Believe me she would."

"She's that independent, that self-sufficient."

"Like Aunt Elizabeth," Marian said, thinking aloud. She looked at Ben and repeated it.

Again, they were waiting for him to reply, all three of them. His impulse was to come right out and tell them—predictably, Marian would surely think—"Thanks, but no," and assume that she would have sense enough eventually to see beyond the house and realize the absurdity of the whole deal. There was still something being left unspoken, he was convinced; something more than mere eccentricity to the Allardyces. But he recognized the look in Marian's eyes; the house had indeed sold itself to her instantly, and it would take more than a blunt "no" to dislodge it.

"We'll think it over," he said as sincerely as he could, "and let you know, okay?"

"But, Ben . . ." Marian said, grabbing his arm. No pout this time; it was genuine protest.

He didn't bother to lower his voice. "Marian. The responsibility of an—" He caught himself, "—elderly woman . . ."

"For *this?*" she broke in, almost embracing the room. "For *all this?*"

Brother nodded confidently to Miss Allardyce who looked away from him quickly. "You won't even know she's here," she insisted. "I promise you. She stays in her room all day. All day."

"Sleepin' most of the time," Brother said.

"And when she's not sleeping, she's working on her collection. Right, Brother?"

He agreed. "Her pitchers. Old photos, she's got thousands of them."

"The memories of a lifetime," Miss Allardyce said.

"It's her hobby," Brother explained, "like mine is my music."

Miss Allardyce's voice dropped. "What music?" she asked.

"My discs, my record collection."

"*That.*" She waved it away. "Give him his Mantovani and his whatyoumacallits . . ."

"Roz here's got no hobbies, no interests at all."

"Some people are too busy being useful for hobbies." They had moved apart for the bickering. "His hobby," she said to Marian and Ben, "is his health, his eternal health."

"You just watch it," Brother said in a fit of coughing that Roz's mention of health seemed to have triggered, "just watch yourself."

She looked away from him. "The people last year—" she said, and Brother corrected her with, "Two years ago, dummy." The coughing fit was passing.

Roz glared. "Two years ago," she said, "—they didn't see her once."

"The McDonalds," Brother remembered fondly.

"Wonderful family," Miss Allardyce said. The voice was rising again, and she was moving back behind Brother's chair.

"Or the time before, as I recall." Brother straightened in his chair, the rattle in his throat gone. "The Doncheys."

"Another wonderful family."

"They were all, Roz, all of them. The Wassoffs."

Miss Allardyce smiled. "And Norton, Brother, remember?"

"Do I? And Spiering."

The names came at Ben and Marian, a whole litany of them that Roz and Brother were calling up with mounting and almost childish enthusiasm: Costanza, Kappes, Whipple, Ferguson, Thorne, Zori, Ableman, Wright, Griffin, Loomie, Costello . . .

They stopped abruptly, and Roz and Brother seemed lost in meditation for a moment.

"Wonderful families, all of them," Brother said, and Miss Allardyce nodded and said, "Just wonderful."

There was a silence. "And now," Brother said quietly, "—Rolfe?"

Miss Allardyce repeated the name, like a prayer. "Rolfe."

The announcement, small-voiced and whining, came from the open terrace door, wrecking the silence: "I fell." He limped two steps into the room, holding up his arms and displaying two scraped elbows. His jeans were torn and his left knee gaped through, ragged and bleeding.

The shock took a while to reach Marian; when it did it jolted her. She cried, "*David!*" and ran to him across the room. "What happened?" She was on her knees in front of him. "My God, baby, what happened!"

"I fell!" he repeated shakily, and her reaction brought on the tears.

Ben was beside her, examining the wounds. "Okay, sport, easy now." He raised the scraped elbows gently. "Easy." Marian had her arms around David. "Is he all right? Ben, is he all right?"

"You want t' wash out them cuts," Brother said. He had wheeled himself closer.

Miss Allardyce snapped her fingers. "Bring him this way, into the kitchen."

Their voices, the rasp and rattle back, were filled with concern.

"He's all right," Ben said. "Aren't you, Dave?"

"I fell on the rocks," he said to Marian where all the sympathy seemed to be. She had taken out a Kleenex and was wiping his elbows, wincing along with him.

"I *told* you," she said to Ben, "he shouldn't have been left alone."

"An accident, that's all," Brother said, leaning forward to see. "Roz here's got a first-aid kit. Go get it."

"C'mon, Dave, alley-oop!" Ben lifted him and Marian grabbed his hand. "What's a few cuts, after all?" He held him tight and moved toward the door to hurry Miss Allardyce.

"It *hurts*," David cried.

And Marian said, for Ben as well, "I know, baby, I know."

They followed Miss Allardyce out of the room, leaving Brother who heard Marian say, "I'm sorry," to Roz, "we should've been more careful."

Brother waited until the voices disappeared and then wheeled closer to the window, pulling his robe closed at the neck. Light was moving above the water like a nimbus, blinding him to the opposite shore. In a while, something shuffled behind him.

"What's all the hubbub?" Walker asked.

Brother didn't turn. They were perfect, the woman especially; a natural. "Boy got hurt," he said to Walker.

"Serious?"

"He'll live."

Walker came to the window. He stopped beside a pedestal supporting a large gardenia plant.

"They takin' the house?" he asked casually.

Brother shrugged. Of course they'd take it. He'd never been wrong yet. "We'll see," he said.

Walker lifted the plant which was stiff, brown, and leafless.

Brother turned his head. "Where're you goin' with that plant?"

"Out to the car."

"Why?"

He nodded in the direction of the door. "Whozis said it was dead."

"Did she?" Brother faced the bay. "Look again," he said.

The base of the plant, just above the powdery soil, was a pale green, and above it, on a dead branch, were two fresh shoots.

Walker looked at Brother's back, then at the plant again, reexamining it. "Now ain't that somethin'," he said.

(4)

The wounds, once Ben had cleaned them, were slight; and although it was Marian who had shown the most concern (so much so that she could barely remember the kitchen afterwards, except that it was huge and bright and wonderfully old-fashioned, with everything double-sized), it was Ben who urged them out to the car, saying, "I think we better get the chief here home."

"He'll be just fine, won't you, sonny?" Miss Allardyce said. "Heck, any boy who can survive New York *City* . . ."

Marian put her arm around his shoulders and squeezed him protectively. He was no longer wearing his wounded expression; the patched knee and elbows were evidence enough. "He just has to get used to the country," she said to him.

"Well, there'll be plenty of time for that," Miss Allardyce said. She reached into a box and pulled out a chocolate chip cookie. Ben was signalling Marian, indicating the door impatiently. "In a minute!" she gestured.

David tried to bite into the cookie, made a face, and then held it out to Marian distastefully. "It's like a rock," he said.

"Probably stale," Miss Allardyce said with a sigh, "like everything else around here. Throw it out."

Ben was holding the kitchen door open. "Let's go, Dave," he said, addressing Marian. When she passed him she slapped his arm and whispered, "Why are you in such a hurry?"

Miss Allardyce turned and pointed to a passageway beside the kitchen. "Servants' wing's through there," she said; "unused, needless to say, except for the old fool. Laundry room, pantry, sewing room, and whatever else you can think of."

She took Marian's arm and led her back to the entrance hall.
Ben had slipped past them, joining David who was limping
toward the front door. "Once you're all set up, there'll be no
need to leave the place; everything's here." They passed beside the staircase which now had a small metal platform with
a folding chair at its foot. "Brother's inclinator." Brother himself was not in evidence. "Dining room," Miss Allardyce continued, "library." Her thumb arched over her left shoulder,
pointing backwards. "Greenhouse through there. A mess, I'm
afraid." Marian remembered the photographs in the alcove,
and of course there was no way she could mention them
without admitting she had been snooping. Miss Allardyce
led her directly ahead, without stopping to open any of the
closed doors. There were six bedrooms on the second floor,
two with sitting rooms. "Besides our mother's suite in the
west wing."

The phrases came back to her, and the incantatory sound
of their voices: way at the end of the house . . . where you'll
never see her . . . never even know she's there. . . .

There were another four above that, if Miss Allardyce
remembered correctly. "Half the rooms I haven't been in for
years; some of them never, would you believe it?" Heat was
oil, tenants' expense; not that they'd need it. There were indi-
vidual heaters in the bedrooms for cool spells. She rattled off
more details: linens, dishes, pots, all provided; the old fool
would show them the pool house and the gardening shed
when they took possession. Sorry, *if*.

Ben and David were still walking ahead; Ben impatiently,
Marian thought—and rudely so, which surprised her; not
bothering to look back or show even token interest in Miss
Allardyce's booming inventory.

"Did you hear all that, Ben?" Marian called.

"I heard," he said from the porch, and bent to check the
bandage on David's knee.

Marian shrugged an apology to Miss Allardyce who dismissed him with a reassuring wave. "He just doesn't want to
seem too interested," she said. "Brother spotted it."

"Let me work on it," Marian said. "Can we call tomorrow?"

"Noon the latest." She stopped her just inside the front door. "We'd hate to lose you, but ... Like I said, there are others."

"I don't think you'll lose us," Marian assured her. "Not if I have anything to say about it."

She smiled and Miss Allardyce smiled back. "I don't think we're going to lose you either." She was giving Marian that close, discomforting look again. "You won't be sorry, Marian," she said. "Believe me." It was her other sound, the voice underneath, and Marian heard rooms and rooms again, and basements and sub-basements, the words rolling inside her with the cadence of waves.

Ben's voice came at them from the edge of the porch. "It's a beautiful house, Miss Allardyce," he said, and the waves stopped inside her. He took a step down, supporting David who laughed when the wood creaked under them. "Thanks very much." It was politic enough, and as far as he was concerned, final enough as well.

She had looked back at the house just once as they drove through the field, then sat back and stared ahead silently. Ben was watching the twists in the road, glancing at her quickly once or twice. He had seen the same expression often enough in the past to realize that she was already rearranging the furniture; casters rolled in the silence and the smell of lemon oil blew in with the hot rush of air.

The car tunnelled through the woods, stopped at the stone pillars, and turned right, onto the dirt road. Ben took his foot off the gas, said "Whew!" and shook his head. "So that's what they mean by the Funny Farm." Marian held the stare, straight ahead and, now that he noticed, somewhat stony. He shrugged, looked furtively left and right, and stepped on the gas pedal hard, spinning the rear wheels and raising a cloud of yellow dust. He released his foot immediately and waited for Marian's reaction.

"You know I don't like games when you're driving," she said icily.

"Sorry," he replied.

The stone wall disappeared behind the foliage. She drew a deep breath to power the words, and finally announced, "You were impossibly rude."

"Was I?" he said innocently. "I wasn't aware of it."

"You could've shown some interest. It was downright embarrassing."

"Honey, you showed enough for both of us," he said, patting her knee for emphasis. "I heard the pitch; I just wanted to get out of there."

"You made that clear enough," she said, shifting in the seat and loosening a bit. "Do you mind telling me why?"

He half-turned in her direction, then brought his eyes back to the road. "Oh, come *on*, babe; you've got to be kidding. Someone ought to go in there with a large butterfly net."

"Because they're a little eccentric?"

"Eccentric?" he laughed. "Honey, that kind of eccentric is out-and-out certifiable."

"They got carried away, that's all."

"Not yet, they didn't; but they will, they will."

"Whatever they are," she said while he chuckled, "it has nothing to do with the house. It's perfect, it's absolutely ideal." He waited for the smile to disappear.

"You're sure about that," he said.

"Of course I'm sure." She drew her leg up under her and faced him. "Ben, I honestly don't see what there is to *think* about. It's exactly—it's *in*finitely more than we were looking for."

"I wasn't looking for anything, Marian. I'm just along for the ride, remember?"

"For once," she said, a little angrily, "be serious."

"All right," he said, "serious." He looked at her long enough for her to bring her hand up to the wheel which was vibrating with the ripples and potholes in the road. "I don't like the house." He said it simply and firmly and—she knew the tone —very seriously.

It hardly came as a surprise to her; his reaction to the house had been as obvious as her own. She forced a laugh anyway. "Don't like it?" she said in disbelief. "For God's sake, *why?*"

David was pushing a half-unwrapped sandwich over the seat and under her nose. "What's this stuff?" he asked.

"Chicken salad," she said quickly, anxious to pursue Ben's absurd statement.

"We got anything else?"

"Shrimp salad." She brushed the sandwich away as David made a retching sound. He sat back and Marian draped her hand over the seat and touched his knee gently. She kept her eyes on Ben.

"There's something weird about the place," he said finally. "Christ, Marian, you must've felt it yourself."

"All right, they're weird, they're crazy," she said for the last time. "But, honey, we're renting the house, not Miss Allar-dyce and her brother."

"The house is what I'm talking about, the whole deal. There's something suspicious about it."

"I call it luck."

"Luck, hunh?"

"Luck. I mean, just to have it fall into our laps like that—"

"Marian," he cut in, "you don't rent an estate like that for nine hundred dollars."

"Why not? Maybe they don't need the money, maybe it's more important to have someone look after the place, just *be* there. That's worth some concession, isn't it? Especially if they happen to be the right people."

"Meaning us?"

"Us. Is that so hard to accept?"

"All right, maybe not. What's a damn sight harder to accept, even from two weirdos like that, is the rest of the deal —the old lady. You don't leave a ninety-year-old woman—"

"Eighty-five."

"A hundred and eighty-five, what's the difference? You

don't leave an old lady with total strangers, and I don't care how right they happen to be. It's A, presumptuous, and B, irresponsible. Christ, do you really want that kind of burden?"

"For that house? Yes, if those are the terms."

"Will you try to see something besides the house. Like who feeds her—?"

"A tray, three times a day; that's all."

"Who cleans up after her, what if something should happen?"

"You heard what they said: we won't even know she's there."

"Whatever those nuts may think, an old woman needs some kind of attention."

"Does Aunt Elizabeth?"

"What has that got to do with it?"

"Does Aunt Elizabeth?" she insisted.

"Aunt Elizabeth is different."

"How do you know that?"

"I know Aunt Elizabeth, which is more than you can say for Mama Allardyce."

"Don't be so flip," she said, and when he looked to see whether she had meant it seriously, she pointed left and said, "Turn here."

They had reached the blacktop perpendicular to the dirt road. He made the turn and caught David in the rear view mirror, his upper lip smeared with mayonnaise.

"How's it going, Dave?" he said.

David said, "Fine," and Marian turned and said, "You liked the house, didn't you, sweetheart?"

"It was okay."

Marian wiped his lip with a tissue. "And you'd learn to be a little more careful, wouldn't you?"

"We gonna buy it?"

"We'd be crazy not to, don't you think?" She was brushing his hair back from his forehead which was damp and a little red from the sun.

"I think we should look at some of the others," Ben said.

Her hand rested on David's head for a second; he moved away and she let it fall. "Why?" she said wearily. "If you don't want that one, you obviously don't want any of them. Like you said, you're just out for the ride."

"If we find something, we'll take it," he said, and for the first time he really meant it, even if it had come out to pacify her. He gave her knee a reassuring squeeze, and when she remained silent, obviously brooding, he squeezed harder and repeated, "Okay, babe? Cross my heart?"

He made the gesture and she faced front, her eyes passing somewhere under his shoulder.

"As far as I'm concerned, we've found it," she said sullenly. "I don't want to see anything else."

"Come on," he said, nodding at her bag. "Dig in and pull out that list."

"I don't want to see anything else!" Marian repeated with a vehemence he had seldom heard in her before.

When, ten minutes later, they passed through the small cluster of buildings again (there was a car parked outside the post office this time, and some activity behind the window of the general store), they were both still silent. David leaned between them and asked, "When's the picnic?"

"Some other time, chief," Ben said.

Marian continued to stare ahead, calling out monosyllabic directions until they reached Riverhead and the Expressway which eventually became jammed with traffic in both directions. At one point she reached into the picnic hamper for a shrimp salad sandwich. She unwrapped it for Ben and held a thermos cup of coffee for him while he inched past construction crews and overheated cars and, near the Nassau-Queens line, a wicked three-car smashup.

He brought up the house once more, apologetically, and was about to catalogue his objections again, but she cut him off with a resigned "It's forgotten." Still, she refused to look at any other houses, and when he said, "Maybe next week then?" she shrugged and replied, "Maybe," with little interest.

It was after two when he pulled into the Bus Stop in front

of their building. He kept the motor running and let Marian out, and David who was going upstairs for their baseball gloves and a softball.

"Hon?" he called out to her, leaning across the seat. "You're all right, aren't you?"

She looked up at the building, counted the eight floors and added two for an even, therapeutic ten, and said, "Of course I'm all right."

He watched her walk away without turning. "We'll be back by four, okay?"

"Whenever," she said. She dodged the kids, the tricycles, the jump ropes and a ball whacking against the side of the building, edged past the knot of women at the entrance, and disappeared inside.

Ben sat up and leaned against the wheel. Forgotten, my ass, he said to himself.

It was the treatment, of course; laid on a little heavier than usual, but following the basic paradigm: distance, silence, a cold plate for dinner. He had pointed it out to her after dinner, misjudging her mood. She flared up and locked herself in the bathroom for ten minutes. He might have given in at that point and called the Allardyces, despite his feelings about the house. Hell, if it was that important to her . . . But his own instincts were still stronger than her stubborn petulance. No doubt she was feeling exactly the same way, and for all the times he had given in—the evidence was ranged around the apartment—she could give in this once.

She was in bed before him and when he leaned over to kiss her, to make one more attempt, her breathing suddenly became heavier and more regular. She was making herself sick, he had told her earlier, all over a lousy house for the summer, and yes, she agreed resentfully, she was making herself sick, she wanted it that much.

It was ridiculous. A *house*, after all.

Ben lay back, his hands behind his head, and distracted himself with the sounds from the neighboring building.

There was a party somewhere above the courtyard; the decibel count would rise until around two when the music would
stop and there'd be ten minutes or so of drunken banter
below the windows. The late movies then, and the accelerated hum of air conditioners, until the string of bars let out
and Northern Boulevard roared with the sound of souped-
up cars and an occasional police siren. Saturday nights, a
whole summer of them, a whole summer of—what? Another
course, another fumbling attempt at his Master's? Scrounge
around for a job teaching summer school?

His will was weakening; he recognized the signs. The
shade moved and he waited for the breeze to pass over him.
When it did, he called "Marian?" quietly. The heavy breathing
lost a beat.

"Does it really mean that much to you?" he said.

Her voice, when it finally came, was very much awake.
"You know it does." She shifted a little away from him. "I'll
survive," she said.

"The question is . . . will I?" He put his hand on her shoulder and let it slide down to her hip.

"It's hot," she said. "Move to your own side."

He didn't and she made no attempt to move away from
him.

"Do you want me to call them?" he asked.

She gave a long sigh and her breath caught, just a little
beyond control. "At this point, Ben, I don't care much what
you do."

Just before noon Sunday morning, the phone rang in the
hall. Miss Allardyce reached it on the second ring, and then
let it ring three more times, until Brother came in from the
living room and Walker from the kitchen. They heard her
say, "Marvelous, just marvelous . . ." and "Brother will be
thrilled . . ." which was all they needed to hear. The first of
July would be fine, and of course they'd all be there and show
them the house and everything they needed to know. When
she hung up, she was smiling.

"Our mother . . . ?" Brother asked, holding out his hand to Miss Allardyce.

". . . is going to be just fine, Brother." She patted his hand reassuringly, and Walker, without waiting to be barked at, went out to the car to prepare it for their biennial trip.

(5)

A few days later they received two hand-written copies of a letter of agreement, signed "Arnold Allardyce," with space for Ben's signature. They would agree to occupy the premises of Seventeen Shore Road from July First to Labor Day, vacating September Third. A check for four fifty should accompany the signed letter; four fifty was payable directly to Arnold Allardyce on September Third. Ben withdrew the money from their savings account, leaving them with a balance of just over seventeen hundred dollars, and mailed a check to P.O. Box 121, Mohonkson, New York.

The letter and the scrawled receipt that followed made it all real to Marian; the house and everything in it was theirs for two months; the grounds and the pool and the beach and the private dock which was useless but nice to have anyway. All her instincts had been right, from the moment she had circled the ad and called Miss Allardyce. Fate, she decided, nothing less. When she told him, Ben said, "Fate, my ass. You're a spoiled brat and I'm a weak-willed pushover." But it had been something close to fate, as much as meeting Ben had been ten years ago. It was only a house and it would only last two months, not a lifetime, but the depth of her reaction surprised even her when she thought about it, which was often. Having met Ben and not having married him was inconceivable to her in retrospect; the same was true of the house. Her mood—black, blacker than she could ever remember—when he had decided the house wasn't for them, was not mere petulance, not the reaction of a spoiled child. The house was absolutely essential, a vital part of herself which she recognized immediately.

She didn't understand it, was surprised that she could even vaguely analyze the complexity of her feelings. But it was true; the house was everything she had always wanted; it was, like Ben and David, a reflection of what she was or could be inside, at her best. And when she repeated to herself, occasionally, "For God's sake, it's only a house," she was either denying the truth or—and this came to her in an ultra reflective moment—minimizing it to still some embryonic fear buried way down inside her. Why did the word "fear" come to her first? Why not "anxiety" which was probably more accurate? The house, after all, was enormous, and, yes, an old woman was something of a responsibility.

If it hadn't been for Ben and his groundless suspicions, the feeling wouldn't have been there in the first place, and the voices wouldn't come back to her every once in a while, and the disconcerting looks. When they did she reminded herself that the Allardyces were old, senile maybe or close to it, insular certainly, and harmless. Besides, as she said over and over to Ben, they wouldn't be anywhere near the house and their summer.

It was anxiety after all, and perfectly natural.

She mentioned none of it to Ben. He wouldn't understand, or if he did, he'd laugh and, worse, say his instincts were truer than hers. Which they weren't. Either way it was none of his business. They had taken a house for the summer and the glosses were purely personal.

Marian had seldom, she reflected, spent so much time inside herself.

Once she rearranged her calendar, Aunt Elizabeth would be delighted to spend the summer, or at least a good part of it, with them. But were they sure they wanted an old lady hanging around all the time? Ben roared and Aunt Elizabeth wondered what she had said that was so funny.

The term was over in mid-June. Ben spent an additional week at school, cleaning up his desk and meeting with the rest of the English Department to plan the fall schedule. He fought with the cretinous Miss MacKenzie over a sophomore assignment, and received a vaguely threatening exhortation from Byron, the principal, about getting on with his Master's. When he got home after the confrontations, he was irritable and distracted, and for the first time the house and the distance and two months of leisurely reading under a tree or beside the pool seemed distinctly attractive to him.

They arranged to have their mail held until they could provide a forwarding address, and after much discussion decided they were "out of town, far out" for the summer as far as their friends were concerned. Selfish or not, they'd have enough to handle without having to gird themselves for weekly invasions. They didn't dare mention the pool and the beach, and the house became a small cottage in the woods where Ben could work up his courses peacefully. Everyone understood, and since Aunt Elizabeth would be with them, the Rolfes would effectively pass out of existence for the next two months.

Marian, both of them were surprised to discover, had no qualms at all about abandoning the apartment and everything she had collected so lovingly. She began to dust every other day and vacuum only twice a week. She'd wash the windows when they got back in September, and the floors could wait as well. The apartment, in her mind, had suddenly become transitional.

July first, they picked up Aunt Elizabeth at eight in the morning. Ben struggled with the luggage in the small trunk of the Camaro and managed to squeeze her one suitcase in. He had attached a rack to the top of the car, which he piled with luggage, tied down, and covered with canvas. It took him half an hour to slip her easel in under the covering and maneuver Aunt Elizabeth, who was thin and amazingly agile for seventy-four and a half (her reckoning) into the back seat crammed with books and shopping bags. David sat in the front, uncomfortably, between the two bucket seats.

"We're like a bunch of Okies," Aunt Elizabeth said, delighted, as Ben started the car. She straightened her dress, a bright silk print, and tied a blue veil over her hair which was silver and beautifully sculpted. Marian asked her if she was comfortable, and she said, "Heavens, no!" She put on a pair of large sunglasses.

"It'll be worth it," Marian promised her, and then groaned and pushed herself closer to the door. "David," she said, "my leg. *Please.*"

By the time they reached Shore Road, everything in Aunt Elizabeth had gone numb. "Except of course my mouth."

Marian was leaning forward anxiously, searching the foliage for the stone wall.

The deserted road reminded Aunt Elizabeth of the driving lessons Ben had been promising her. "I've renewed my learner's permit," she told him. "I'm determined this time."

Marian said, "Slow here, Ben."

"I must say," Ben said, "I admire your persistence."

"My persistence is the reason I've flourished this long."

"You've just got to learn to relax at the wheel."

"I'm always relaxed at the wheel. I get nervous inspectors. The last one never took his hand off the door handle. 'Young man,' I told him, 'I've been taking this test for nine years. I know exactly what I'm doing.'"

The wall had appeared, and soon after, the twin pillars.

"Here we are, Ben!" Marian said. He had seen them and already slowed the car.

"I trust myself more than some licensed drivers," Aunt Elizabeth continued, and her voice had become grating and distracting to Marian who watched the dipping road as Ben drove between the pillars. "Mrs. Brinkman, for instance. Backing out of her garage the other day . . ."

"Isn't this lovely, Aunt Elizabeth?" Marian cut in.

Aunt Elizabeth looked out at the shrubbery which had grown much thicker and closer to the drive. "Yes, just lovely," she said, and then rested her hand on Ben's shoulder. "Her car shot forward, Mrs. Brinkman's, and bang! right into the side of her house."

"She get killed?" David asked.

"Let me finish. Hit the side of her house and then jerked back, all the way to the opposite curb." She was illustrating the motion with her hands. "You follow?" she asked David.

"That kill her?" he asked.

"Wait. Made a perfect U-turn, and then smashed through Mrs. Monsees' bay window, straight into the living room." She tapped Ben's shoulder for emphasis. "Hitting, I might add, poor Mrs. Monsees who was on the phone at the time."

She giggled and Ben said, "Oh, come on, Aunt Elizabeth," skeptically. They were reaching the end of the woods.

"It's the truth, Benjie," she said, trying to control the giggle.

"That must've killed her," David said.

"There it is!" Marian said. "Look at it, just look at it!"

Aunt Elizabeth looked and said, "Good God!" She raised her sunglasses, was silent for a long moment, and then repeated it. "*Good God!*"

The garage doors were closed, with the huge old Packard nowhere in sight, and so were the French windows lining the terrace, and all the other windows in the house. Ben honked the horn once as they pulled up in front of the steps.

David said, "There are sixteen of them," and Aunt Elizabeth groaned.

"You can avoid them by going around the side," Marian said, "toward the terrace."

Ben turned off the ignition. Marian was watching the front door which remained closed while they climbed out of the car stiffly.

"Looks deserted," Ben said.

Marian searched the face of the house, her eyes once again stopping at the large rounded bay. "It can't be," she said, moving toward the steps. "They probably didn't hear the horn."

"I can't get over it," Aunt Elizabeth exclaimed, pulling back her shoulders and stretching. She paced to get the circulation going, taking in the grounds and the house rising high above her.

Ben was untying the canvas cover. "Okay, Dave," he called, "let's get to work."

When she reached the top of the steps, Marian saw a bulging envelope resting against the base of the door. It was addressed to "Mr. and Mrs. Rolfe" in Arnold Allardyce's large and florid hand.

Oh, no, she thought as she lifted it and felt the ring of keys inside.

Sure enough, they had gone. "Hi Folks," the letter began, and went on to describe, most apologetically, how the damn travel agent had messed them up, miscalculating their schedule by a full day. There was a map of the house enclosed, mimeographed and quite detailed. "Boy," "Aunt," and "Master Chamber" had been inked in. Marian flipped through the pages of instructions and the list of names (grocer, plumber, electrician, doctor, even their insurance agent).

"What's up?" Ben called from beside the car.

She came to the edge of the porch and tried not to hesitate or betray her own surprise and annoyance. "They had to leave," she called back.

"Leave?"

He dropped the canvas and climbed past Aunt Elizabeth who had puffed her way up eight steps. Marian handed him the letter.

" 'Enjoy the house,' " he read aloud, incredulously, " 'and don't worry about anything. Arnold and Roz Allardyce.' " He looked directly at Marian and said, "Jesus Christ!"

"I know," Marian agreed, "it's crazy. They *did* try to get us though."

"They couldn't have tried very hard." He scanned the list of names. "What if something goes wrong? Where do we reach them? *Jesus!*" he repeated.

"Well," Marian said as decisively as she could, "obviously nothing's going to go wrong." She was looking at the map with Ben. "Our Mother," she noticed, was mimeographed across two rooms at the western end of the house. Marian recognized the position immediately; her window would be the rounded bay.

"I was wrong," Ben said; "they're a couple of steps beyond weird." He folded the papers and stuffed them into the envelope. "What about the old lady?"

"I'd better look in on her," Marian said. The keys, nine or ten of them, were all neatly labelled. She picked out "Front Door."

"You do that," Ben said sarcastically. "She's all yours."

"Rub it in," Marian said, sticking the key into the lock.

"Oh, I intend to," Ben said. "Here." He handed her the envelope and turned to help Aunt Elizabeth up the last few steps.

"I won't have to do this again, Benjie, will I?" Marian heard her say as she opened the door and stepped into the hall. "Ever?"

The double doors to the left and right of the entrance hall were closed, and the passage leading to the kitchen and servants' wing in the rear of the house dark and silent. She remembered, as if over a month hadn't passed, the chandelier, still cloudy in the light streaming in from the open door and the fanlight, and the Persian rug, still rolled against the wall. The mirror that had been hanging over the Regency console had been removed, leaving a tall rectangular shadow and a circle of white plaster, the size of a bullethole, in the pale green wall. She hadn't remembered the pictures, old Italian prints, flanking the highboy against the opposite wall; but one of the two Chippendale wingchairs was missing, leaving the wall particularly naked and unbalanced. The console's clock, gold and elaborately scrolled, read two-thirty which was wrong; the grandfather clock just before the passage at the opposite end read seven.

Marian checked her watch; it was almost ten-thirty. The Allardyces' letter had been dated July first, which meant they had left the old lady that morning.

Brother's inclinator, with the seat pulled up, was at the foot

of the staircase. She walked past it and up the carpeted steps
which curved and climbed to a long, broad hall, cut with four
doors on either side. An enormous oriental rug, faded and
frayed, travelled the length of the hall whose walls were covered with fabric, a green and gold pattern, worn and curling at
the seams, and in one place hanging like a wide, colorless frond.

Marian checked the map and followed it down the corridor, passing another tall clock in a finialed Baltimore-type
case, this one reading eight. She could hear Ben and Aunt
Elizabeth dimly in the hall below.

"They do crazy things sometimes, old people," she heard
Aunt Elizabeth saying.

The second door on the right, according to the map, was
hers and Ben's, opposite was David's, and next to his, Aunt Elizabeth's. The rooms, which she looked into just briefly, seemed
bright and spacious, their light spilling into the corridor. She
spent more time in front of an incredibly beautiful bombé cabinet of burled walnut; behind the glass which had a long hairline crack were several pieces of rose medallion, and several
blank spaces as well. There were pictures on the walls, lush
landscapes most of them, and more smudged rectangles and
nail holes where there had once been pictures. Midway down
the corridor was a green striped Empire sofa, and opposite it a
pier-glass-console combination with a great silver candelabra.

At the end of the corridor, and indicated on the map, were
five wide steps leading to the west wing of the house which
could be closed off by shutting the white double doors. Marian
climbed the steps and found herself in a small dark hall, about
ten-by-ten. There was one door, directly ahead. On either side
of the door were pedestals supporting huge Canton bowls.
"Our Mother," the map said; a bedroom and a sitting room
were indicated beyond the door.

Marian folded the map, cleared her throat, and knocked
lightly. The hall was absolutely quiet and airless; whatever
light there was came from the main corridor, and if the doors
were closed there would be none at all.

She waited, and then called, "Mrs. Allardyce?" There was

no reply. She pushed the door and called again, through the narrow opening.

The old woman was obviously in her bedroom which should be to the left of the sitting room and, Marian reminded herself, locked. "Always," the voice came back to her, "our poor, gentle darling . . ."

She opened the door wider and stepped into the room which was large and dim, with two pencil lines of bright sunlight cutting through the not quite closed drapes. To her right, and with a suddenness that startled her, was an enormous table draped with velvet, burgundy like the drapes, and filled with framed photographs. The table covered half the room, stretching back to the rear windows which would overlook the lawn and the bay. It was a great field of photographs, faces as far as she could make out, each of them framed differently in silver—square, round, sunburst, some larger, some mere cameos. "The memories of a lifetime," Miss Allardyce had told her. The light catching the frames was hypnotic.

The sound as well, which she had just become aware of: a very low and steady hum, barely audible, emphasizing the silence, like her own breathing. Still not moving, with her hand on the knob, she let her eyes range over the sitting room to trace the sound.

The door to the bedroom was in the left wall. Near it was a wingchair, gold brocade, facing the pictures on the table; a small tea table, set with a tray, stood in front of the chair. There was nothing else in the room except for the rug, a ruby-colored Sarouk, patterned in rose and gold.

The sound seemed to be coming from the bedroom. She moved toward the door, very quietly. It was the room, she told herself, that was intimidating: the stillness and the half-light and the hum. Initially, that's all; she'd get used to them, and if she felt a little nervous now and entertained a brief second thought about the responsibility of an old woman and a house she hadn't even begun to explore, it would all pass soon enough, and become familiar and comfortable.

The hum that drew her to the door at the end of the sitting

room had become deeper and stronger, but almost imperceptibly so. It was the door itself that caught her attention now. It
was white, and framed within the narrow, smooth border was
an intricate pattern of lines and curves carved into the wood,
so delicate in the room's dim light that she hadn't noticed the
design until she came within a few feet. Swirls and garlands
were cut into triangular panels that met in a small, raised pistil.
She moved closer and the design became more intricate and
abstract and impenetrable: a globe, a web, a sunburst, a maze,
a slab carved with ancient pictographs.

Marian stopped just in front of the door and, impulsively,
raised one hand, letting the tips of her fingers pass lightly over
the raised surface. Immediately, she could feel the vibration
passing through her. She lifted her other hand and slowly
started to bring her face closer, turning so that her ear almost
touched the door. The sound moved against her hair, deep and
unrecognizable, an abstraction like the carved braille flutter-
ing under her fingertips. Her fingers moved slower and then
stopped, and the palms of her hands were flat against the door,
and her ear pressed against it. Restful, so suddenly restful, not
listening, not touching, barely aware of pushing herself closer
into the door which was warm and fragrant, smelling of
green. And the hum had deepened and broken into the sound
of her own heartbeat.

She tried to fight the wave of drowsiness that had come
over her, to open her eyes, and thought, One minute more,
just one minute more. And then tried again and saw the small
ridges of white pillowing her hand, and heard the sound and
felt the wood against her cheek. And, *My God, what am I doing?*
she said to herself—several times before she summoned the
strength to pull herself away from the door.

How long had she been standing like that? She turned,
startled, and waited for the room to work itself back into her
consciousness: the wingchair, the tray, the photos, all of them
shadowy; and with relief, with great relief, the open door leading to the corridor and the staircase and Ben and David and
Aunt Elizabeth.

However dark the room was, and airless, and intimidating, however hypnotic that insistent hum, she couldn't have been asleep on her feet, not that suddenly and completely. What in hell had happened to her?

She turned to the carved door again and stared at it. A trick? Some weird kind of optical illusion?

Whatever. She tried to dismiss it. Three hours sleep last night, if even that; packing, the tension of closing the apartment, remembering everything. The past week had been one long headache, literally. Nerves, anticipation; excitement, too much—Ben had said it several times. So she blacked out for a second. There'd be two months, two beautiful months to insulate the nerve ends.

She had come up to check the old lady, she reminded herself. She raised her hand to knock, hesitated, moved to the smooth frame of the door and knocked. The sound was dull, inaudible, she would think, over the air conditioner or whatever it was humming in the room. She knocked again, harder but no louder. Her knuckles hurt. The door had to be solid, unusually heavy.

She waited, and then closer to the door, called, "Mrs. Allardyce?"

She knocked again, waving her hand to fan the knuckles. "Are you all right, Mrs. Allardyce?" she called louder. "It's Marian Rolfe." She assumed the old lady had been told about them, but added anyway, "We're the people who've taken the house for the summer." There was only the hum in reply. (*Was* it an air conditioner? She'd have to check the west window of the bedroom.) "If there's anything you need . . ." Marian said, letting her voice fall.

The old lady was probably asleep; she'd show herself when she was ready, although Miss Allardyce had said the people last time didn't see her once. Marian herself would prefer it that way.

She gave the door one final long look, without touching it, and then moved away, stopping to pick up the tray which held a blue Spode plate and egg coddler (the egg half eaten), an untouched wedge of toast and a silver spoon; the napkin, linen with lace trim, was unfolded. Miss Allardyce had prepared her: the old woman ate little, some days nothing at all, surviving, her daughter insisted, on sheer will and, less mysteriously, whatever she might have cached away in her room. Marian's grandmother had done the same, she recalled: the bottom drawer of her dresser had to be emptied regularly of candy wrappers, stale cookies and dried sausage skins. ("Emphatically *not* the same," Miss Allardyce had said when Marian told her.) In any event, whether she ate or not, the silver tray was to be carried up three times a day: egg for breakfast, soup for lunch, a single piece of chicken and a green vegetable for dinner. At nine, twelve and six.

Marian balanced the tray, listening for a sound or some movement behind the bedroom door and looking at the vague faces watching her on the table. Was the room always this close? Surely a little more light, a bit of air; she could always close the windows again and draw the heavy drapes if Mrs. Allardyce preferred. She lay the tray down and went to the window, parting the velvet drapes which were heavy with dust. There were thick curtains against the windows, blurring the sun to a white haze. Silk damask, gold tinted, shone on the walls. She went to the second window, and when she spread the drapes, motes filled the light which fell over the silver frames on the table and bounced against the walls and the ceiling.

Marian was beside the table. She let her eyes travel over the photographs which, like the pictures in the alcove downstairs, were a mixture of sepia and color and black and white. Each of them was of a single figure, some full length, some of faces only; every age seemed to be represented, every style of dress, from turn of the century, or earlier, up to the present. She bent closer, awed by the display, by the incredible variety of faces and the delicacy of the frames, no two alike. There was a color shot of a beautiful young woman, unsmiling, and next to her an older woman in a thirties-style dress, staring blankly into the camera, and a man, Ben's age, with a peculiar, almost stunned expression; an infant with her eyes closed, and older children, all of them strangely unsmiling. And as she looked over the table, she realized that none of the faces was smiling, not one of them. The expressions were uniformly, and chillingly, blank. And one of the faces, an old man's, was looking out at her with what had to be outright terror. Like that boy's. And the child near the edge of the table. And the woman wearing the old fashioned bonnet whose picture, a cameo, she reached down for. When she touched the frame, the picture fell forward with a small metallic cry which made Marian gasp and spin around to look at the carved door. It was closed and the only sound the insistent hum. Her fingers, she found, were trembling. She moved them slowly toward the cameo, waited, and then uprighted the picture quickly, pulling her hand away as though she had touched something painful or repellent.

Miss Allardyce's soft phrase came back to her again: "the memories of a lifetime." It did nothing to soften or clarify the expressions frozen on the table, or make them less unsettling.

Ben stood at the top of the stairs, a suitcase in either hand, and called, "Marian!" down the corridor. Where the hell was she? The inclinator whirred behind him, mounting the steps with Aunt Elizabeth and David; he was half-seated on her lap, their backs to Ben as they rose. Ben said, "Christ!" under his breath, dropped the suitcases, and started to walk down the corridor when he finally saw Marian in the distance. She was closing the double doors behind her and coming down the steps.

"Where've you been?" he yelled, and Marian replied with a loud "Sssshhh!" fifty feet away.

The inclinator stopped behind him and David cried, "Again! Again!"

"We've been up twice already," Aunt Elizabeth said. "It's making me giddy."

"Come on, real fast this time." David pressed a button and they started to descend again.

"David, no," Aunt Elizabeth protested, and laughed.

Marian reached Ben; she was carrying Mrs. Allardyce's tray.

"Is she okay?" he asked.

"She's asleep." She looked over his shoulder at the heads sinking below the stairs. "That's not a toy, David," she called. "Up, and off."

"What did I tell you?" Aunt Elizabeth said, still laughing. She pressed the Up button.

"Did you see her?" Ben asked.

"No." She was balancing the tray and pulling the map out of the waist of her skirt. "She's all the way at the end of the corridor," Marian said. "They were right; you probably won't even see her."

"Crushing," Ben said.

David and Aunt Elizabeth were climbing out of the inclinator. "The stairs back there are out of bounds," Marian announced. "To everybody but me. Do you hear that, Dave? Absolutely out of bounds at all times." She waited for each of them to nod, Ben included and Ben especially; she'd prefer he didn't see the photographs or the carved door or anything to bring out the inevitable "Weird." She was unfolding the map, the old man's face still clear in her mind, and the woman wearing the bonnet. "We're in there," she said to Ben, nodding right. "David across, and then Aunt Elizabeth."

"Nice and cozy," Aunt Elizabeth said. She had been looking up the stairs which wound, narrower, up to the third floor.

Ben went for the suitcases. "How about bringing up your games?" he said to David who started to climb into the inclinator again until Marian ordered, "Walk!" He bounded down the stairs.

Aunt Elizabeth stopped in front of the tall clock which read eight o'clock. "None of the clocks are working," she said. "Pity; they're all so lovely and expensive."

"They just need winding," Marian said. They were moving toward Aunt Elizabeth's room. "Just wait till I get started."

"She's just itching to get into her kneepads and her jock-strap," Ben said, and Aunt Elizabeth said, "Benjie!" and laughed disapprovingly. "Guarantee you don't see her before Labor Day."

Marian, who was still carrying the tray, gave him a nudge with the side of her knee. "You play with your toys and I'll play with mine," she said.

Aunt Elizabeth looked down the corridor before following Ben into her room which faced, beyond a large and dying elm, the vast field sloping away from the front of the house. There was a huge fourposter and a silk-covered chaise in the room, a fanback Windsor, and several early Primitives on the walls which delighted Aunt Elizabeth as much as the ancient gas heater in a corner of the room. "I haven't seen one of those in years," she said, and then hugged Marian and Ben, saying, "Thanks for having me, my darlings. It's going to be a perfectly lovely summer."

Ben carried the last of the suitcases up to his and Marian's room which, of the three, was the largest, the most beautifully furnished, with, Marian pointed out to him, an extraordinary Queen Anne highboy carved with a sunburst pattern, and a rare Newport desk. The room looked north, toward the bay.

He was changing into a tee shirt and chinos when she came into the bedroom.

"Put your pants on and come with me," she said excitedly.

"An eighteenth century pottie, right?" he guessed, pulling on a pair of tennis sneakers. "Signed, of course."

"You'll see," she said. She had already changed into jeans and one of his old button-down shirts; the sleeves were rolled up and the tail hanging loose.

She bounced down the stairs ahead of him and led him into the kitchen, moving with assurance through the passageway, past the table piled with their pots and shopping bags, to the large double refrigerator. "They're weird, right?" she said, grabbing the handle; "dirty-crazy and not to be trusted." She waited for him to come in front of the refrigerator, and then, with a flourish, pulled it open, exclaiming "*Voilà!*" and, as she pulled the second door open, "*Voilà* again!" The shelves were packed with food, all of it, she pointed out, fresh, specially laid in for them. There was a large cooked chicken and a strawberry pie, and several bottles of champagne chilling; and when she grabbed his hand and took him into the pantry, he saw shelves laden with canned goods and liquor and soft drinks, and the freezer as well was packed with steaks and roasts. She waved the damp note she had found in the refrigerator.

"All ours," she said; "look."

Compliments of Roz and Brother, Ben read. *Use it all. Please.*

"There's enough food here for the whole summer," Marian said, closing the freezer lid. "I feel so guilty. I mean, they certainly didn't have to do *this*." She moved closer to Ben and wrapped her arms around him. "Say it," she teased him; "eccentric, suspicious."

He let his eyes travel over the long shelves thoughtfully, then put his arms around her, smiled and kissed her.

"This kind of eccentric," he said, "I suspect I can live with."

By lunchtime, Marian had washed as well as she could the wrought iron table with its chipped glass top, and the four chairs. She helped Ben move them from beside the French windows to the rear of the flagstone terrace where they would have a sweeping view of the lawn beyond the stone balusters and the glistening bay. She found a bright red tablecloth and a set of blue ironware; looked through the pantry drawers for a set of everyday tableware and found three separate sets of beautifully patterned silver. She chose the simplest for outdoors, as well as four crystal tumblers and three champagne glasses. When it was all set up, with the roast chicken set in front of Ben's place and the bottle of champagne on a small glass teacart, she called, "Ready!" through the kitchen door and waited for them to find their way to the terrace.

David said "Neat!" and Aunt Elizabeth breathed in the air deeply, repeating "Lovely, lovely," despite the weeds growing through the flagstones and the broken balusters and her chair which wobbled threateningly beneath her. Ben opened the champagne and Marian beamed as he raised his glass and said, with no trace of sarcasm, "To our summer. The four of us."

"And Roz and Brother," she added. "Our benefactors."

"Our benefactors," Aunt Elizabeth said.

They took a sip and Ben raised his glass once more. The voice, when it came out, was pure Roz Allardyce. "And our mother, God save her . . ." He made a sweeping gesture with his glass, ending in the direction of the upper windows. "Wherever she is."

And Marian, who could seldom remember being so totally content, went suddenly pale and almost dropped her glass. "My God!" she exclaimed. "Her tray! I completely forgot." She pushed her chair back and ran toward the kitchen door.

"Aw, hon?" Ben called. "Can't it wait?"

She had closed the door behind her.

(6)

Ben was already in bed, reading a book of Kenneth Patchen poems, when she came into the room. The covers were pulled all the way down, and the windows were open, shades up, curtains moving lightly in the breeze. There was nothing but black space beyond, no lighted windows, no wall of white brick; and, blessedly, no sound.

"What took you so long?" he said, closing the book on his chest.

She smiled wearily and said, "Things." She had checked all the windows, doors, lights, moving easily through the rooms which had already become almost as familiar to her as their four rooms on the other side of the moon. Last of all, she had gone down the corridor to the sitting room, drawn the drapes and left a small lamp burning. The tray had been still untouched, like the tray that afternoon—which, she assured herself, she was not to worry about.

She went into the bathroom and left the door ajar.

"Dave's bugging me about that pool," Ben said. "I ought to have a look at it tomorrow."

"There's a page on pools," Marian said behind the door, referring to the lists of instructions the Allardyces had left. "I almost dread it, y'know? You'll have to lay down the law to him; no pool unless one of us is around, no beach either."

She closed the door. Ben placed the book on the night table, pulled off his shorts, and lit a cigarette. He stretched out and let the breeze pass over his body. Marian came out of the bathroom in a short blue nightgown, thought, *Oh, no, Ben, not tonight, please,* when she saw him naked, and delayed getting into bed as long as she could, adjusting windows, inspecting the gas heater ("Are these things safe?" "We won't be using them."), and passing her hand reverently over the wood of the highboy.

"Come to bed."

She went to the windows again, luxuriating in the space and the quiet. "I could get used to this very, very easily," she said, and then took several deep breaths, rising on the balls of her feet. Ben watched her and spread his right hand over her side of the bed, smoothing the tight, cool sheet.

"Bed's comfortable," he said softly. "Just hard enough. Come and try it."

She took her time, walking barefoot over the vast needlepoint rug, and then slid in lazily on her stomach, her face away from him.

"You're right," she said, muffled.

His hand moved through her hair and under the top of her nightgown, rubbing her back. "You're overdressed," he said, and she made a small, sleepy sound, burrowing deeper into the pillow. He slid his hand all the way down, and then under, spreading his fingers over her stomach and working them lower. He had moved closer to her and his fingers slipped between her legs, rubbing very gently. She raised herself and he pressed closer, and when she felt him, hard and moving against her, with his lips on the back of her neck, she said,

"No," almost soundlessly, "Please no, honey." She let him pull the loose nightgown off and turn her on her back, and when he slipped in, she locked herself around him and closed her eyes. And at first she pushed up and let him drive himself deep into her. His face was buried in her neck, and then his mouth was covering her ear and the sounds were hot and wet and suddenly unpleasant. He was hurting her. She tried to move her head, to push her body deeper into the mattress, away from Ben. Her eyes were open, watching the shadows on the ceiling, and she had stopped moving under him altogether. And when he raised his face and pleaded, "Come on, baby, come *on*," with a deep, almost punishing thrust, she kept her eyes determinedly on the ceiling and pushed up against him with no pleasure at all, with only an awful burning sensation. His back had become wet and sticky under her hands, and she dug her nails in so that she'd feel only the tips of her fingers, not his skin which had never been repulsive to her before. He was pushing in deeper and quicker, with the pleas becoming more intense, and all Marian could think was, "Let him come, for Christ's sake let him come. Now."

He cried out when he did and she pulled his face against her shoulder to cut off the sound. And later she gave him the obligatory assurance that, yes, it had been as good for her; and smiled and touched his face when he said, "Christ, the place really works after all."

Marian waited for him to fall asleep. Then she crept out of bed and took a shower with the bathroom door closed, scrubbing away at whatever was left of the city.

The next morning was glorious, beautifully clear, with a nice, constant breeze blowing in from the bay. David and Ben woke at eight, Aunt Elizabeth a little later; none of them had ever slept as well. Neither had Marian, she told them, though actually she had slept fitfully, getting up around three and sitting beside the window. At one point she had gone out into the hall and looked toward the closed double doors, barely visible beyond the light of the lamp outside Aunt Elizabeth's room.

There was no sound anywhere in the house, and the distant hum she had heard, standing outside her bedroom door, had to be imaginary, suggested by the stillness and the vague whiteness in the distance. Associative: sitting room—hum (just as, for Ben, the apartment in Queens was always associated with the smell of lemon oil). Obviously the old lady was on her mind for some reason; she must have been, if Marian thought about it, while Ben was trying to make love to her; like some disapproving presence, as formless and pervasive as an imaginary hum.

She had come back into the room, closing the door on the sound, and when she saw Ben she felt a pang of guilt. Wonderful, she had lied to him, when if anything it had been unpleasant, almost unbearably so. His body, which she loved, as well as the physical act. *Why?*

She had watched him sleeping for a long while, and then touched his body lightly—his chest, and then very lightly, the hair below his stomach. She kissed the tip of his shoulder which was warm and sweet-smelling, and then, still sleepless, got out of bed again and came down to the kitchen. Light was spreading above the trees to the east, and she brought her coffee out to the terrace and watched the sun come up, tugging every now and then at the weeds growing between the flagstones.

When Ben came down, Mrs. Allardyce's egg was boiling on the stove and Marian was rearranging shelves in the pantry. She brought his breakfast out to the terrace, then David's, then Aunt Elizabeth's. At eight fifty-five precisely she left them chattering away brightly and carried Mrs. Allardyce's tray up to the sitting room. She opened the drapes, turned off the lamp, and lifted the untouched dinner tray, resisting the impulse, which was even stronger than it had been last night, to go near the carved door.

Ben and David drove to the post office to arrange for a box, and Marian and Aunt Elizabeth had another cup of coffee on the terrace. ("Death," Aunt Elizabeth intoned with a fist pressing against her chest, but she drank it anyway.)

"How's the town?" Marian asked Ben later.

"Swinging," he said. He put the bag with a carton of cigarettes and two quarts of milk on the table. It would hold them for the rest of the week. "We are in the middle of nowhere, but nowhere."

"I like the idea," Marian said.

They set up a schedule: mail pickup, milk and incidentals once a week. Television would have to replace the daily *Times*; Sundays, if Ben got ambitious, he'd drive to Southold.

"Were they friendly?" Marian asked.

"The natives?"

She nodded, putting the milk away, and Ben said, "Not especially."

"Did you tell them who we were?"

"No. Should I have?"

"Friendly relations with the locals. Can't hurt."

"Next time." He was peeling a banana. "Incidentally, who are we supposed to be?"

"The Rolfes," she announced impressively, spreading her arms and then wrapping them around him. "Of Land's End, and Heart's Desire, and all that sort of thing. Think of something smart and intimidating."

David stuck his head into the kitchen. "What about that pool?" he said to Ben.

"Canada," Ben said to Marian. "We'll call it Canada."

Whatever doubts Ben had had about the house, nothing happened to corroborate them, not that day, or the next, or the day after that. The sun seemed to shine brighter each day, and the huge house was becoming more familiar and comfortable and manageable. Marian had been right: the tension poured out of him like sweat and all he had to do was jump into the warm bay and let it wash off him, effortlessly. He managed to get the pool's filter going, briefly and not very effectively, following the typewritten instructions, and found the net and vacuum in the poolhouse. David would have to content himself with the beach until all the debris had been worked out of the pool. Ben looked at the chaise they had dragged from the recesses of one of the garages, and the faded beach umbrella growing out of a rusted table, saw books on the table and a rum collins and long shaded afternoons on the tiled surface, and found himself growing just as impatient as David. He could, too—get used to it very, very easily.

They explored the grounds, Ben and David, with Marian stealing a moment from the house occasionally, while Aunt Elizabeth set her easel up on the terrace and began to paint the view, a massive sunhat shielding her eyes from the sun. The picture started out accurately enough, with nice modulations of green and blue and brown; and then a lighthouse materialized halfway across the bay, and the white dot of a cabin cruiser, and children playing on the beach, watched by a thin woman in an enormous straw sunhat. She would call it, she told Ben, *L'Été*, or *The Summer*.

She waved at them from the terrace as they walked to the stone jetty where David had fallen. Beyond it the beach ended against a cliff-like rise too steep to climb, although David tried, and then Ben.

The grounds were hemispherical, within the line of beach and the great curve of woods. They found the remnants of a tennis court, and much more interesting, an old cemetery with tilting nameless tombstones, way off to the west, beyond a grove of trees. The grass was low and sparse in some places, coarser in others; the earth rose irregularly, and some of the graves seemed fresher than others, though "fresher" probably meant generations old rather than centuries. Ben could eventually make out the traces of ALLARDYCE on two or three of the stones.

David found it absolutely spooky and fascinating. They'd come back some night when there was a full moon, Ben told him, hunching up his shoulders and making a crazy Igor-like face, and watch to see what rose from the graves. A whole horde of ghost-like gorillas, probably, all of them on blood-stained two-wheelers.

"Three-wheelers," David reminded him. And when Ben

started to limp toward him, David backed away.

"Where are you going, little boy?" Ben asked, all twisted and grunting.

David kept his eyes on Ben. "Find the bike," he said, moving back faster. "It's a whole lot scarier than this stupid place."

Ben straightened up and smiled. "That's enough scary stuff for today." He put his arms around David. "Let's go check on that crummy pool." Which was fine with David.

For the last time, she told herself, there's absolutely nothing to worry about. If there were some complaint, or anything at all wrong with the old woman, she'd certainly find some way to communicate with Marian. The soup was cold, the spoon and napkin exactly where Marian had left them.

What was she living on?

Once or twice the awful thought came into Marian's head that Mrs. Allardyce wasn't living at all, she was dead behind the carved door. Or if not dead, then some kind of terrible joke the Allardyces were playing on her, the ultimate catch: there was no Mrs. Allardyce. If only she'd give her some slight sign to ease her mind, to make everything as perfect for her as it obviously was for Ben and David and Aunt Elizabeth.

Gradually, her concern was bringing her up to the sitting room more than the three times required each day. She'd stop in first thing in the morning and last thing at night; opening the drapes and putting out the light, and then closing them and putting it back on. If she had to come upstairs for anything, she'd visit the sitting room before going back down. Peer in, pause, listening for a footstep or the click of a door, and then leave. By the third or fourth day she was leaving excuses to climb the long circular staircase on the bureau in her room or the bathroom shelf or the hamper: rings, her watch, a tissue, a blouse for the laundry room. Eventually she dispensed with the excuses.

The old lady, the well-being if not the existence of Mrs. Allardyce, was becoming an obsession.

The room itself had become less discomforting; she was scarcely aware of the hum anymore, and the collection of photographs was now extraordinary rather than chilling. It was only the carved door and the deepening of the hum as she approached it, the impulse to touch it and lose herself in its puzzling intricacy, that she found mystifying and intimidating.

Of course, she said nothing to Ben who expressed polite disinterest every once in a while. If he asked, the old lady was either asleep or had said something to Marian from behind the closed door. "In your average old lady's voice," she told him, at which he said, "By cracky!" and hobbled off without any further questions. A few times he saw Marian carrying the uneaten food back to the kitchen. He'd shake his head sympathetically and parody what he assumed was an old lady's belch.

He was happy, which was the important thing, even in bed, although that was taking more and more effort on Marian's part. It would pass, she was sure; what she was going through now was some kind of metaphysical period.

She was pouring the soup down the drain when he bounded into the kitchen with a tennis-anyone? gesture. He was wearing shorts and a terrycloth pullover. His face and arms were burned a light pink and the wide smile dazzled her.

"When're you coming out to play?" he asked her.

"Soon. How are the folks?"

"Busy, busy." He took two cream sodas and a ginger ale out of the refrigerator. "I swear, Aunt Elizabeth just dropped another ten years."

Marian smiled and washed the plate. "And you were the man with all the misgivings."

"That's right." He pulled the tabs on the soda cans. "I'm still waiting for the piper to come skipping over the hill." She took the tabs off the counter and threw them away. "Look," he said, grabbing her hands, "how about doffing those work weeds and donning a pinafore? You can dust and sweep and oil all you want when the sun goes down. It's a smashing day, babe."

"I will, as soon as I get that room ready for you."

"What do I need with a stuffy room? I can work as well outdoors." He made his voice deeper, imitating Mr. Byron: "If indeed, work seems feasible at all."

"It's a perfect room." She was talking about the library. "You can barricade yourself in and get away from all of us."

"Like you've been doing?"

"I have *not*." Her voice wavered a little and she tried to suppress the guilty smile. "I've just been . . . straightening up a bit."

"Uh-hunh," he said. "And the place is beginning to smell of lemon oil."

"I'm enjoying myself."

"Yippee!" he said; "ninety rooms to take on. Christ, the lemon oil alone'll break us." He drew her closer and let his eyes travel over her face. "Paleface," he said affectionately. "You'll never change." He saw something on the side of her head. "Correction," he said, raising his hand.

"What's wrong?"

His fingers were touching her left temple. "You're getting old, baby," he said with quiet sympathy.

"A gray hair!" she said, appalled. Her eyes were straining left.

"More than one." He was separating the strands.

"Ben! Stop kidding."

"I'm not kidding." He turned her head and examined the right side, saying, infuriatingly, tsk-tsk-tsk-tsk.

"Clown," she said, pushing him away. Then, more emphatically: "Beast." She headed for the powder room outside the kitchen.

"I think it's kind of sexy, myself," she heard Ben calling. When he realized how upset she might be, he added, "You can barely see it, babe. Honest."

She turned on the light and slammed the door. There was one . . . two . . . Her fingers swept through the hair on her left side. Four . . . five . . . My God! And the other side as well. She hurried out of the room, bumping into Ben who was actually laughing, the bastard, saying something about vanity, vanity. "Oh, shut up, smart-ass!" she called over her shoulder. She went upstairs to her own bathroom for the hand-mirror, focusing it on the medicine cabinet. Nothing on top or in the back, thank God; just a thin streak on either side, and like he said, barely noticeable in her light hair. *But there.*

She came out of the bathroom and sat, stunned, on the edge of the bed for a couple of minutes. Ben was calling her downstairs. She waited for him to give up, then went back into the bathroom. She pulled out some of the gray, grimacing terribly, and then tried to cut the rest. She combed her hair, covering whatever gray she had missed.

Before she came downstairs again, she went into Mrs. Allardyce's sitting room. And for the first time actually sat. In the gold brocade wingchair.

Sunday morning, before breakfast, Ben announced that he was going to Southold for rolls and *The Times*. Marian told him to forget the rolls, she was baking cinnamon bread; all they needed was milk. By the time he reached Mohonkson, he had lost interest in the papers and the fifteen mile drive (in, vaguely, *that* direction, according to the monosyllabic proprietor of the general store). He picked up the milk and drove back to the house. Today, July Sixth, was finally Pool Day.

"You haven't come across a pair of pruning shears, have you?" he asked Marian in the kitchen. She was wearing her eternal shirt and jeans.

"In the whaddayacallit—the garden house," she said. "Why?"

"I've got to do something about that driveway. Bushes are growing like crazy."

"Now who's becoming proprietary?"

"It's a question of passage," he corrected her. "Besides, I scratched the car."

"That's better than losing it," she said, and stuck out her tongue.

He made several whipping gestures with appropriate

sound effects, lashing her back as she knelt in front of the oven. The smell of cinnamon filled the kitchen.

"Jesus," he said after a moment, "you're really at home."

"Aren't you?" She rose and brushed her hair back from her temples; the motion was becoming a nervous, self-conscious habit.

"*I* know the idyl's got to end eventually; that's the difference," he said.

She went for his eyes with her nails, kissed him grudgingly, and said, "Gather the tribe, please."

David came to breakfast with his flippers on and his face-mask, making a fish-mouth at Aunt Elizabeth who assured them all that she was wearing her new bikini, which was *brazen*, under her sleeveless white dress.

"Thank God for those Swiss doctors," Ben said. "Admit it, that's what keeps you going."

"Swiss doctors?" Aunt Elizabeth raised her sunglasses. "You mean those fiends with their monkey glands and placentas?" She screwed her face and made a gagging sound. "You don't seriously think that, Benjie."

"There's got to be a secret somewhere," he said, sliding a knife through David's grapefruit.

"There is," she said: "Riotous living." She had survived, she reminded Ben, two husbands, rest their souls—the second four years younger than herself.

"Anybody on deck at the moment?" Ben asked.

She lowered her glasses. "Not with my record, there isn't."

Marian was walking across the terrace, carrying the electric percolator, and David, who was still deep underwater, turned to her slowly and opened and closed his pursed lips. "Where's your bathing suit?" he asked behind the mask.

"Sounds remarkably like a real fish, doesn't he?" Marian said as she sat down.

"Daddie's got his on," David continued. "And Aunt Elizabeth's got a brazen bikini."

"So's your old lady," Ben said, "a brand new one, as I recall."

He passed him the grapefruit and tapped the glass of the face-mask. David pushed it up to his forehead. "When do I get to see it?" Ben asked her.

"I'll have it on in time for the first dip," she said, raising her right hand and adding, "Promise," when Ben looked at her skeptically. "No cleaning, no potting around the greenhouse; just a long, lovely day in the sun. Okay?"

Ben scooped some scrambled eggs onto his plate. "I'll believe it when I see it," he said.

"How come you're always *clean*ing?" David asked. "It's the country, isn't it?"

Ben nodded with satisfaction. "You tell her, Dave."

Marian turned to Aunt Elizabeth with an uncomprehending look. "Have I really been making myself that scarce?" she said.

"They're pulling your leg, dear," Aunt Elizabeth said, patting her hand. "I think what you're doing for the house is admirable."

"Thank you." She dug a silver serrated spoon into her grapefruit. "Now eat your breakfast, both of you."

In all probability she would have been there, at the pool with the rest of them, even though she ought to have been making some sense out of that greenhouse, which she'd at least attempt, eventually, or the disarray in the living room (most of the pieces, on closer inspection, were in shocking condition, and none of them where she would have placed them). She would even have put off that huge closetful of china and the cabinets filled with dull crystal—a crime, all of it—slipped into the bikini and shut them up for the day, son as well as father. But when she went into the sitting room for the breakfast tray, she saw that it had finally happened: the tea table had been moved a bit away from the wingchair, the napkin, unfolded, was draped across the tray; the egg had been cracked and (she checked) partially eaten, and so had one small wedge of toast.

If there was relief in Marian's reaction, there was gratitude as well. The old lady was alive, she actually existed behind the carved door; there was no need to mention her growing concern to Ben, which she would have had to have done soon, and raise again the suspicions the house had so beautifully dispelled.

Marian had brought the tray up at nine and it was a little after ten now; Mrs. Allardyce might have just left the sitting room, she would certainly be awake. Marian looked at the door, aware again of the hum. Today the pattern emerged as a stylized sunburst; yesterday it had been clearly, to Marian, a map of the heavens, with the Big Dipper and all the other constellations. It was the angle, she decided, the degree of light that determined the image; marvelously, as marvelous as anything else in the house. (Where had it come from? It suggested Egypt to her, or one of those elaborately carved Hindu temples.)

As fascinating as it was, what was beyond the door was more important to her right now; she'd see it eventually, she was sure, and meet the elusive Mrs. Allardyce, despite what she'd been told about the previous families. Should she push it? Go up to the door, knock, and try to communicate with her again? It was just curiosity of course, nothing stronger. Perfectly natural: what sort of person had accumulated the treasures that filled the house and that were now, tragically, crumbling from neglect? And what kind of woman was it who could inspire such reverence, whether it was eccentric or not? Marian could still hear their voices, the Allardyces', a decibel below the hum.

She stood for a long while beside the wingchair, staring at the door; one hand passed idly back and forth over the fabric. The reverence—and she was aware of it in herself every time she approached the room, feeling it intensify whenever she moved nearer the door—the reverence had been infectious; it was based, when she analyzed it, on nothing more than an idea and a house filled with its manifestations.

Somewhere beyond the closed windows she thought she heard David's voice calling her. She didn't move, except to bring her hands up to her head and brush the hair back against her temples. It was strange how the room insulated her; David, for the moment, seemed as distant to her as the sound of his voice. The hum was closer, more insistent.

Marian brought her hands down to the tray. Had Mrs. Allardyce noticed?—it was polished, gleaming under the blue Spode; not at all the way Marian had found it. She lifted it, jiggling it deliberately; and pointlessly—the sound would hardly penetrate the thick door. She waited, listening for some recognition beyond the door. And if it didn't come, it would, whenever the old lady was ready. "Our darling," she remembered, and when she looked down at the remnants on the tray, she could see her, frail and white and trembling, and "Our darling" became appropriate and touching. She repeated it: our darling.

She moved quietly away from the chair, and as she did she could hear David's voice again. The windows beyond the table of photographs overlooked the rear of the house and, off to the right, the pool where the calls were coming from. Marian moved past the rows of faces; they were clouding with dust, she noticed, and there was dust on the velvet covering as well. Her collection; she could hardly be expected to take care of it herself, an eighty-five year old woman. David had stopped calling and Marian turned back before she reached the window. She looked over the vast, shadowy emptiness of the room. Did Mrs. Allardyce really prefer it this way? There had been no complaint when she'd opened the drapes and aired the room before. Marian lowered the tray. Something against the bare, long wall to the left possibly—a table with a vase of flowers, just to brighten the room. There were roses growing beside the garage. She'd appreciate that.

But after. First she'd dust each of the picture frames and run a soft brush over the burgundy velvet. It might take her the rest of the morning, but she'd appreciate that as well, the old darling. Ben wouldn't, and neither would David; but there was a whole summer to fool around in the pool anyway.

David had let out one final, noisy *"Maaa!"*, spinning with

the effort, when Ben, at the opposite end of the pool, called, "Okay, Dave, cool it."

"She said she'd come swimming," David said. The face-mask was hanging loose around his neck and he was holding his flippers. The concrete perimeter of the pool, cracked and irregular in many places, was hot and bumpy under his feet.

"If she comes, she comes," Ben said. "You know your mother." He was drawing the long poolnet, its webbing mini-mally effective, over the surface of the water at the deep end of the pool. The house, huge and bright with sunlight, was about two hundred yards distant, sprawling above the sweep of lawn. There was no sign of Marian, which didn't surprise him.

Aunt Elizabeth was sitting under the faded beach umbrella across the pool where Ben had set up the table, chaise longue and chairs they had found in the garage. A rubber whale was growing in her hands as she blew into the nozzle.

"How's your wind holding out?" Ben called to her.

She pinched the nozzle which whistled as she took it from her mouth. "Not what it used to be," she managed to say between gasps.

"You smoke too much," Ben said. She had a cigarette each morning with her second cup of coffee, and another with her six o'clock martini (half vodka, half vermouth), using an elegant ivory holder.

"I know," she called back. "I drink too much and I'm a lecherous old lady. I'll never make eighty."

She examined the whale, which was still loose and sickly, drew a deep breath, and sputtered life into the nozzle. David was behind her, pulling on his flippers. He stood up quietly, raised the facemask, and began to move toward her, his arms outspread like some creature from beneath the sea. When he was directly in back of her, he laid a slimy hand on her shoul-der, heavily, like he'd seen the Mummy do on television, and made a scary sound which caused Aunt Elizabeth to shriek and let the whale fart its way out of her hands.

"*David!*" she cried, bringing her hands to her bosom. The

whale, flat and lifeless, had come to rest beside the edge of the pool. When she caught her breath, she shook her head and said sadly, "All my effort, all that precious wind." David lumbered after the whale with stiff gestures and the same menacing face.

The water was still a not very appetizing brown, with patches of blue where the paint had not worn off the bottom and sides of the pool. The filter had given out again, and Ben had used the net to skim off most of the dead leaves and bits of grass and debris he had found floating. The pool had been filled, according to the instructions, just before the Rolfes had seen the house for the first time. Filled, Ben assumed, with no attempt to clean out the year's accumulated waste, some of which he could still make out in the pool's dim bottom. "It figures," he had decided, remembering the Allardyces, which he did—deliberately—infrequently.

David was close to the edge at the low end. "Now can I go in?" he said impatiently.

"In a minute," Ben replied, working the net.

"If you put chlorine in," David suggested, "it kills all the germs."

"Who's worried about germs?" Ben said, plunging in the net. "It's that lousy sea serpent I'm after."

David examined the water more carefully. "*Really?*" he said.

"Really."

Aunt Elizabeth nodded when David looked to her for confirmation. She was making another attempt at the whale.

Ben looked toward the house once more. It was too far to be sure, but he thought he saw a window being raised and Marian's figure, briefly, way at the west end. Marian or not, she had obviously found something to occupy herself somewhere in the house. To hell with her. He flipped the net onto the grass bordering the concrete rim of the pool, and said, "Okay, chief, get your tube on." There was another one, a small yellow tire all blown up, at Aunt Elizabeth's feet. David pulled it around his waist.

"What about the sea serpent?" he asked, a little dubiously.

"Must be out to lunch," Ben said. "Stay down at the low end."

David readjusted his facemask, called a muffled "Lookit me!" to Aunt Elizabeth and then ran clumsily toward the pool. He jumped into the ankle-deep water as Aunt Elizabeth called "Bravo!" and kicked his way farther out, slapping the water with his green flippers.

"Come on in!" he called to her, and she waved in reply, breaking off suddenly and shouting, "Watch out, Davey!"

Ben was running along the edge, toward the middle of the pool. David saw him leap, grab his knees, and cannonball in, hitting David with the spray. David squealed delightedly, and when Ben began to swim toward him, making threatening sounds, he squealed louder and pulled his feet in the opposite direction.

"Faster, Dave, faster!" Aunt Elizabeth was calling.

Ben grabbed a flipper, tripping David whose face hit the water. When he surfaced, Ben was swimming away, making triumphant sea serpent sounds. David dragged himself toward Aunt Elizabeth at the low end, saying, "Close call, close call."

Ben reached the center of the pool, his hands churning the water around him and sending waves against the worn rubbery lining. He raised himself, grabbing a mouthful of air, and then plunged down, his bottom, green and white stripes, sticking up and disappearing, and then his feet.

Light rippled around him, blue and gold, and as he plunged lower, a dull brown. Something was gleaming ahead of him, in the deepest part of the pool. He kicked himself lower, toward the discolored wall, and when he felt the pressure growing inside his lungs, he reached out and scooped up the source of light. It was a pair of eyeglasses, the frame rusted, one lens intact, the other shattered. He bent and pushed himself upwards, holding the glasses carefully.

David was lying on his stomach in the shallow water, waiting for Ben to reappear. He had taken off his yellow tube. Aunt Elizabeth, who had finally finished inflating the whale, held it up for David's inspection.

"How's that?" she said.

"You can use it," David replied. "I really don't need a tube. I can swim already."

"No, you can't," Aunt Elizabeth said, tossing the whale into the pool. "But I'm sure you will, before the summer's over."

David said, "Wanna bet?" He covered his face with the mask and began to flail away from her, his knees touching the floor of the pool.

Ben surfaced under the rickety diving board. He shook the water out of his ears and eyes and held the glasses close to his face. The frame was silver under the rust; the prescription, from the unshattered lens, very strong. There was a small jagged hole in the middle of the second lens, with a cracked web filling the frame, as though something had been plunged through it. The idea made his right eye tear. He turned the frame, examining it; there'd be a few small splinters of glass somewhere at the bottom of the pool. Possibly; if it had happened in the pool, whatever it was that *had* happened. He looked around for something to explain that small break in the lens, something jutting, and when he realized what it was he was trying to reconstruct, ghoulishly, a chill ran through him. The glasses must have fallen on the concrete ledge or dropped into the pool. But if that was so, why had they been left there? He brought both elbows up to the ledge to support himself, and the more he puzzled over the glasses, the more troubling they became, which, he made himself realize, was the way his mind usually worked. The curse of the footnote.

He heard Aunt Elizabeth in back of him: "David, that's deep water. Now you stop showing off."

Ben turned and saw David attempting to swim, with splashy, uncoordinated strokes, to the center of the pool where the water would be over his head.

"Ben?" Her voice shook when she raised it. "You tell that boy to come back here."

"All right, Dave, that's it," Ben said, and when he kept coming toward him, Ben placed the broken glasses close to the ledge—in plain view, where they obviously hadn't been when they were stepped on or kicked or whatever—and called out again, "That's far enough, chief. Back."

He either didn't hear him above the clumsy sounds he was making, or he was disregarding him. "Okay, wise guy," Ben said, and began to swim toward him with long, easy strokes. David saw him and stopped; when he stood up the water reached the top of his shoulders. He pulled the mask away from his face to let the sound out, his legs pedalling under him, like he'd seen Ben do. "I told you I could swim," he said breathlessly, in Aunt Elizabeth's direction.

"I believe you," she said. "Now come back where it's safe."

About ten feet away from him, Ben said, "Rule one: three foot limit; everything else is out of bounds."

David pulled the mask down and let it hang from his neck. "But I can *swim*," he protested.

"That so?" Ben said, and then he disappeared below the surface, and David could see his body, with the green and white trunks, waving underwater with the ripples and the light, and moving closer to him. He lifted his flippered feet higher, trying to float the lower part of his body and beat Ben to the low end. He was winded, sinking a little with each hard stroke and tasting chlorine somewhere in back of his nose. He turned, and as he did, something slippery touched his ankle. Then he yelled, delighted, and tried to step away from the flat shape with the pulled-back hair moving slowly around him, below his knees. Ben's hands were around his legs and David yelled again; Ben's head passed under him, forcing its way between his legs, and David could feel something strong supporting him and lifting his feet off the concrete floor. His voice rose and shook on a long, uneasy *"Ohhh . . ."* as though he were about to topple. Ben was lifting him higher and higher out of the water.

"The sea serpent!" he yelled to Aunt Elizabeth, grabbing onto Ben's forehead to balance himself.

"Thought you'd get away, hunh?" Ben said, bobbing under him. He added, "Wise guy," in an okay-let's-put-the-gloves-on tone David recognized, and then began to turn slowly, plotting something. David saw Aunt Elizabeth, who was playing appalled, and the house, and the trees and the wide bay where they'd gone swimming up until now. The water slapped Ben's stomach lightly, and David gripped his shoulders harder with his legs. He was going to flip him, like he'd done in the bay. When he saw Aunt Elizabeth again, he called out, "Help!"

Ben continued to turn silently, catching his breath and squeezing the water out of his nose, and when David looked down he saw a funny, mischievous expression on his father's face, as though he were building up to one tremendous "Boo!"

Aunt Elizabeth was watching them in the shade of the umbrella, saying "Watch it, Davey," and laughing encouragement. And then it seemed to her that Ben had lost his footing, although David could feel the shoulders tilting backward and Ben's hands pushing up against the bottom of his feet, with no warning, no warning at all. David smashed into the water and disappeared for a few thrashing seconds.

"Oh, Ben!" Aunt Elizabeth said, disapproval in the laughter.

David surfaced, coughing, and he could barely hear Ben say, "How's that grab you, hunh, Tarzan?" He turned his back to him, rubbing his eyes which were burning. A fly or a bee was buzzing around his head; it hit him and buzzed louder until he shook it loose, and when it came back, he aimed a gush of water at it, and at Ben who lowered himself and pushed toward him, shark-like. David was trying to stand. Ben was behind him and all around him, making bubbly noises, half-water, half-air. David slapped at the water and made it foam, swinging around to keep Ben in sight.

"Had enough?" Ben said. "Enough?" He kept coming at him, grabbing at his waist, and though David tried to smile in the spirit of the game, his mouth was filling with water, making him gag. And while he didn't mean it, Ben was beginning to hurt him, his fingers pinching his waist. David said, "Ow!" and then, "Come on, Dad, that hurts."

"What's the matter, can't you take it?" Ben said.

"All right, you two," Aunt Elizabeth said, and her voice

had become more commanding, "that's enough now. David, you're turning blue."

"Tell him to leave me alone," David called back.

"Benjie," she said, "you're worse than a child."

"What does she know?" Ben said and then plunged under again. David felt his hands spreading his legs and Ben's head under him, and once again he was being lifted, a little more shakily this time.

"No more, Dad," he said, but Ben didn't seem to hear; he was moving backwards into the deeper water which he had warned David against. David held on tighter, his fingers digging into the sides of Ben's face. "I give up," he pleaded, and Aunt Elizabeth could hear the fear that had come into his voice. "Dad, I give up," he repeated, more insistently.

"Ben, you're frightening him," Aunt Elizabeth said, leaning forward in her seat, and when Ben continued to move toward the center of the pool, she stood up uneasily and said, louder, "Did you hear what I said?"

"I've got him," Ben assured her. "You're not afraid, are you, sport? Not while I've got you."

His hands were cupping the bottom of David's feet, and David could feel the upward pressure beginning again. "Lemme go," David said. "I don't like this kind of game."

"Why not?" Ben said, and he was breathing hard too, "Why don't you like it?"

And before David could say anything, Ben brought his hands up with a jolt and slammed David backwards into the water.

Aunt Elizabeth was at the edge of the pool. "What's wrong with you?" she shouted angrily. Ben was watching for David to come up. "Ben! Do you hear me?"

He disregarded her, and when David came gasping to the surface, he shouted, "Here he is, here he is!" and lunged at him and pulled his hands away from his face. "Had enough? Had enough, chief?" he asked and something terrible had come into his voice, something punishing. David was trying to force the water out of his throat. "No?" Ben said. "A little more?" And to Aunt Elizabeth's horror, he lifted him and flipped him again.

"What are you doing?"

And then again.

She was standing helplessly on the ledge, her hands raised to her mouth. *"What are you doing?"*

"Just a little roughhouse. Right, Dave? Right?" David was choking, the water boiling around him as he tried to pull away from Ben. The facemask had come off, its band wound around David's wrist. "Davey knows it's all a game," Ben said, and all Aunt Elizabeth could hear was the awful threat in his voice and David's choking sounds. He grabbed for his arm and his leg. David kicked himself free, and then Ben grabbed again and started to lift him, and David, with more strength than he had ever used in his life, swung his arm viciously to protect himself and slammed Ben in the mouth with the mask.

Aunt Elizabeth had taken a step down, into the pool, speechless, as Ben cried out and dropped David. He covered his face with his hands, rocking up and down in pain. David pushed himself away, stumbling to the end of the pool while Ben stood rocking silently. Aunt Elizabeth's face had gone white, and when David reached her and threw himself against her, struggling for breath, she could barely hold him for the trembling in herself.

Ben had bent low, his hands still pressed to his face. Blood was trickling through his fingers and falling into the water, spreading itself and dissolving. He lowered his hands slowly and looked at the blood, then up at Aunt Elizabeth and David whose body was shaking with great sobs.

The water smacked against the sides of the pool, and it was a long while before Ben could find the voice to call, in fear and disbelief, "Dave . . . ?" And then again, "Dave . . . ?" On the second one, barely audible, the voice snapped, like something in his head.

(7)

There was a dream—the playback of an image really—which had been recurring, whenever he was on the verge of illness, ever since his childhood. The dream itself was a symptom of illness, as valid as an ache or a queasy feeling or a fever. The details were always the same: the throbbing first, like a heartbeat, which became the sound of a motor idling; then the limousine; then, behind the tinted glass, the vague figure of the chauffeur.

He could trace, with some certitude, the genesis of the nightmare, or the image. When he was young, he had seen a black limousine idling outside his building, in the rain. There had been a death in a neighboring apartment, the first death he could remember hearing about, and the limousine had come for the family. The sound stuck in his head, and the image, all black and gray, and even now if Ben were asked: What's death?—he'd have to say a black limousine with its motor idling and a chauffeur waiting behind the tinted glass. Only half joking, or a quarter.

On the two occasions when he had been given an anaesthetic, it was the same image, appearing at the last moment of consciousness, that had finally put him under.

It had come to him again tonight—at least the beginnings of it: the throbbing, like a first, alarming wave of sickness. It stopped as soon as he opened his eyes—the sound did, anyway; the throbbing persisted as a sharp pain between his eyes, somewhere in the middle of his head. He got out of bed quietly and paced a while; then went downstairs and paced a while longer on the terrace, looking in the direction of the pool which was invisible beyond the dark slope of the lawn.

When Marian found him, he was sitting in the living room, just outside the lamp's small circle of light. She was wearing a green silk robe over her nightgown.

"How long have you been down here?" she asked him from the doorway, and she made it sound very gentle and sympathetic.

"I don't know," Ben said. He was playing with a cigarette, shaping the lighted end in the small rose medallion bowl he was using as an ashtray.

"It's after two."

"Is it?"

She was obviously intruding, but she came toward him anyway, the silk billowing. "Did you sleep at all?"

He shrugged and said, "Some."

"Want to come back and try some more?"

"In a while, maybe."

She stood beside him for a moment; his upper lip was split and swollen, and he was having trouble drawing on the cigarette. "Must you smoke?" she said.

"Why?" he asked, without looking up. "Is it wrong for the room?"

She smiled and let it pass, lowering herself in front of the armchair and laying her hand on his bare knee which was sticking out from under the terrycloth robe. A breeze blew in through the open terrace door, smelling of rain. Marian gripped his knee and then ran her hand down his leg, soothingly. "Brooding about it isn't going to help, you know."

He waited before he said, dully, "What is?"

"Look," she said, and her hand tightened on his leg for emphasis, "can I say it again? It was bound to get out of control sooner or later. I've seen the way you two fool around. You're too rough. How many times have I told you that?"

"This wasn't the same thing," Ben said, as though he had already said it several times that day.

"Ben, of course it was. The roughhouse just got out of hand."

"Roughhouse, hunh?"

"That's the word."

"You weren't *there*, for Chrissake." He stubbed his cigarette roughly, splitting it, and Marian tried not to be distracted by the rose medallion bowl, or the tiny heaps of ash on the surface of the table which was japanned maple.

"No," she admitted guiltily, "I wasn't there."

"I can't get it out of my head," Ben said. "Christ, it's all I can think about."

"That's just the trouble," Marian said.

He leaned forward and reached for her wrist. "I swear, Marian, I don't understand what happened to me out there. Maybe I blacked out or went crazy or something, I don't know—but I couldn't control myself, I didn't know what I was doing. Hell, it's worse. I *did* know, and I couldn't stop myself. That's the most frightening part of it. *Why?* Why would I want to hurt my own son?"

"I told you, Ben, that's ridiculous."

"It's not," he insisted, "it's the truth. I wanted to hurt him. *Davey*. Jesus! What if I—?"

"What if you *nothing*," she cut him off. "Ben, look—David is all right." She was speaking clearly and deliberately, as if there were a hospital bed between them. "He's all right."

"How can he be all right after what I tried to do to him?"

"Darling, that's all in your mind."

"It's *not* in my mind." He pulled his hand away suddenly and then brought it up to his mouth and rubbed his upper lip with that painfully reflective, distant look she'd seen in him all day. The breeze was constant now, rising and moving the heavy drapes, faded blue, which she intended to change eventually or at least attempt to repair. He was silent a long while, and so was Marian, listening to the wind and the metallic tap of a chain against a lamp bulb. Finally, Ben asked, very quietly, "What did Aunt Elizabeth tell you?"

Marian shrugged. "Nothing more than you heard her tell me," she said. "Sometimes you're worse than a child yourself; you don't know when to stop." She smiled. "Amen."

If it was a lie, then it was one that had to be closer to the actual truth. Aunt Elizabeth was, after all, seventy-four; there had to be some inaccuracy in what she saw and heard, and said (on occasion she rambled, Marian had recently discovered). What she *had* said, when Marian had pressed her, approximated what Ben himself was saying now. Except for his deliberately wanting to hurt David. She never even suggested that; and if she thought as much and were keeping it from Marian—if that suspicion was what had sent her to her room and kept her there for a good part of the day—well, it made no more sense to Marian than what Ben, overwhelmed with guilt, had somehow brought himself to believe. Insanely. The idea was inconceivable.

"And Davey . . . ?" he asked quietly.

"Resilient," she said; "you saw that." Ben had avoided him until Marian had literally pushed them at each other, and the embrace was, for Ben, premature and painful. Later, resilient or not, David bolted down his dinner, and instead of spending the evening in front of the television set in the library, went up to his room.

"As far as he's concerned," Marian continued, "it's exactly what I said it was. The roughhouse got out of hand; you tried to teach him a lesson and you went too far, both of you. Which is all that *did* happen, whether I was there to see it or not." She waited for Ben to react, and at least she had penetrated enough for him to look at her; in his face she could read, if not immediate belief, then something like a plea for reassurance. She touched his lip very lightly. "He got himself a good scare and you got yourself a fat lip. Let's leave it at that and not spend the rest of the summer brooding. Okay, darling?"

The smell of rain had grown stronger, filling the room. In a minute it would pour, and while she kept her eyes on Ben's face and continued to touch him tenderly, she couldn't help thinking, *Windows; which windows were open?* And at the same time, *Why should something like that distract her now?* She tried to put it out of her mind, and with it the sudden, unnerving thought that she might be minimizing the incident for the sake of the house, to protect their summer. But what she had been saying to Ben was sincere, unquestionably sincere, she assured herself. The idea that he would hurt David was absurd, and it had to be somehow providential that she hadn't seen the incident (thank God for Mrs. Allardyce) and could be reasonable about it and objective.

She brushed her hair back against her temple, repeating the motion several times. Ben watched her and then ran the back of his fingers against her hair.

"What if it's not a joke anymore, Marian?" he said. "Not another car incident, or keys, or missing exam papers. What if it's finally happened . . . ?" He snapped his fingers. "Just like that. Hell, how long can you be on the verge of it?"

"Of what?"

"It's called a breakdown."

"Oh, for God's sake, Ben—"

"I blacked out, Marian." He leaned closer and looked directly at her. "Whether you believe it or not, that's exactly what happened. I didn't know what I was doing."

"And you don't know what you're saying now either. It's the same thing, isn't it? And if I let it go, you'll brood over it and embellish it until you really make yourself sick over it. The knots, honey—they're all packed away, remember? We left them back in town with the Byrons and MacKenzies and the piano and The Supervisor." She touched the arm of the chair which was covered in yellow damask and lifted her eyes to the fretted valances over the windows. "This," she said, with that reverence that always came into her voice when she spoke about the house, "this is where we came to unwind." She got up slowly and held her hand out to him. "Come and sleep with me."

It had happened, though, and exactly the way he remembered it, whatever she chose to believe. And if all the knots had been left behind, well, one of them had managed to slip past the double pillars.

He took Marian's hand and held on for a moment. "It'll pass," he said. "Just give me a while longer."

"Promise?"

It came down with a strong rush of wind before he could reply, hammering on the metal chairs and the glass-topped table out on the terrace. "My God," she said, "listen to it!" She slipped her hand out of his and walked quickly to the open door. It was coming down even harder now, the wind blowing her hair and her robe and filling the room with a green, steaming smell. Marian pushed the glass door closed and watched the rain stream against the panes.

"We need it," she said. "Everything outside was bone dry." The dim lights across the bay had disappeared completely.

Ben hadn't moved. She came back to the chair and said, "I've got to get those upstairs windows," apologetically.

"Go ahead," he said.

"You'll be all right?"

He nodded and smiled up at her. "I won't do anything to wreck your summer. Promise."

"*Our* summer," she said. She bent and kissed his forehead. "It was all working so beautifully, Ben. Everything we could ever want." She searched his face; the look was just a little less inward. "Trust me. Please?"

"Get those windows," he said.

She left the room quickly, pulling the silk robe around her tighter.

Ben lit another cigarette and sat listening to the sounds outside, steady, muted by the glass. The pool came into his mind again, and the image of David slamming backwards into the water. And Aunt Elizabeth standing at the other end, the water covering her shoes. He tried to call it all back, to reconstruct what might have been in his mind during that terrible five minutes or ten or whatever. It was still blank. A part of his mind, like something separate and beyond his control, had closed itself off from him. And if it should happen again, and again . . . ?

The rain continued to beat down against the windows and the flagstone, and poured with a steady rhythm down the gutters. And for a few moments then, the sounds blended, and if he listened closely Ben could make out a low, steady beat, like a throbbing, outside the windows which were dark, like tinted glass.

When Marian woke up the next morning, Ben was sleeping soundly beside her. She raised the windows on bright morning sunlight (it had rained through the night) and an incredibly sweet, fresh smell, put on her shirt and jeans, and left the bedroom. David's door across the hall was open; she went in quietly, opened the window and covered him with the sheet he had thrown off. Aunt Elizabeth's door was closed.

The dinner tray in Mrs. Allardyce's room had been untouched. In six days she had eaten, if that was the word, just once, and carrying up the tray and then bringing it down again was becoming an almost ritual gesture for Marian. Yesterday, rather than pour the untouched soup down the drain, she had reheated it and drunk it herself. She'd do the same with the chicken today. Somehow it made Mrs. Allardyce's fast less disturbing to her.

There were puddles on the terrace, where she brought her eye-opening cup of coffee, and the lawn reaching down to the bay sparkled, a little greener than it had been. The pool was off to the right, the poolhouse just partially visible below the rise. She placed the cup on the balustrade and found herself walking over the cool, wet grass toward the pool—toward the incident really. She stopped suddenly on the small rise.

The water had overflowed the pool a bit, running over the concrete border and into the grass. It was clear in the pool, bright turquoise, and the metal rails descending were polished and shining. The concrete border was level and uncracked, and a wide swatch of grass around it, which had absorbed the overflow, was a deep, rich green. Marian moved closer, fascinated by the transformation.

She could hear the filter from the poolhouse humming steadily, with the same sound, only stronger, that she recognized from the sitting room. Ben had been struggling with it vainly for days, she recalled.

She walked around the perimeter. The debris had all been filtered out overnight, and finally she could see clear to the bottom which, like the sides, appeared freshly painted. She went closer and almost stepped on something near the edge

of the pool. She bent and picked up the pair of shattered
eyeglasses Ben had retrieved, and examined them. Ben wore
reading glasses, not at all like them; and while Aunt Elizabeth
should, she didn't. Marian thought about slipping them into
her pocket—that was pointless; instead she threw them into
the trashcan beside the poolhouse. The pool itself was absorbing all her attention.

How could it have happened so suddenly? The rain? The
filter which had fallen into gear at last, on its own? That might
explain the clarity of the water, possibly even the lining of
the pool which may have been caked brown by the dirt. But
the pavement, she *knew*, had been cracked and uneven. She
searched for some traces, pausing at the rails which had
become steady and unrusted. There were, of course, any
number of explanations. (She had once heard, from friends
of theirs in Valley Stream, of a backyard pool rising ten feet
out of the ground at one end, with the spring thaw. This was
the same thing, in reverse. Wasn't it?) Any number of explanations, and reasonable, all of them. And all of them, she realized, she was rehearsing for Ben, if he should see the pool,
which she would prefer he didn't.

Why?

She brought Mrs. Allardyce's breakfast tray up earlier than
usual, as soon as she had hurried in from the pool. She closed
the door behind her and set the tray down.

There was a table now, along the left wall, which Marian
had brought up from the living room where it had been hidden
near the greenhouse alcove. It was small and exquisite, with
a scalloped top formed by the odd turreted frame; on it was
a tall Sèvres vase filled with roses from one of the few bushes
that were blooming. There were roses in the Canton bowl as
well, and clouds of asparagus fern. Marian had placed it, on
its pedestal, beside the carved door.

The room calmed her almost immediately. Despite the
intimidation she had felt initially, the sitting room, separate
and quiet except for the soothing hum, was becoming the
one part of the house where she felt most completely at ease

and most private. To Marian it had become the very center of the house, the room closest to the core, just as the rounded bay, somewhere beyond the carved door, was architecturally the house's unifying principal. Everything about the room had become pleasing—the light, the peace, the vast, empty stretches which seemed to be waiting for the imposition of some personality.

She moved around it, turning off the night lamp and opening the drapes, and with every motion a bit more of the uneasiness she had felt beside the pool passed away. She skirted the table where the photographs stood polished and rearranged (by her) on the velvet covering.

From the rear windows she could see the pool, a bright turquoise rectangle, framed with white. She looked at it a long time, brushing the hair back against her temples. There was a transformation, that was clear enough; but from the vantage point of the sitting room, there was more wonder than shock or surprise in her reaction. The pool was now exactly as it should have been all along, and that, some part of herself insisted, was the most important consideration.

She turned away from the pool and looked across the room at the intricate rose window the door's carved pattern had become.

But there was another part, another voice, still filled with shock and surprise, that was resisting the insight and clarity the room was trying to give her. There had been the incident with Ben and David, and then the transformation, overnight.

It was absurd, totally unreasonable, to associate the two; as absurd as Ben's retelling of the incident. And to accept it would be to accept the presence of some inexplicable malevolence. And what then? Flight? Give up the house? *The house?*

She lifted her eyes to the cornice above the door and the gold silk covering the walls. What sort of malevolence could there be in something so perfect, something that could draw her so irresistibly, until it seemed almost an extension of herself?

It was Ben's failing: seizing on something, magnifying and distorting it; manufacturing complexity.

The pool was as it should be. And maybe if she stared at the door long and hard enough and lost herself in the hum, she'd accept it without question, for the wonderful mystery it might be.

Ben slept late. Marian had over an hour to put the finishing touches on the large, panelled library she was setting up for him. She put the textbooks he'd be using on the oval Hepplewhite desk, beautifully grained mahogany with a red leather top, and on the Hepplewhite library table in the center of the room, under the gilt-bronze chandelier. The center of the ceiling was coved, set off by a circular band of stucco molding. She unpacked his set of Arden Shakespeare, even though there were several impressive sets, large and beautifully bound, in the bookcases that lined one end of the room; Chaucer, and commentaries on the *Canterbury Tales*; and a whole brace of nineteenth and twentieth century novels, some of which Marian had read.

She wanted everything just right for him, a perfect retreat out of bounds to all of them. And whether it was the work that was absorbing her, or the reassurance she had found in the sitting room, the mystery of the pool seemed less pressing at the moment. She accepted it, and the only possible difficulty would be Ben's reaction to the transformation. If somehow she could manage to keep him away from it, or at least prepare him.

She met him in the entrance hall where the rug, another project, was still rolled against the wall.

"Morning," she said, studying the mood.

He said, "Morning," and reached out and hugged her. "I overslept."

He was holding onto her, tightly. "You were out cold when I got up," she said. "That's a good sign." She drew back a little. "How are you feeling?"

"Better," he said, dismissing it. "David up?"

"Nope. Just me. I've been puttering around for hours; inside, outside." She moved away and reached for his hand. "Want to see?"

She led him toward the study, wondering whether she should mention the pool. What could she say? That she'd been out, polishing the rails; that she'd managed, with a fumbling competence that shocked her, to get the filter going, and it was incredible the difference that made?

She said, "Close eyes," when they reached the library door, opened it and said, "All yours," watching with pleasure as he examined the books and ran his hand over the polished wood of the desk. "Like it?"

"It's great," he said, and finally there was a full, untroubled smile.

She pointed to a table beside the window. "Typewriter's there, paper too. Your attaché case is next to the desk." She pulled open drawers, cataloguing, "Yellow pads, pens, writing paper, envelopes. That television goes; I'll set up something in the servants' quarters. It's wrong for the room anyway, you should forgive the expression." She came up to him and threw her arms around him, rubbing her fingers against the back of his neck. "Nothing to distract you, nothing to disturb you. Your very own turf."

He tightened his lips and nodded, impressed. "Now," he said, "if we could just think of something for me to do."

"You've got loads to do. There are two new courses, and if Byron's pressing on that Master's, well, now's as good a time as any to start thinking about it."

"You don't just think about a Master's."

"Whatever you do with it. I'm dumb, remember?" He smiled again and she said, "Do that a little more around here, hunh?" She kissed him, and what kind of malevolence could there be in a house where she felt such warmth and tenderness? "It's okay, Benjie, isn't it?"

"The room?"

"Everything. Yesterday's such a long time ago that I'm not even sure it ever happened. Let's start all over, hunh?"

He raised his eyes and looked at the rows of leather-bound books. "It's a good room," he said. "Thanks."

They heard Aunt Elizabeth's voice calling down the corridor: "Anybody?"

"In here," Marian called back; "Ben's study."

She appeared in the doorway, carrying the almost-finished watercolor she'd been working on; her other arm was around David's shoulder. He was carrying her paint box. She nudged him into the room.

"David's decided to take up painting," she announced. Her voice was strained and her face pallid under the large sunhat. "We're off to search out a view after breakfast. Isn't that so, David?"

He said, "Yes," shyly, sneaking looks at Ben and trying not to look too hard at the bruise on his face. Aunt Elizabeth gave him another small push.

"Isn't this nice?" she said, inspecting the room. She had slept fitfully and it showed in her walk as well.

"And out of bounds to all of us," Marian warned. "Daddy's got work to do."

"Marvelous room," Aunt Elizabeth said, "good vibrations. Don't you feel that, David?"

David said, "Uh-hunh," and stayed close to Aunt Elizabeth, shifting the paint box to his left hand.

Ben held out his hand, a little stiffly, smiled, and said, "Come on in, Dave." Marian and Aunt Elizabeth watched without saying anything. David took a few hesitant steps forward, and when Ben asked, "Friends again?" he nodded very positively, as though that's all he'd been waiting for, and threw himself into Ben's arms, really meaning it this time.

Marian let out a relieved sigh. "Hey, everybody!" she called out, "I've got a great idea. A picnic lunch; someplace we haven't even explored yet. Maybe that rickety old summer pavilion."

"With a game of softball," Ben added. "How'd you like that, Dave?"

David said, "Great!" enthusiastically.

"Girls against the boys," Aunt Elizabeth said, and Ben clapped his hands and said, "We'll clobber them, right, Dave?"

"Right!" David said, and softball struck him as a really fine idea, better even than painting with Aunt Elizabeth. Either way, he wouldn't have to go anywhere near the pool.

She had, as she suspected, been magnifying the problem. Ben didn't see the pool, not that day which was warm, cloudless and perfect for a picnic. ("It's worth the whole summer, isn't it?" Marian said, lying back on the grass; "just this moment?" Ben agreed.) And not the next day which was gray and threatening; providentially, as far as Marian was concerned. He began to spend his time in the library, more and more each day. And while the dark mood had passed, she noticed a certain distraction in him which she attributed to whatever he was working on behind the closed library door. She mentioned it at one point and he said, "I didn't sleep much last night," and changed the subject.

Aunt Elizabeth finished her seascape, *L'Été*, which she would show to Mrs. Allardyce whenever she might appear. She set up her easel near the summer pavilion for a picture to be called *Temps Perdu*, or *Time Past*. It would be moody and impressionistic, she decided, "representing loss." She avoided the pool, and so did David who became briefly interested in his painting lessons, then bored, wondering where all the neighborhood kids hung out, and why hadn't they been smart enough to bring his bike with them for the summer. He spent a good deal of time in the sewing room where Marian had sent the ancient television set. Once, Marian took time out from the greenhouse, which she had finally gotten to, and watched him try to swim in the bay. Ben had said, "No. Busy," through the closed door when she had asked him to come along.

Once again, just as Marian began to feel some concern about Mrs. Allardyce, she found the napkin unfolded on the lunch tray, and the soup dish nearly empty.

She stayed in the sitting room for hours at a time, locking the outer door now, even though no one had come near it in the nine days they'd been in the house. Mrs. Allardyce remained invisible, and there was still no sound but the hum behind the carved door. The room had been empty, shapeless except for the wingchair and the table of photographs (which Marian arranged and rearranged with endless fascination). And of course the door. She was filling it now, shaping it, with no interference, with a silence that had to indicate approval on Mrs. Allardyce's part, shaping it to her own taste. She had carried up small consoles and endtables and enameled chests from other parts of the house; and Chinese bowls and vases, Dresden figurines, and delicate Venetian glass, most of which had been hidden in closets or coated with dust.

She had even steeled herself one morning and gone down to the basement which, as the Allardyces had said, went on and on, with narrow passages and sub-basements and locked steel doors. It was dark and damp and frightening, with sheeted, spectral heaps shadowy against the stone walls. As she suspected, there were treasures among the broken tables and andirons and piles of ancient magazines (and, spookily, rusted wheelchairs, two of them). She salvaged a round Italian mirror in a gilded frame, a beautiful rococo piece, which she hung in the sitting room and flanked with bronze wall sconces.

It never occurred to Marian to question the reason behind the activity, or the secrecy of it all. It was giving her pleasure and enormous satisfaction; the most complete expression of her responsibility to the house and to Mrs. Allardyce. And if it should manage to draw the old woman out of the bedroom finally, that would be gratifying of course, but purely incidental. Or reasonably incidental.

Ben, fortunately, was spending as much time in the library, and David had rediscovered his "Hot Wheels" toy and, miraculously, was reading for something approaching pleasure. Gradually, they were finding a routine, casual and refreshing, and gradually too the pool incident would fade completely, and that would become part of the routine as well, with enough time elapsed to make the transformation less conspicuous; she hoped.

Marian never left the grounds. Once or twice she thought about a trip, preferably secret, to the local drugstore, wherever that might be. There was a bit of gray now, easily concealed, at the base of her neck. The problem was becoming less momentous, however, the more she got involved in the house.

Ben went into town once during the week, for milk and the mail (the larder, packed with the Allardyces' beneficence, was holding up beautifully). When he returned he found Marian winding the clocks and actually succeeding in making the brass Regency clock on the mantel work for exactly three minutes; the "Hallelujah!" died on her lips.

"I'll get it eventually," she swore; "all of them."

Ben had that same, vaguely distracted look. He was complaining about the driveway again. "It's barely passable," he said.

"So you've told me. Why not fool around with the clippers?" She pinched his cheeks. "Get rid of some of that scholar's pallor."

He found the clippers, spent a few hours trimming the foliage, and then, overwhelmed by the magnitude of the job, gave up. He wondered what the hell they would do in a week or so.

"Hole up and disappear," Marian said later. "Everything we need is right here."

From the way she said it, Ben couldn't quite tell whether she was kidding or not.

One night, toward the end of their second week in the house, Marian came into the bedroom late—after midnight; she had been working in the sitting room since nine. The lamps were on beside the bed; Ben's side was rumpled, with a paperbound copy of *The American* open, print-side down. His clothes were thrown on the chair—pants, shirt, shorts; the bathroom was empty. Marian started to unbutton her shirt, walking toward the window.

The past two nights, when she'd finally come to bed, he had been asleep; both times she was aware of movement in the middle of the night, and when she stretched out her right arm, he wasn't beside her. He was, he admitted, sleeping badly; but it would pass.

The outside lights, she saw from the window, were on, flooding the terrace. When she looked down and couldn't find him, she buttoned her shirt again and went downstairs.

There was a breeze on the terrace and the lights across the bay were soft and blueish. She could hear leaves and the sound of crickets. She called, "Ben?" very lightly, several times, and was about to go in and check the library, when a bit of light appeared in the distance, below the rise of lawn. He was at the pool.

She left the terrace and walked across the lawn, out of the light spilling over from the terrace, faster as she approached the rise.

There was a single lightbulb on, hanging at the door of the poolhouse which was gray and shadowy against the vague outline of trees. Ben was standing at the edge of the pool, his white terrycloth robe catching the pale light. Marian stopped and watched him for a moment; the uneasiness about the pool, which she had all but forgotten, settled in her stomach again. But just briefly: the water was dark, flecked with bits of moving light, and the rails and concrete border barely visible. She called out to him, her voice sounding unnaturally loud in the silence.

"I didn't feel like sleeping," he explained when she had come beside him.

She looked up at the sky and the stars she could see all the way to the horizon. "Beautiful, isn't it?" she said. "Just like Northern Boulevard."

The water was lapping the side of the pool, lazily. Ben was silent, not moving, and Marian tried to divorce what she had seen in daylight from what was visible now. The filter working in the poolhouse was the only aspect of the transformation that might draw his attention.

"For a minute I got worried," she said, and slipped her hand under his arm. "I'm hooked, I suppose; I don't like going to bed without you."

He half-turned to her. "That's what I've been thinking lately."

She made the pause long enough to seem contrite. "I'm sorry, darling. I got involved as usual." Her head touched his shoulder. "Be patient with me. You know what I'm like with a new toy." She caught a view of the house behind them, distant but still massive, with the floodlights fanning upward and washing the gray shingles white.

"I don't know what you're doing," he said, still staring at the water. "Christ, it's a rented house, it's two months . . ."

"Don't remind me." He had said it casually, with no particular emotion, but there was resentment under the long pauses, she felt, and her closeness seemed discomforting to him. She wrapped her arm around his, tighter, and there was no response. "Is that what's behind all the heavy thoughts? The fact that I've been spending a lot of time with the house, not enough with you?"

"There are no heavy thoughts, Marian."

"Sure about that?"

"Sure." It was his drop-it tone, and he punctuated it with a little pressure around her arm, like a reassuring pat. He moved away from her, walking along the edge of the pool and looking at the water as though something had been lost in it and might suddenly reappear, luminous in the darkness. He stopped. "It's a while since I've been down here," he said.

"I know." It was that too, then; still. The scene of the imaginary crime. An inflection could trigger it all over again. She walked up to him. "Silly, isn't it? I mean, how many people *dream* of having their own pool?"

"And how many people . . . ?" he thought about adding, but dropped it and said, "Filter's going," instead.

"Yes," Marian said.

"How'd you manage that?"

"I haven't the slightest idea. Pushed a button, turned a knob, and gave it one hell of a kick. Sheer coincidence." She waited for some kind of skeptical reaction; when it didn't come she continued, more confidently: "I also polished the chrome, plucked the weeds and scrubbed the concrete." She sniffed loudly. "Smell it? The lemon oil?" At least he was smiling. "It's lovely now. We really ought to think about floodlights or something. Like that pool in Bermuda. Remember?" She wrapped her arms around him again, swaying. "Perfumed nights. Water lapping sensuously in the dark. Hot stuff, all of it." Her hands had slipped under the robe, touching his stomach; she rested her face against his back. "Benjie?" she said. "A deal? You don't lock me out and I won't lock you out. No secrets, no dark thoughts. That's for mushrooms. What is it, baby? Just once more."

She could feel him take a deep breath, under her hands, and then feel the sound of his voice against her face. "I wanted to come down here," he said, "just to see if I could."

"And?"

"I could, it turns out. That's some kind of progress, isn't it?"

"I thought there'd been more. I thought we'd forgotten all about it."

"We tried. Sometimes ... sometimes I get this feeling there's a small button somewhere on me. Red, if I want to elaborate it. And on this button there's a label ... 'Self-destruct.' And it's got to be on the bottom of my feet or on my rump, or someplace where it gets used a hell of a lot."

"I haven't found it," she said. Her hands slid under the top of his suit. "And I know all about the bottom of your feet." She squeezed a bit of flesh and said, "You're getting flabby," which made him turn with a nice, deflated smile. "That's all I'm worried about."

He put his arms around her and pulled her closer. "And you're getting grayer by the day."

"That's middle age for you."

"Poor Marian, poor little hausfrau—"

"Don't make fun." She buried her face against his neck. How much grayer? She hadn't looked today.

He shook his head sympathetically and she could feel the muscles in his neck tighten. "You really stuck yourself with something of a kook. A loser."

"You're not a loser. As for being a kook, well, that makes two of us."

"That it does," he said.

"It *is* better though, isn't it, Benjie—kook to kook, if that's all that's available? Better than moody walks in the dark?"

He drew back from her, looked directly at her, and said, "It's better. When it's available."

"It's always available." She snapped the elastic on his suit. "Your suit's on. Why not jump in something wet?" He looked at the pool. "It's just water. Honest."

He let her push the robe off his shoulders.

"Go on, Ben. It'll be lovely."

He turned and she held the robe while he pulled his arms out of it and went to the edge of the pool. He was pinching his nose nervously. She watched him hesitate, draw in a mouthful of air, hesitate again, and finally plunge in, hitting the dark water as hard as he could. "That's it," she said, relieved, "that's it."

He surfaced at the other end, a dim, sputtering head, and two white shoulders. He pushed himself forward and swam back, cutting through the water almost soundlessly. Marian met him at the edge as he lifted himself out, throwing his right leg over the side.

"Better, right?" she said.

"Better." He was shivering, breathing hard.

She crouched beside him and wiped his face with the robe.

"It's warm," he said, "soft." He lay back, pillowing himself on the robe. Marian ran her finger down his chest, drawing letters lightly.

"And simple, wasn't it, after all?"

He was still drawing deep breaths, his chest rising and falling rapidly. He said, "No."

She lay on her side, beside him, with her face on his wet shoulder. They were silent a while and then Marian mentioned the apartment and the piano and the bowling balls on the ceiling, and wouldn't it be funny, and appropriate, to look back at the house and find the Supervisor perched in one of the windows, and did Ben really miss any of it, and of course he didn't. What was there to miss? What, when you came down to it, had they left behind that was worth missing, measured against what they'd found here? And whatever they said sounded intimate and secret in the silence, and true, with nothing but that enormous sky over them. She could feel him loosening, and herself as well, and it was like those first dips in the bay for him, refreshing and therapeutic. So therapeutic that his hand started wandering over her body, under her shirt, and he swung his right leg over her.

"None of that stuff now," she said.

He said, "Why not?"

"Because we're relaxing."

He kept his hand where it was, with an occasional foray under the bra which she didn't resist immediately.

"Don't you miss it occasionally?" he asked.

"Let you know when I do, okay?" She slapped his hand and sat up, shaking her hair loose and then smoothing it back against her temples. "God, that water looks good," she said.

"Why don't you try it?"

"I don't have my suit."

He raised himself on one elbow and played with the back of her hair. "Go bare-assed," he whispered loudly.

"Ben!" She looked at the house as though it might have overheard him.

"Why not? There's no one to see."

"I couldn't."

"It's a great feeling."

She thought about it briefly, inclining her head like a scale. "It's late," she said, rejecting the idea. "We really ought to be getting back."

"Getting back to what? Christ, I really am competing with

a house." He sat up and scrutinized her. "You're a prude at heart. That's something I never knew before."

"I'm not a prude."

"Then go bare-assed."

She sighed, relenting a little.

"What if I go first?" Without waiting for a reply, he reached down and pulled his trunks off. The pavement was cool under him, and smooth and even, which didn't seem to strike him as odd. "That make it easier for you?"

"This is awfully adolescent," she said, just on the edge of a protective giggle.

"Well," Ben said, "consider the source." He reached for her shirt and started to undo the buttons. Marian offered no resistance, but she found herself stealing self-conscious looks at the house and the two windows at the very end with their soft red glow. Her shirt was open. She looked down, said, "Oh, why not?" finally decisive, and slipped out of it; then stood up and took off the shoes and jeans, turning her back to the house while she undid her bra.

"Everything," Ben ordered when she hesitated. "Drawers too."

"Will it aid in the therapy?"

"It'll aid a lot."

She shivered when she got them off and leaped into the pool clumsily. Ben grimaced and shook his head, feeling the slap of the water against his own stomach. When she surfaced undamaged he called, "Okay?"

"Fine," she called back breathlessly. He dove in.

She was gliding toward him. "Sometimes," she said, raising her face out of the water, "you manage a good idea or two."

"Feel liberated?"

"Very."

She turned gracefully and began to swim the length of the pool, feeling the water, just nicely cool, between her legs. Ben swam beside her, turned with her under the diving board, and then quickened his stroke, fading in front of her.

Marian swam facing the house, barely stirring the water. He was waiting in the center of the pool, the water just below his chest. He bent when she reached him and leaned back, letting her body slide against his, and then wrapping his arms around her.

"All we need," he said, "is something lush on the sound-track."

She relaxed against him. "Wonderful, isn't it?" she said, a little winded; "not having to dodge bodies or contend with transistors? No beefy types kicking sand in your face and winning me. Ever think we'd live in such luxury?"

"I never gave it much thought," Ben replied.

"Why would they give it up, I wonder—the Allardyces?"

Ben made a sound of distaste at the mention of the name. He had put them very effectively out of mind.

"They've been very good to us," Marian said in protest. "Where are they, do you think?"

"I never gave that much thought," Ben replied.

He raised her to a standing position and moved back a bit, passing his hands over her shoulders and then down to her breasts. She watched him without moving, part of her enjoying the sensation and the novelty of being naked beside him in the pool, another part self-conscious and very much aware of the house behind them.

"Seems like an awfully long time between visits," he said quietly. "I've missed them."

He pressed closer. Her hair was flat and straight, her eyes larger and bluer, even in the dim light. He gave her a long, quiet look, very close now, and kissed her. She felt him moving against her, and as the touch became more pleasurable and seductive, the uneasiness welled up inside her. When he tried to kiss her again, her arms stiffened against his chest.

"None of that stuff now," she whispered.

"Who's to see?"

Her eyes narrowed a bit, playing suspicious. "There wasn't any kind of ulterior motive in all this, was there?"

"Like what?" he asked innocently. He bent low, bringing

the water up to their necks. "Just a little harmless water sport, something to get the circulation going."

"My circulation's fine."

"It's mine that I'm worried about."

She wriggled free and swam a few sidestrokes away from him, while he called, "Hey!" and "Come on, babe, why ruin the mood?"

"What one of us needs, I suspect, is a nice cold shower. Great for the circulation." She slapped water in his direction and backed away toward the polished rails.

Ben turned his face and held his hands out against the spray. "Tell you a little secret," he said; "one of us has been taking nice cold showers. Lots of them lately."

"Poor baby." She scooped one last handful at him and pulled herself up out of the pool while he lunged and caught at the water. He called her back in and she said, "Not on your life." She scraped the water off her shoulders and arms and began to wring out her hair, leaning sideways, with her back to the house. Ben wound his arms around the rails, which were firm, and if he was aware of anything unusual, the game Marian seemed to be playing halted any comment.

"You were the one with romantic ideas," he reminded her. "Bermuda?"

"That," she said, gesturing toward the middle of the pool, "is not what we did in Bermuda."

"A chaste kiss," Ben said; "What's wrong with that?"

"It's not the kiss that stirred me; it's the underwater liberty."

"Christ, you sound like a schoolgirl. We're married, remember?"

She picked up his robe and asked, "Can I use this to dry?"

He climbed out while she rubbed herself. She was bending, drying her legs. Ben came closer, the water rolling down his body, and pulled her up gently by the elbow.

"I don't get it," he said. "I'm not saying it's got to be fireworks after nine years, but—at least a vestige of excitement. Hell, we've got a year or two before the climacteric."

She let him brush the wet strands of hair away from her face and pass his thumbs over her eyebrows.

"I keep trying to figure out what it is that's made me so repulsive all of a sudden."

"You're not repulsive," she said, "you're incredibly sexy." She gave him a quick kiss on the mouth, and to Ben it was like a pacifier plugging an infant.

"Do you mean that, Marian?"

"I mean it."

"And the—what do we call it? The distance . . . ?"

She lowered her eyes to the robe bundled in her hand. "If I've been out of it a little . . . I'm sorry." She looked up again and smiled. "Change of water maybe, change of clime."

"Any chance of getting a little more reassurance than that?" His hands were moving against her back, and Marian responded by nodding at the terrycloth robe.

"Let me finish drying," she said. "I'm all goosebumps."

"Sure it's the cold?"

"Positive."

His hands continued to caress her back. "Ben honey," she started to protest, "this is hardly the place—"

"You name it then. Where *is* the place?" She raised her eyes and sighed. Ben's voice became very soft and pleading. "A little reassurance, Marian . . . ?" His arms tightened around her and his lips brushed her neck and then opened on her mouth. Marian drew in her breath sharply and turned her face away from him. "You're impossible," she said, trying to make it sound light and teasing, and giving his back a weak hammering with one fist.

"Just a little," he said again. His mouth was on her ear. She tilted her head and brought her shoulder up against the side of her face.

"Behave," she said, with that same uneasy lightness, and what did he have to do to make her take him seriously, to realize that he did need her, did need the reassurance?

He started to guide her off the concrete ledge and onto the grass, where it was soft and darker. He could feel her stiffen and a tightness creep into her voice. "Ben, please," she said, "I really don't want to."

"Why not?"

"I just *don't*."

"We won't do anything," he whispered; "promise. Just lie together, like before."

He held her closer, his hands covering her back, and for just a moment she felt herself loosening, until the house appeared above his shoulder, and the red draped windows, like a floodlight suddenly let loose on them. She said, "Ben . . ." and it came out like a warning. Her eyes were fixed on the windows, and if she concentrated hard enough she could see the carved door beyond the windows and hear the hum, like the sound of the filter somewhere behind her. And what she wanted more than anything right now was somehow to be able to project herself into the peace and insulation of that room, to elevate herself above his touch and the stifling closeness.

She felt the grass under her and Ben's weight forcing her down. She said, "Ben!" even more urgently, covering the sound of her own name and whatever it was he was pleading. He was lowering her to the grass, very gently, and then it was wet and cold against her back and his full weight was on her, holding her to the ground. She raised her eyes, searching through the blur of stars for the house, like some magnetic pole; and then it was there again, above her in the distance, with the two windows hanging like votive lamps.

She brought her arms up, gripping the back of his shoulders, and his skin was hard under her nails. She twisted under him, trying to pull back, and her voice rose with the movement, saying, "Not here. You can't. *Not here*." He had squirmed between her legs, the pleas more insistent, and for all the strength above her, gentler and more vulnerable.

"Don't you understand?" she cried out. "You can't. *You can't!*"

He stopped moving suddenly and looked down at her. Marian closed her eyes on his face. "*Please!*" she whispered. She felt the weight lift and slip off her, silently. When she opened her eyes, his back was to her; he lay absolutely still, one hand under him, the other clutching the grass. She tried to rise, then fell back with the effort and stared at the sky for a few seconds, listening to the filter working in the silence, and the sound of Ben's deep, even breathing.

She got to her feet, embarrassed again by her nakedness, pulled on the terrycloth robe and gathered up her clothes. She stopped to look down at him, brushing the still wet hair back against her temples.

"I'm sorry," she said quietly.

His hand moved against the grass in a gesture of dismissal. "There's nothing to be sorry about, Marian." The voice was spent and toneless.

"It's just that . . ." She stopped, wondering whether she should say it, whether the feeling that something between them had terminated would pass eventually. She said it anyway: "It's not the same."

"That happens, I suppose," Ben said casually. He raised himself slowly and faced the pool. "Once again I seem to have gotten carried away. I ought to look into that, I suppose." He half-turned. "I promise I won't put you in that kind of situation again. Go back to the house, Marian."

She waited for him to say something more, something that might trigger sorrow or guilt or whatever it was she should be feeling. He said nothing, and nothing sympathetic was triggered.

Marian went back to the house; to their bedroom first. The thought that Ben might come in made her apprehensive and uncomfortable. She left the room and went into a bathroom adjoining one of the vacant bedrooms, where she showered for a long time. That night she slept sitting up, in the gold brocade chair, in peace and insulation.

She had wrapped the untouched chicken and the string beans in tinfoil (it would be her lunch) and was lifting the egg coddler out of the boiling water when David came into the kitchen. He kissed her good morning and took a package of Yankee Doodles out of the breadbox.

"That your entire breakfast?" she asked.

David said, "Yup," and started to go to the television set in the sewing room.

"It's not even eight o'clock," Marian said. "What could possibly be on TV?"

"Cartoons," he said.

Marian lifted Mrs. Allardyce's breakfast tray. "Take a napkin," she called out to him. "And watch crumbs, please."

Their bedroom door was closed when she went to the sitting room, and thankfully, closed when she came out ten minutes later. She would have to face Ben eventually of course. How? Pretend nothing had happened, or whatever had happened was a momentary aberration on both their parts? It had all been clear enough to her last night, in the sitting room. It wasn't now, and unfortunately a large part of her life would have to be lived outside the confines of the sitting room. How had it happened; how could she find herself, all of a sudden, sheltering two such distinct and contradictory personalities? And if it continued, then how to resolve the problem? Choose? How could she, when the choices themselves were still so indistinct.

She was giving herself problems, manufacturing complexity again, and when she came downstairs she heard the blare of the television set with something approaching gratitude. Anything, even an annoyance, as long as it distracted her.

She walked faster toward the sewing room and the loud cartoon sound effects. She stopped in the dim passageway running the length of the servants' wing and glared into the room. David was sitting directly in front of the set, too close as always, with the remnants of two packages of Yankee Doodles in front of him.

"Will you lower that set please, honey?" she said. "And you're too close; move back." He turned down the volume and pushed himself back a few inches. "I hate to be a pest, but how about cleaning up that mess?"

"I will," David said, absorbed in the cartoon which was Japanese, of all things, and violent.

"Now," Marian insisted.

He muttered a complaint, scooped up the papers, and walked past her heavily, toward the kitchen. He was barefoot but Marian couldn't find the energy for another nagging comment. Besides, something in the passageway had caught her eye—a closet which she must have seen before even though she couldn't remember it immediately. The door was slightly ajar, and immovable when she tried to push it closed. She flicked on the light in the passageway—a low-watt naked light bulb which would have to go, but fast—and opened the closet door.

Even in half-light, and unpolished, the collection was staggering: felt-lined shelves filled, *crammed*, with silver—salvers and punch bowls and vases embroidered with enameled flowers, and tea sets, and filigree-work baskets. And gold as well—brass, she thought at first, but no, gold: candlesticks and service plates with elaborately worked rims, and goblets —ten, eleven, twelve of them—large, like liturgical chalices, and an exquisite pitcher carved with pendent grape clusters. And more, a quietly glittering mass of it, packed into the dark recesses of the closet.

The discovery overwhelmed her, the suddenness of it. And the wave of depression that had come over her when she left the sitting room, the troubling thought of facing Ben and trying somehow to repair the damage of the previous evening—it all dissolved in front of the incredible richness she only had to reach out to touch. She would have seen the closet eventually of course, and investigated it, but to have come upon it just then, so accidentally—what could it be but providential, like so much else in the house?

She lifted the pitcher like something consecrated, passing her fingers over the curve of the handle and the scalloped rim.

"Beautiful," she said aloud, "absolutely beautiful . . ."

And if there was anything to depress Marian at that moment, any one thing in her life she could truly regret, it wasn't the distance she found growing between Ben and herself, or even that disturbing, contradictory presence slowly rooting itself inside her; it was the simple fact that in less than two months now it would all, cruelly and unfairly, pass back to the Allardyces.

David came back into the passageway, and Marian found herself holding the pitcher closer, protectively.

Ben drank his breakfast, juice and coffee only, standing up in the kitchen. He could hear the television set in the sewing room, and footsteps travelling from the rear passageway to the dining room, with an occasional metallic sound. Marian must have heard the coffee cup rattling or the sound of the refrigerator being closed; she called, "Ben?" from outside the kitchen and he called back, "Yes."

She peered in, and there was just a slight pause before she said, "I'll have your breakfast in a minute."

"I'm having it," Ben said, holding up the coffee cup.

"Nothing else?"

He shook his head, and there was another pause.

"I'm involved at the moment," she explained.

"Go ahead," Ben said, and when the door swung closed after her he realized that, as painful as it might be, what he should have said was, "Got a minute?" or "Can we talk about it?" Marian obviously wasn't ready, and if his instincts were to be trusted, neither was he.

He poured the rest of his coffee into the sink and waited, staring out the kitchen window. The sounds continued busily in the dining room. Finally, he called out to her, "I'm going to work on that driveway," and Marian said, "Good idea," without coming into the kitchen. When the door opened, it was only David who asked, "Can I come and help?"

"You'd just be in the way, chief," Ben said, looking beyond him into the passageway. "Help your mother."

David made an unpleasant face and slapped a bare foot against the linoleum floor which was worn, faded and gleaming with fresh wax.

"Anything you want done here?" Ben tried again.

"Nothing," Marian called back.

Ben left through the outside kitchen door while David grumbled, bored and abandoned.

He gathered the scythe, clippers and a large hacking knife, all of which he had sharpened recently, into the car, and drove the winding half mile or so to the narrow opening in the woods. The house slipped in and out of the rearview mirror, smaller and smaller, until the car turned left, into the field of high grass, and it was gone. Out of sight and for a few hours, hopefully, out of mind.

He had been thinking about it more and more recently, the house, finding the old suspicions returning, and with them a growing conviction that, however ambiguous the evidence might be, there was something inimical to them in that house. Or to him. Something almost chemically antipathetic in the atmosphere of the place. It was unreasonable, of course, an improbable assumption; it was after all a house, a rambling mass of stone and wood shingle, and the only accusation he could level at it (at a *house*) was that it had furnished them with a pool and Marian with a houseful of expensive toys to work into an obsession.

As absurd as the feeling was, it was preferable to the alternative which was, as he had told Marian, that he was on the verge of a breakdown. What else would explain the blank he still drew whenever he tried to recreate the incident with David, or the loss of control last night, or the sleeplessness and the waking fantasies bordering on hallucination? The fact that he couldn't work, that when he closed the library door, his mind seemed to turn itself off and two pages out of three of a simple sophomore-level novel would be lost minutes after he had read them? Or that he would seize upon the excuse of a *house* to quiet his fears?

He had reached the opening in the woods. He turned off the ignition and stared into the driveway which rose and then turned out of sight. And if there was anything he wasn't up to at that moment, it was climbing out of the car and hacking away at that jungle.

He did, after a while, trying to find the spot he had been working on a few days before. Wherever it was, it had covered itself over again.

The base of the foliage had spread well over the gravel on both sides, leaving an opening just wide enough to accommodate the small Camaro. Even the area at the end of the drive, which Ben remembered as relatively open and thin, was wild with new growth. Overhead the branches grew into a lowering ceiling of green, completely blocking out the sun.

He had taken off his shirt and hung it on the car aerial, and pulled on an old pair of gardening gloves. He used the clippers first, working on the thinner branches sticking out over the gravel. The sweat began to fall into his eyes, clouding them, and to pour, cool, down his chest and sides. He worked the clippers faster, feeling the sweat and the pull in his arms and in the back of his legs. How long was it since he'd done something purely, invigoratingly physical, something not confined by the walls of a classroom or an apartment? Shelving his mind for a while, whatever was left of it, and using only his body which had actually been good at one time and without the slight thickening he was beginning to notice around the middle. (Marian had noticed it as well last night, during the cock-teasing.) It was therapeutic: the effort, the sound, the branches falling away, and that blessed emptying of his mind as he cut deeper into the drive.

He dropped the clippers and picked up the knife, hacking away at the branches which rustled above him and fell cracking into the gravel. He had been right: some time away from the house was what he needed to clear his mind, away from Marian, David even, from the pool and the bedroom and that suffocating study she had set up for him with all the best intentions in the world. Pretend the vines and branches were the tangle that had somehow begun to grow around his brain.

His brain, his mind—why this obsession with it? The self-destruct syndrome all over? Think your way into a breakdown? If he truly lived in his mind, if it were being taxed by something a little more elevated than what the sum of his life really was—

The knife sliced through the vine growing over the drive and stopped. There was a sound somewhere in front of him —a car moving over the gravel and heading toward him. The sweat rolled into his eyes. He listened. Visitors? Not likely, though the idea, after almost two weeks of isolation, was appealing. A wrong turn, more likely. He straightened and passed his arm over his eyes. The sound came closer, unmistakably a car; he could hear branches scraping against the sides. He lowered his arm and when he opened his eyes it was all a green blur, except for the vague black shape which had maneuvered the turn and was creeping forward, crushing the gravel beneath it. And then it stopped, no more than ten feet away. All he could hear was the sound of the motor idling. Even without seeing clearly he knew what it was, from the instinctive reaction of his body to the sound.

A trick, he told himself, an hallucination—if he could just rub the sweat out of his eyes and catch his breath it would disappear, and the sound with it.

He dropped the knife and pulled off his gloves, rubbing his fingers into his eyes. It wasn't there. He knew that. It didn't exist, not outside those childish and unreasonably frightening nightmares. There was absolutely no way something could creep back from the distant past and be real; or out of the tiny, vulnerable part of his brain where the image had lodged itself. And be real and no more than ten feet away from him.

He opened his eyes. It was there. So clear, so palpably real, with the branches pushed forward around it. He could reach out and touch it, touch the chauffeur behind the tinted glass.

It's not there, he repeated to himself. And if it was the child in him that had called up the image, then it was reasonable to speak to that part of himself and say, "It's not there, and if something is really not there then you can't be seeing it." Pick up the knife and continue to clear away the branches.

He did, with his back to the car, hacking away at the foliage as if there were nothing making that steady throbbing sound in the driveway. He cut faster, moving closer to the sound and blocking it out of his mind, until he felt the bumper pressing against the back of his leg.

(8)

The occasional spells of dizziness were the result of too much sun, nothing more. Yesterday, for example, she had spent a good three hours painting on that unshaded stretch of lawn, which she realized was foolish even if it did provide the most attractive view of the summer pavilion. As for the pains in her legs—and no, she was *not* becoming a complaining old woman—she should hardly have expected to keep up with David who, on their daily walks, bounded over the lawns inexhaustibly. She napped in the afternoon—a novelty for Aunt Elizabeth—because she was tired, and she was tired, healthily so, because her days were full: painting, exploring the grounds, with or without David (she still avoided the pool area with its troubling memory), reading, writing letters, and occasionally helping Marian with the housework (the luxury chores were hers—polishing the silver, arranging the roses and wildflowers in vases which then seemed to disappear).

The aches and the weariness, which she never bored anyone with, were, paradoxically, a sign of bracing physical and mental activity. And the only concession to them she'd permit herself, besides the daily nap, was a weakening of the proportions of her six o'clock martini with Ben; one-fourth vodka now, three-fourths vermouth, and heavy on the rocks.

Getting out of bed that morning had been something of a chore; and after breakfast she wanted nothing so much as to come back up to her room and lie down, without closing her eyes, for an hour or so. She fought it and spent the morning on the terrace instead, reading Lana Turner's biography (if Ben hadn't gone to clear out the drive she would have continued with *The Portrait of a Lady*, his recommendation, but *Lana* was less taxing at the moment, and spicier).

Since Ben hadn't returned by lunchtime and Marian was involved somewhere else, as usual, Aunt Elizabeth kept David company for a quick lunch in the kitchen, and came up to her room immediately afterward, using the inclinator on the stairs, as she had been doing for the past three or four days. Once she had closed the door, however, the idea of taking to her bed and probably sleeping away the afternoon struck her as weak and self-indulgent and unpleasantly old womanish. She opened the door again and looked around the room for something to distract herself. There was a letter to answer, and her journal (days behind in entries), both of them requiring more ambition than she could summon at that time. She saw the finished watercolor, *L'Été*, propped up on the chaise, and as soon as she saw it she thought for some reason of Mrs. Allardyce.

Almost two weeks and they still hadn't met. The old woman, Marian had said at one point, had a fascinating picture collection. Aunt Elizabeth's painting was primitive and hardly fascinating, but it was an appropriate way to introduce herself. And it wasn't merely nosiness on her part (not completely, anyway); more an act of courtesy, long overdue. And if it would somehow alleviate the enervation, the creeping weariness . . .

Aunt Elizabeth held the picture at arm's length, decided it wasn't all that embarrassing, and carried it out of her room.

The double doors at the end of the corridor, up the five steps, were closed. Would she regard it as an intrusion? Marian had said the area was out of bounds, but that was obviously for David's benefit. A lonely old woman? She'd welcome the company.

Aunt Elizabeth stopped in front of the pier-glass-console and passed a hand over her hair which, she noticed, could use some attention: it looked thin, shapeless, and the gray was washing out to an old lady's white. Beauty parlor, next week —wherever the nearest one was. As a matter of fact, she'd suggest it to Marian as well; her hair was becoming noticeably gray at the temples, which was a shame in such a young, attractive woman. A nice outing, a few hours away from the house, with Aunt Elizabeth treating. It was the least she could do for all the hospitality, though of course she'd show her gratitude with something more elaborate once they all returned to the city.

She continued toward the double doors, stopping to catch her breath at the foot of the short staircase (*one* cigarette from now on, with her martini). She gripped the bannister, and her arm began to shake with the effort of pulling herself up the stair; there was lead in her shoes. One step, pause; another, pause again, a little longer. She held the painting more securely, thinking, "For heaven's sake, Elizabeth, what's wrong with you? *Up.*" When she reached the top step she was winded. She leaned against the wall until the slight dizziness passed and she was breathing more evenly. If it weren't so ridiculous it would be alarming: five steps and she was on the verge of collapsing. Will, Elizabeth, *will;* age is a state of mind. She pushed herself away from the wall, raised her hand which was small and pallid, and knocked. She held her hand against the door, looking at it; the skin was loose, the bones prominent. But steady, still. She knocked again, waited, and then began to turn the knob.

"Mrs. Allardyce?" she called softly as she opened the door; "May I come in?"

She heard an inner door closing, and then the knob was pulled out of her hand and Marian stood in front of her.

"Marian, I didn't know you were in there, dear."

"Straightening up," Marian said. She kept the opening narrow. "What is it?"

"I thought it was about time I introduced myself," Aunt Elizabeth said and paused for breath; "to our benefactor."

"She's sleeping," Marian said.

"Oh. That's too bad." She raised the watercolor. "I thought she might enjoy seeing my picture."

Marian looked at the painting briefly. "I'm sure she would. When she's awake."

Aunt Elizabeth was trying to see beyond Marian. "She sleeps quite a bit, doesn't she?"

"Quite a bit," Marian said.

"When do you think I might see her?"

"That's hard to say. She very seldom leaves her room." Aunt Elizabeth lowered her voice and gestured toward the area in back of Marian. "Is she sleeping there?"

"No," Marian said, "that's her sitting room."

"With her picture collection?"

"Pictures?" Marian seemed surprised.

"You said she collected pictures. That's why I brought this."

"Her photographs, you mean."

"Oh," Aunt Elizabeth said, "photographs."

Marian brushed her hair back from her face. "Aunt Elizabeth, I'm right in the middle—"

"Yes, dear, I'm sorry; I didn't mean to interrupt anything."

Marian smiled politely; her voice lightened. "Everything under control downstairs?"

"David's playing on the terrace, Ben hasn't come back yet."

She smiled again and closed the door another inch. "I'll be out in a while. Lamb for dinner, all right?"

"That's fine," Aunt Elizabeth said. She started to turn away, then stopped. "Tell me—you've met her of course? Mrs. Allardyce?"

Marian hesitated, quickly adjusting something on the inside doorknob. "Yes," she said, and then looked up at Aunt Elizabeth again. "Several times now."

"What is she like?"

Marian shrugged. "Very old," she said.

"That's not saying much; there's old and there's old. Did she speak to you?"

"Casually, yes. 'Good morning' and 'How are you all enjoying the house?' That sort of thing. I'm sure you'll meet her eventually."

"I'm prying, I know," Aunt Elizabeth said. "It's just that I'm curious. A woman that age—she's what? Eighty-three?"

"Eighty-five."

"Eighty-five. And very independent, I'd think."

"Very."

"That's admirable."

"She's certainly that," Marian said. "And terribly shy. I think we should all respect her privacy."

"Of course."

"It's probably upsetting enough to have me coming in and out."

"Oh, I wouldn't dream of upsetting an old woman," Aunt Elizabeth assured her. "You'll tell her, though, that I came to visit?"

Marian nodded. "I know she'll appreciate it."

"And any time she'd like some company—"

"I'll let you know," Marian said. "Be careful on the steps." She lowered her eyes as if guiding Aunt Elizabeth's feet.

"Go back to your work, Marian," Aunt Elizabeth said, and waited for the door to close so that Marian wouldn't see how absurdly difficult five small steps had become for a woman who just two weeks ago . . .

The thought, puzzling and disturbing, was interrupted by the sound of the lock.

He had dropped the knife in the bushes, when the presence had become intolerable, had left the scythe and clippers somewhere near the end of the driveway, and walked to the Camaro parked in the shade. Slowly and without looking back, as if nothing were behind him. He remembered pulling his shirt off the aerial, and the comfort of closing the windows on the sound of the motor idling; and then driving the short distance back to the house. Immediately, he thought. But when he found himself parked on the thin gravel paving in front of the garage, the inside of the Camaro had become airless and suffocating, the steering wheel hot enough to burn the palms of his hands, and his shirt and chinos were dark with sweat stains.

Mommie was busy somewhere, David told him when he

reached the terrace, and Aunt Elizabeth had gone up to her room right after lunch.

"Lunch?" Ben said incredulously. "What time is it?"

"I don't know," David said. "Two maybe. How'd you get all sweaty?"

Ben repeated it soundlessly: "*Two.*" He moved away from David who was sitting on the floor in the middle of a network of orange plastic tracks that curved and looped over the flagstone; he was holding a small metal racing car.

"Wanna see something neat?" he said to Ben. He placed the car on the highest point of the track which was draped over one of the metal chairs. "Look at this, Dad." When Ben turned he released the car, sending it flying, like a roller-coaster, down the dips. David embellished the sound with a guttural roar that exploded joyously when the car jumped a curve and crashed against the flagstone.

"You need more track," Ben said distantly.

"A lot more," David agreed and crawled over the stones, which Marian had already weeded several times, to retrieve the car. "Can we get some?" When he looked up, Ben had left the terrace.

The kitchen clock, the simplest in the house and the only one that worked despite Marian's efforts with all the others, read one-twenty. At least two hours, then, were blank, lost; totally, as hard as he tried to retrace the morning. Maybe he'd left the house later than he remembered, or spent more time working on the driveway, or stopped the car some-where on the way back. It was still blank, or vague at best, and the only memory he could call up with certainty was the sequence of the hallucination. Nothing else in retrospect was as real.

He heard Marian somewhere near the terrace saying, "Hi, sweetheart, how're you doing?" and David replying, "Okay. Except I need more tracks." A minute later the door to the kitchen swung open behind him. There was a brief silence before she said, a little too cheerfully, "My God, somebody here's really been working!" She came in and let the door swing closed. Ben went to the refrigerator for a cream soda, keeping his back to her.

"I think I might've overdone it," he said, and it surprised him by coming out normal and even.

"That's a lot of driveway," Marian said.

"Afraid I didn't get very far, despite appearances." He held up the can. "Want one?"

"No." He could feel her watching him. "You didn't get too much sun, did you?"

"Some." He went to the sink and pulled the tab off the can. "We're going to have to get someone. I can manage the power mower but that jungle's a bitch."

"We'll get someone then. I'll check the list."

He felt controlled enough to face her. He turned and toasted her with the can. Marian nodded. She was standing in the middle of the kitchen, watching him silently; one hand played with the sleeve of her shirt, a yellow and green boat-neck which she either had or hadn't worn that morning—he couldn't remember. Ben took a long drink, and when he lowered his arm she was coming toward him and he could see her eyes filling suddenly. He put the drink down on the counter and held her as she buried her face in his chest. She said his name, calling him "Benjie," and again how sorry she was about last night, could he ever forgive her? The words dissolved into quiet sobbing. "Okay," Ben said, "okay . . ." His arm curved around her shoulders tighter, and something selfish started to creep into the compassion he was feeling for her. He shut his eyes, trying to block out everything but the close warmth and the comfort of feeling her against him. And when she said, "You know how much I love you," he brushed his lips against her hair, nodding "Yes."

"And nothing will change, Ben, nothing between us will ever change."

"Why should anything change?"

She raised her face to him. "It won't. Because you're all that means anything to me . . . you and David." She reached for his hand and squeezed it. "You know that's true, don't you?"

"Of course it's true, Marian."

"God, how I've wanted to say that to you today. I've been absolutely miserable." She took a tissue out of her pocket and wiped her eyes and nose.

Ben pushed the hair back from her face. She lowered her hand and forced a weak smile. "Are you okay now?" he asked.

"Better," Marian said, drawing in a long shaky breath.

Should he bring it all out, he wondered; tell her about what had happened to him, as calmly and with as much sense as he could? Bring her to the driveway and show her where the limousine had appeared, point out the tire tracks and the spot where somehow two hours of his life had been wiped away?

She was saying something, tugging at his shirt. "What?"

"Good way to catch cold."

"I'll go up and change," Ben said. The shirt was sticking to him, cool in the draft coming through the open window.

Marian stuffed the tissue back into her pocket; her eyes were red and shining, and there was still a quaver in her voice. "Can I show you something first?"

She took his hand and led him in the direction of the dining room, and still he wondered—should he tell her? The door was closed.

"Close your eyes," she said. He heard her turn the knob and call, "Ready." He opened his eyes and saw the table stretched out to its full length and covered, every inch of it, with freshly polished silver. And the other stuff—gold?

"Gold it is," she assured him, and her eyes were shining even brighter now, her voice controlled and level.

Ben gave a low whistle and moved nearer the table.

"Incredible, isn't it?" Marian said.

"Where'd you find it all?"

"A closet; just today. I spent all morning polishing it."

He walked the length of the table. It was an awesome collection. And for some reason what Marian had said a few minutes before came back to him: "I've been absolutely miserable."

As sincere as he knew she'd been, he stopped and looked back at her, for even the slightest corroboration of just how miserable she might have been.

They slept together that night, and Marian made a point of coming into bed while Ben was still awake. He was wearing pajamas, tops as well as bottoms, which he seldom did, as if to reassure her that for the time being at least it would be by appointment only.

Again, he wanted to tell her, but how? She was propped up on the pillow beside him, with a gardening book open on her lap, and talking about the progress she was making in the greenhouse. At least she'd cleared away some of the debris— and would he remember to take it to the garbage pit tomorrow and burn it? The plants had been separated into "possible" and "hopeless" categories; and while her gardening experience had been limited to some apartment plants, she had been unusually successful with her philodendron and dracaena, and with a gardenia and Boston fern as well, both of which, she informed him, could be bitches.

He was only half-listening. How to tell her? "By the way, Marian . . ."? Or "Marian, I'm frightened . . ."? Or "Marian, I'm not sure, but . . ."? And *why*? What could he expect her to do— reason away the fears, encourage them; agree with him that, yes, there was something inimical in the house conjuring up these phantoms to torment him, and of course there's nothing to do but pack up immediately, and find some nice doctor for him to see? The more he thought about it, the more confusing and incoherent it all became; and that itself became one more frightening realization. Thinking, simple reasoning was at times impossible, and his brain, when it did function, distorted reality. At times, he reminded himself; there were lucid moments. But which ones were they?

Marian had turned out her light. She said, "Goodnight, darling. I'm beat," leaned over and kissed him.

"Sleep well," Ben said, and watched her turn her back to him and pull the sheet up to her neck.

He leaned back and reached for a cigarette. The James novel he'd started reading a few days ago was on the night table; twenty-odd pages—the extent of the work he'd done on his new English IV class. He tried to recall what he'd read and then flipped through the opening pages for confirmation; at least it hadn't all gone.

The light was hurting his eyes, aggravating the headache he'd developed after dinner. There was a slight throbbing now just above the eyes. He put out the cigarette and the light, and kissed the sheet covering Marian's shoulder. She was asleep.

He tried lying on his right side and then his left and on his stomach, pressing his forehead into the pillow to numb the throbbing; when he lay on his back he heard it, just as he'd expected, somewhere under the bedroom windows. If he gave in and went to the window he'd see the limousine, he knew, even though there was nothing below but the terrace and the lawns sloping down to the bay. He shifted to his right side and lay his hand very lightly on Marian's hip. He could see a line of light beyond her, at the bottom of the closed bedroom door.

If he could sleep, if it would just come. The throbbing had separated itself from the pain in his head; it was outside. Would it stop if he went to the window and acknowledged it? The pain with it? And let him sleep? He closed his eyes and moved lower in the bed. His feet were sweating, and the palms of his hands; he could feel a tightening in his groin. How could she be asleep, breathing so evenly?

Who was it in college—Hoffman? Last day of the course. "Ladies and gentlemen, one word of advice: always get a good night's sleep." Thank you, Dr. Hoffman.

It came eventually; fitfully, a few minutes at a time—not sleep, but a dulling grogginess that, paradoxically, sharpened his senses, chambering sounds. The throbbing still, and then something else—a ticking somewhere beyond the closed door. Louder, more regular, and gradually replacing the sound under the windows. Ben's eyes opened again; he raised his head and the pain sharpened above his eyes. The ticking was in the hall, and when he looked in the direction of the sound he saw a shadow passing slowly across the thin line of light at the bottom of the door; someone moving up the corridor toward the old lady's room. He listened for footsteps or the creaking of floorboards. There was only the steady ticking. He passed a hand over his forehead and then got out of bed carefully, trying not to jog the pain. The windows were near his side of the bed, about ten feet away. Was it still there or had it disappeared with the sound? He struggled with the impulse to go to the window; took a step toward it, and then turned abruptly and headed for the door. The ticking was outside—the hall clock. He opened the bedroom door and saw the pendulum swinging in the glass case. There was nothing else; the hall was empty, the double doors at the end closed, Aunt Elizabeth's as well. And David's, whose door was never closed.

Ben walked across the corridor quickly, disregarding the pain and the swinging pendulum. As soon as he put his hand on the knob he smelled the gas rising from under the door. He twisted the knob and pushed against the door, and then again, and then with all his weight, shouting, "David! David!"

The door snapped open and he rushed into the room, ripping at his pajama tops and covering his face against the fumes. He threw aside a chair and ran to the bed, shouting David's name as he reached down and scooped him up, dragging the covers with him. Marian had come to the door and then pulled back suddenly.

"What is it?"

When she saw Ben lifting him and carrying him toward her, and David with his eyes half-closed and twisting in Ben's arms, she came into the room with a cry.

"Get out of here!" Ben yelled at her, pushing her back toward the door.

"My God! Is he all right? Ben! Is he?"

She followed him into their bedroom. Ben lay David on the bed and went to the windows, throwing all of them open. When he came back to the bed Marian was leaning over him, helplessly, rubbing his face, his hands. David's eyes were open; he was gagging. Ben lifted him again and carried him to the window, holding his head out and saying, "Come on, Davey, breathe in deep, deep. *Marian.*"

She was beside them, repeating, "Is he all right?"

"Hold him. Like this." He put her arms around him. "That's it, Dave," he said, "that's it."

He left them and went back into David's room, throwing on the light and going for the gas heater which was hissing at one end of the room. He covered his face again and reached for the knob, twisting it shut and cutting off the sound. All the windows were closed; he flung them open and then came out of the room, pulling the door shut behind him.

Aunt Elizabeth was standing in their doorway, her robe drawn tightly around her. "What is it?"

"Nothing," Ben said, moving past her. "He's going to be all right."

Marian was leaning beside David at the window. Ben put his arms around him, pressing his chest lightly. He looked up at Ben; his lips and chin were wet and trembling; he gagged and then started to cry. Ben thrust his head out the window again and said, "You're going to be okay . . . okay, Dave."

"Is he?" Marian formed the words silently, grabbing Ben's arm.

Ben looked at the back of David's head and nodded, too tentatively, to reassure her completely. He said, "Call a doctor."

She rose to her feet, repeating, "Doctor . . ." vaguely, and then she remembered the list downstairs on a kitchen counter. She hesitated, looking anxiously at David, and the enormity of what might have happened hit her suddenly. She began to cry and knelt beside him again. "I don't understand," she said, "I just don't understand how it could have—"

"Get that list and call a doctor!" Ben yelled at her, and she saw his eyes close against something inside him and his body tense. He turned away from her. "Go ahead," he said; his voice had faded to a whisper.

Aunt Elizabeth was wringing her hands in the middle of the room, staring at the window. Marian passed her without speaking, and as she left the room heard her saying, "Ben . . ." in a small, trembling voice. She went down to the kitchen and found the list, sliding her finger down the page until it reached W. G. Ross, M.D. She dialled shakily, and while she was waiting for the phone to be picked up—four, five, six excruciating rings—the clock beside her in the entry hall chimed the half-hour. All Marian heard was an angry voice saying, "Dr. Ross."

He had asked her, brutally direct—first, was he breathing, and second, was he conscious; and if he was, then there was nothing to be done, certainly not at one-thirty in the morning. "Nothing?" she had protested, and the voice had become surlier, repeating, "Is he breathing okay?" Then fresh air and sleep for now, and he would see the boy in his office at nine in the morning. "If it was a gas heater, then it's either fatal or it's not fatal," he had assured her; "nothing in between. Have the boy get some rest."

He was conscious and he was breathing regularly, Ben told her. He made David walk to the bed—unsteady, but he was walking. Marian covered him and sat beside him for a while, watching him sleep on Ben's side of the bed. She rested her hand lightly on his shoulder. His breathing was deep, and, yes, regular, and he stirred when she pressed her lips to his forehead which was cool, not feverish.

Ben had gone into David's room. "It's off," he said when he came back; "It'll be all right." That was all. He went to the armchair next to the window, sat, and propped his feet up on a hassock.

"But *how*, Ben? I don't understand."

"Get some sleep," he said. He closed his eyes and sank deeper into the chair, rubbing his hand across his brow. The pain was back, more intense; it had probably never even gone, if he weren't too drained to remember.

"Ben?" Marian called uneasily. "Is there something you know?"

"I don't know anything at all right now, Marian." Nothing at all except, thank God, there were still some of those lucid moments left. But not now; all he wanted was the comfort of the word—*nothing*. Nothing. Turn off the pain and think *nothing*.

Marian watched his hand fall and dangle over the arm of the chair. She got up from the edge of the bed, smoothed the covers over David, and crossed to her own side. She looked from David to Ben, and then around the room distractedly, as if she were trying to trace a sound or a memory or a fragrance. Her eyes stopped at the closed door and she remembered: Mrs. Allardyce. *Had she heard?* Had the noise reached the sitting room? Until that moment she hadn't even thought of her; and while the inattention—if that's what it was—was justified, *still* . . . not even to have thought of her.

They were sleeping, both of them. She walked quietly to the door, and her excuse for opening it and leaving the room was not simply the responsibility of a helpless old woman, but that ticking out in the hall which she was hearing for the first time.

Coincidence, she said to herself. Firmly. Coincidence as well with all the other clocks she hurried downstairs to check. Nothing more. And if there was any doubt, any feeling of dread; if she remembered saying even once, *"My God"*—then the remembrance was lost after a while in the solace of the sitting room, where the hum and the patterns in the carved door could elevate even the sound of a clock ticking to a benediction.

Ben called her from the village the next morning to tell her that the doctor—a cantankerous old man even by day—had looked David over, and the recovery, as far as he was concerned, was complete. Ben was taking him to Southold to hunt up a toy shop and a new "G.I. Joe" outfit. They'd be back by noon. He added, cryptically, "How's Aunt Elizabeth?"

"She's not up yet," Marian said.

She understood what might have been in back of his concern later, when Aunt Elizabeth found her in the greenhouse. She knocked on the glass door timidly, and Marian, who was loosening the soil around the large skeleton of what was once a wax begonia, beckoned her in. Aunt Elizabeth pointed to the doorknob and shook her head. Marian dropped the spade and opened the door for her, twisting the knob to test it.

"It wasn't locked," she said to Aunt Elizabeth, and walked back past rows of orange and blue pots, most of them holding lifeless brown stumps.

The windows, the lower panes at least, had been cleaned, the broken pots removed, and all the "possibles" lined up neatly on the shelves and the long tables.

Aunt Elizabeth was making her way slowly to Marian's work area, scraping her feet against the thin gravel floor.

"Have you had breakfast?" Marian asked.

"It's too late for breakfast," Aunt Elizabeth said. "I overslept shamefully."

Her voice had changed; it sounded strained and quavery. Her face, when she came closer, was pale, with dark circles around her eyes.

"How is David?" she asked.

"Better. With that kind of thing it's either one way or the other. Thank God it turned out the right way." She packed the dirt around the plant and watered it.

"You can't imagine how frightened I was—to see him like that. My Davey." Her voice shook even more; she steadied herself against the table.

"So were we all," Marian said. "If I keep myself busy enough I can try not to think of it. He's all right, thank God."

She squeezed past Aunt Elizabeth for the plastic bag of potting soil. The change in her, close up, shocked Marian. She was trembling, the skin on her face and neck was loose and so thin that it seemed almost transparent.

Aunt Elizabeth wiped her eyes. "Marian?" she said hesitantly. "I didn't . . . I didn't touch the heater."

The statement took Marian by surprise. "Well . . . of course you didn't, Aunt Elizabeth."

"If I did," Aunt Elizabeth continued, "I'd certainly remember."

"No one said you did."

"I just covered him, that's all."

Marian stopped. "Covered him?" She looked at Aunt Elizabeth. "What are you talking about?"

"It was cold. Sometimes I'll look in on him. And if he's
thrown off his covers . . ." She was forcing the words out
slowly, the effort leaving her breathless.

"You were in David's room? Last night?"

"I told Ben. Sometimes I can't sleep and I'll—"

"Wait a minute," Marian interrupted her. "*When* were you
in David's room, what time?"

"I don't remember exactly." Her lips were dry, trembling.

"And Ben knows this?"

"I told him, last night. You'd gone downstairs."

Marian remembered asking him whether there was something he knew; he'd disregarded the question. And even this
morning it had been some kind of freak accident, or David
himself had turned the heater on and was too frightened to
admit it immediately. Why hadn't he told her about Aunt
Elizabeth?

"What exactly did you do in his room, Aunt Elizabeth?"

"I told you—only covered him; he'd thrown his blanket
off." Her hand came up to her other arm as if to ward off
the remembered chill. "It was cold, this house has gotten so
cold . . ."

"Nothing else?"

"No."

"The windows?" Aunt Elizabeth shook her head. "The
door? David's door is never locked, never even closed. It was
locked last night; Ben had to force it open."

"I didn't touch the door."

"It couldn't have closed itself."

Marian was looking directly at her; Aunt Elizabeth avoided
her eyes. "I might have . . . closed it . . . without thinking."

"All right, think *now*."

"I don't remember." She shook her head suddenly. "No, I do, I do. There was a draft. I thought by closing the door . . ."

"What else do you remember?"

"I couldn't have locked it. Why would I do that?"

"All right, you didn't lock it, it locked itself. What about the windows?"

"The windows were open."

"They were closed when Ben went in there; tight."

"Then David might have closed them."

"David was asleep."

"Before he fell asleep."

"And then he opened them again before you came in. Make sense, Aunt Elizabeth."

"How can I make sense when you're shouting at me? I can't think when you shout like that."

"I'm not shouting."

"You *are* and you're accusing me of—I don't know *what* you're accusing me of."

Marian lowered her voice pointedly. "I'm not accusing you of anything. Isn't it reasonable to want to know what caused that heater to go on?"

"Ben never once implied I was responsible."

"*If,*" Marian said, her voice rising above Aunt Elizabeth's, "if I'm implying that, I'm also implying that it was an accident; it certainly wasn't done to hurt David."

"Hurt David? Me?"

"Accidentally, I said."

"Not even accidentally." She was fumbling in her pocket for a handkerchief, her knuckles white and bony, cadaverous almost.

"There's no sense in pursuing it. It's over, he's all right." She watched Aunt Elizabeth dab at her eyes. Her dress, a short-sleeved cotton print Marian had seen her wear before, hung shapeless from her body. She was suddenly very old to Marian, so old that it seemed like an illusion. It might have simply been the fact that she wasn't wearing makeup or that her weekly trips to the hairdresser had been suspended. But the trembling, the change in her voice?

"Where's Ben?" Aunt Elizabeth said. "Ben will believe me."

Marian sighed with resignation. "I believe you too."

"You don't," Aunt Elizabeth said and pulled her elbow back, out of Marian's reach.

"We'll just have to be more careful, that's all." She had taken the gardening gloves off; she started to slip them on again.

"Of me?"

"You're seventy-four, Aunt Elizabeth."

"What does that mean?"

It hadn't struck Marian as cruel, merely honest. She wished now she hadn't said it. "We all forget things," she said.

"I don't forget things, Marian," Aunt Elizabeth said weakly. "I know what I do."

"Of course you do," Marian said. "Let me get your breakfast."

"I don't want any breakfast." She turned to leave. "Please tell Ben I'm in my room."

"I'll bring it to your room if you want."

Aunt Elizabeth stopped; her hand went down to the table for support. "Just like you bring it to her room—the other old woman? Please don't bother, Marian."

He had awakened with the pain above his eyes, and the aspirin hadn't helped, nor the dark glasses he'd worn for the drive to Southold and back. At one point on the road he'd had to stop the car, not only for the pain, but for the sudden, momentary blurring of his vision. It passed, but the pain persisted.

He spoke above it, telling Aunt Elizabeth, "I've never known you to blubber like this."

She was sitting on the edge of the chaise in her room, twisting the handkerchief in her hands. Ben was beside her, with his arm around her shoulders very lightly, as if the slightest pressure might weigh on her insupportably. Even the pain couldn't distract him from the change in her.

His words brought the handkerchief up to her eyes again. "I'm sorry, Benjie, I can't help myself. She had no right to talk to me that way."

"She was upset, she didn't know what she was saying."

"I'd die," Aunt Elizabeth said, touching his knee for emphasis, "*die* before I'd do anything to hurt Davey."

"I know that and so does Marian."

"Does she?"

"Of course she does. You know how Marian feels about you, Aunt Elizabeth."

"I don't know how Marian feels about anything anymore. Except this house."

Ben was silent. "That's not like you either," he said quietly.

"I'm sorry, Benjie. She's gotten me so upset I don't know what I'm saying."

"Look," Ben said, "you two have never had words before. Why, all of a sudden?"

"Ask Marian."

"I did ask her, exactly that. It's possible, isn't it, that you misinterpreted what she was saying?"

"I know what I heard, same as I know what I do. I may be an old lady, Benjie, but that doesn't mean I've lost all my marbles."

"You're not an old lady," Ben said. He looked at her hair, so fine it was almost transparent; the scalp showed underneath, white and lifeless. When had it started? Or was this too all in his mind? "Stop thinking yourself into old age, hunh?" He squeezed her hand affectionately.

"I am old, Benjie," Aunt Elizabeth said.

"Old, my ass. All you need's a little touch-up paint."

She gave him a small, wet-eyed smile. "Tomorrow maybe."

"Why not now?"

She sighed and wilted beside him. "I don't have the strength at the moment." She looked longingly at the bed and started to raise herself, leaning on his arm. "More than anything I'd like to be able to get into that bed and close my eyes for just a while. Like a very young lady," she assured him, "who's just suddenly so tired. Help me, Benjie?"

He found Marian preparing Mrs. Allardyce's lunch tray in the kitchen.

"David's on the terrace," she said, "with a *book*. He says it stinks but he seems to be plugging away. The 'G.I. Joe' was good for twenty minutes. How much did you pay for it?"

"I forget." He told her about Aunt Elizabeth, and Marian, without any wasted motions—hot soup into blue Spode bowl—said, "If I hurt her I'm sorry. The fact is she *was* in his room."

"Why would she lie, Marian?"

"She's not lying; she just doesn't remember what she did. She didn't, then she did close the door, and the windows, and—" Marian dismissed it with a wave. "Face it, darling, Aunt Elizabeth is getting old."

"She wasn't 'old' back in town."

"No, she wasn't," Marian said; "and we didn't live with her then either." She placed the bowl on a plate and moved them onto the silver tray, adding an immaculate linen napkin and a silver spoon which she held up to inspect. "We saw her once every week or so then. Usually fresh from the beauty parlor."

There was a deliberateness in her last statement which seemed especially intended for Ben. "You've seen the change?" he said.

"I've seen it," Marian said. "She's letting herself go. She has been ever since—" She caught herself and repeated the phrase, shrugging it off: "Ever since."

"Ever since what, Marian?" The pool. Neither he nor Aunt Elizabeth had ever mentioned it. Was the memory of it as painful and obsessive for her as well, still? And could a shock like that have done it, or at least started it?

"Ever since we took on country ways," Marian said lightly. She placed a Venetian bud vase with a single yellow rose on the tray. "She'll be fine, once she begins to recognize her limitations. Seventy-four is seventy-four."

"Go up and talk to her, Marian," Ben said.

"I will, darling," Marian said. She lifted the tray. "Later."

He brought his hand against the edge of the tray. "Now. For me?"

"Ben, I'm late," Marian protested. "As soon as I've—"

"I'll take that up to the old lady." He tried to take the tray away from her.

"What are you doing?" She held it tighter, instinctively protective, and with a threat in her voice and face that the quick, nervous laugh failed to cover.

"It's important that you talk to her now," Ben said.

"I'll talk to her later," Marian insisted, and looked down at Ben's hands on the tray. "Now, darling—*please*." He let go of the tray and the threat softened to an ingratiating smile, playfully scolding. "My responsibility, after all," she reminded him. She kissed the air between them and left Ben in the kitchen.

Aunt Elizabeth's door was closed when Marian passed it. She might have been too harsh with her, though probably not as insensitive as Aunt Elizabeth had no doubt made out to Ben. She should have realized that age was Aunt Elizabeth's vulnerable point and any reference to it would bruise her vanity. She took the keys to the double doors and the sitting room out of her pocket. She'd go in to see her later and apologize.

Marian climbed the five steps and unlocked the outer door, steadying the tray quickly as the bud vase slid toward the Spode bowl. She pulled the key out and left the door open behind her.

Vulnerable: the word came back to her. Ben and the pool; why had she even hinted at it? Not deliberately certainly, not to hurt him. She tried to remember the context as she turned the key to unlock the sitting room door. If it had come out as a taunting reminder, that had not been her intention. How could it be?

She entered the room and the silver vases, the gold pitcher and candlesticks she had found yesterday glittered in the room's soft, peaceful light, and for the moment crowded Aunt Elizabeth and Ben and what Marian had or hadn't said out of her mind. She carried the tray to the tea table, set it down, and then turned slowly, surveying the room—from the carved door (gold faceted today, a huge medallion) to the bowls of flowers and candelabra set on polished tables to the mass of faces graced now with vases filled with wildflowers. She started to move toward the pictures and then stopped suddenly and spun around to face the door she'd left open. Ben was watching her silently.

She felt her heart jump. "My God!" she cried. She looked quickly at the carved door, and then back at Ben, her voice hushed. "You frightened me."

He was coming into the room, which made Marian hold out her hands, cautioning.

"Please, darling," she whispered, moving toward him, "she doesn't like anyone in here."

Ben stopped and looked slowly around the room. "Where is she?" he asked with something more than simple curiosity.

Marian's voice became even softer. "In her bedroom." She nodded at the carved door. "Asleep."

Ben listened to the hum. "What's that noise?"

"I don't know; air conditioner probably. It's in her bedroom."

She had slipped her hand through his arm and was trying to guide him back to the door. He moved away from her and walked toward the bedroom, following the sound of the hum.

"Exquisite, isn't it?" Marian said as Ben looked at the carvings in the door.

"It's something," he said. He began to trace the pattern, and Marian found herself tensing, as though his fingers were moving over her own body.

"Come on, Ben," she called softly, "let me lock up."

"In a minute," he said. He walked slowly across the room, stopping at the gold pitcher which he remembered seeing the day before. "You brought it up here," he said.

"Yes." He seemed surprised. "I showed it to her yesterday," Marian said defensively. "She asked me to leave it here. The candlesticks as well." It came out effortlessly, and however right it seemed in view of the intrusion, it was a lie, which disturbed her.

"You see her regularly?" Ben asked.

"Fairly," Marian said, and that disturbed her as well.

He was moving toward the photographs, and Marian felt herself tensing even more. "Her collection," she said, keeping her voice low. She came beside him. "Fascinating. People she's known all over the world. It's her whole life, these pictures." She saw him lingering over a photograph on the edge of the table—a child unsmiling. Marian tugged at Ben's arm. "It's very personal, darling; one of her crotchets, I'm afraid." She tugged again. "I know this would upset her."

Ben looked at her, and though she was trying to cover it with a smile, he saw the face over the tray again. "What are you so nervous about?" he said.

"I'm not nervous. I told you, she doesn't like anyone in here." She pulled the keys out of her pocket. "Can we leave now?"

"I've been curious about this room," Ben said.

"Well," Marian said with a sweep of her hand, "you've seen it."

"Why do you keep it locked?"

"She prefers it that way."

"And she gave you the keys?"

"They were in the envelope the Allardyces left."

He was beginning to walk across the room, thank God, toward the door. "Were the keys you used to wind the clocks in there too?" he asked casually.

Marian hesitated, just briefly. "The clock keys were in the cases, most of them. Why bring that up?"

"I just wondered if you wound all those clocks."

"Of course I did. You've seen me doing it."

"They're working now, you know. How'd you finally manage it?"

"Persistence. Look, this is beginning to sound like the third degree."

"I don't mean it that way," Ben said. "You just seem to know more than any of us around here." He nodded at the tray beside the wingchair. "Her lunch is getting cold. You'd better call her."

"She'll come out when we leave. Can we now?" Ben didn't move. "God, you're acting strange. I've told you, honey, she doesn't like anyone in her room."

"Except you."

"Except me, yes." She looked at the carved door again, anxiously. "We agreed, didn't we—she's my responsibility?"

"You think maybe she's become too much of a responsibility, Marian? The house too?"

"I'm not complaining, am I?"

"No," Ben said, "you're not."

"Then don't you." She came closer to him and gave him a long, overly exasperated sigh. He stared at her, and though she could see her face in the pupils, the eyes seemed turned inward. "What is it, darling?" she whispered. "Tell me."

It had happened again, very briefly—the sudden blurring, the wedge of pain between his eyes. He winced and felt her hands on his face.

"Ben?"

Her features slid back onto her face.

"How important is it to you, Marian? This house?"

The questioning, the almost belligerent way he had come into the room should have prepared her. It hadn't and she could feel her throat tighten around the reply. "Important enough, I guess. Why?"

"If I asked you to," he said very slowly, "would you give it up?"

"Give it up?"

He nodded, and when she asked, "Ben, are you serious?" he nodded again.

"*Why?*" Her voice caught on the word.

"You can ask that, after what happened here last night?"

"Last night?"

"What if I hadn't reached David in time, Marian?"

She shook the thought out of her head and said, "Don't even suggest something like that." Then, trying to keep her voice steady: "What has that got to do with the house, with leaving? Look, I can't believe you're serious."

"I am, Marian."

"Ben, Aunt Elizabeth *admitted* she was in David's room—"

"—and everything else that's been happening to us here, Marian—is that Aunt Elizabeth's fault as well?"

"I'm not blaming Aunt Elizabeth, and I'm certainly not blaming a *house*. Honey, I don't even know what the 'everything else' is supposed to be."

"How could you, Marian? You've become too obsessed with it all to see anything else clearly."

"I am *not* obsessed with it."

"What would you call it then?"

"Just what it is: a responsibility."

"One that's a hell of a lot more than you thought it would be."

"Whatever it is, it's mine as long as we're here." She paused and let him see how wearying it all was. "Ben—do you know how ridiculous it sounds? To read threat into a house. If I don't see it clearly, isn't it possible there's nothing clear to see?" She passed her hand over his hair. "And maybe whatever you think is happening, is only happening *here?*" She was rubbing the back of his neck. "In your mind?"

"Would you give it up, Marian?" he repeated. "For me? Whether it's in my mind or not, would you give it up?"

"Are you asking me to do that, Ben?"

"*Would* you?"

"It's everything we've ever wanted," Marian said faintly.

"Everything you've ever wanted, Marian."

"For us." She looked at him silently for a long while and then rested her face against his shoulder, watching the carved door behind him. "Of course, Ben," she said. It was hardly a whisper, almost indistinguishable from the sound of the hum. She fixed her eyes on the center of the medallion, projecting the same thought over and over: Don't let him ask it, don't let him ask it . . .

"Something's happening to me, Marian." She heard him far away.

"Yes, Ben?"

"I don't know how to describe it."

"Tell me."

"Things are . . . real to me . . . that I know don't exist. So goddamned real. There are times when I just can't control what comes into my head. It's become terrifying." He was holding her closer; she felt his head bury itself against her. "It's like . . . hallucinating. I know it's not there . . . and yet it's real. It's never happened before, Marian, never before this house. It *is* the house. As crazy as it sounds, I know it's the house."

Her fingers moved slower, soothing, against the back of his neck.

"How is that possible, Ben?"

"I don't know."

There was no reason to disbelieve at least part of what he was saying; but belief or not, or sympathy, or fear—they were all swirling around somewhere beyond the periphery of the medallion. And as much as she tried to feel them, the only thing that was working on her emotionally was the thought that he would ask her to give up the house. "If it were true, darling," she said, "if I could believe what you're saying— God, don't you think we'd leave? I'd drag us all out of here so fast. But it's a house, nothing more than a house. And if everything is suspect all of a sudden—from me all the way down to the ticking of a clock—well, forgive me, Ben, but isn't that part of the hallucination as well? Trust me, darling. There's nothing here to threaten us. Nothing." She waited and then asked him again: "Are you asking me to give it up? All of it? Is that what you want?"

He said "No" finally; not said it, merely indicated it by leaving her question unanswered and listening quietly to Marian's renewed promises and the assurance, repeated several times, that there was nothing wrong with him. It was everything from too much sun to not enough sleep; it was imagination and tension and all the residue of the city; their adjustment to the house, the responsibility of it; and, yes, if it had to be brought up again, the reverberating shock of the pool incident. And all the rest of it. He was not losing his mind. He was not on the edge of a breakdown.

Ben left the room eventually; possibly no more reassured, but at least the question of giving up the house had been suspended, and that had to be some kind of progress; there had to be some slight validity in what she was saying.

The house. The word he'd used: *obsession . . .*

It delayed itself until she was alone again, with the sitting room door closed; and at first the realization jolted her like a shock wave: the house was insinuating itself into the deepest part of her being; it was taking possession of her. So completely that she couldn't say with certainty what her life would be like, even with Ben and David, if she were confronted with the terrible choice of giving up the house or not giving up the house. How could she, in view of the mystery of it, and the approbation it showered on her so constantly—in every room, more and more, in the grounds and the pool and even the clocks ticking? Like the Allardyces had suggested, it was coming alive, bit by bit, and all through her.

She could read confirmation in the lines and curves cut into the door, and hear it in the voice of the room, and the peace that had replaced the shock wave, descending on her like grace.

It was mid-afternoon when Marian came out of the sitting room. The security and peace—the feeling that what she was being called upon to do was right, was morally defensible— faded with the click of the lock; reality obtruded, and with it an edginess, a sudden loss of clarity. She had lied to Ben, and however noble the reason, she had never deliberately done that before. Of course he had put her in that position; worst of all, he had made her confront the fact that her life might slowly be divorcing itself from his. And while there might be strength to face that awful possibility in the sitting room (where, at one point, she even recognized it as a kind of elevation), the sitting room was behind her now, the insights locked inside. And what a minute before had been enlightenment could become, if she let herself dwell on it, moral upheaval; and edginess, panic. Unless she found something in the house—the greenhouse, the terrace, whatever—to distract herself.

Aunt Elizabeth's door was still closed, thankfully, and so was the door to Ben's study. She looked out the kitchen window for David; his book was on the terrace, with the "G.I. Joe" and the tangle of "Hot Wheels" equipment.

David. David. If ever there were the question of a choice, then wouldn't David be involved? And if David were involved, then how could there possibly be any choice?

She went outside and scanned the rear lawn for him. (It was greener, the shrubs growing fuller.) She called, "David?" and walked the length of the terrace. She called again, and heard him say, "Coming!" from the living room. Then she heard a crash of glass in the area of the voice.

She rushed into the room and saw him standing, very frightened, above a shattered crystal bowl.

"It slipped!" he said.

"*Slipped?*" She was staring at the pieces scattered over the Aubusson. "What were you doing with it?"

"Nothing." He backed away. He'd been holding it in front of his face, scanning the room and watching the distortion through the base of the bowl.

"That bowl was precious," Marian said. "Look at it!"

"It just slipped," David repeated. "I didn't mean to break it."

"I don't care what you meant." She fell to her knees and spread her hands helplessly over the broken crystal.

"Daddy can glue it maybe," he said.

Marian closed her eyes tightly and heard her voice rising, trembling with emotion. "I've told you—you're not to come into this room."

"There was nothing to do," he whined.

"I don't care," Marian yelled across the room. "You are not to touch her things!" She hammered her fist against her knee. "Ever!" Again. "Ever!" and again. "*Ever!*"

When she opened her eyes he was gone. Marian bent forward and began to gather up the pieces gently. The knot she had felt inside herself when she left the sitting room tightened, and she began to sob. For the bowl at first, and then David, and then herself.

She was still sobbing when she found David later, sitting in the middle of the steps in front of the house. He started to rise when he saw her, but she put her arms around him and sat beside him.

"Forgive me, baby," Marian said. "Whatever I said in there, I didn't mean any of it. Please forgive me."

David tried to move away a little. "It's okay," he said weakly.

"No, it's not. I was terrible to you." She rubbed her face against his hair. "We're going to go in there right now and we're going to touch everything we can find in that crummy house." She held him at arm's length, waiting for the pouting look to disappear. "Even break stuff if you want. Okay?"

"I don't want to break anything," David said.

Her hands framed his face, making him even more uncomfortable. "Because I love you," she said with an intensity that was almost as frightening as the sound of her voice in the living room. "More than her, more than her house. More than anything. You know that, don't you, sweetheart?"

When she finished, the knot, inexplicably, was still there.

At five to six she knocked on the door of the study. There was no reply. She opened it and peered in. Ben was asleep on the couch, his arm covering his face. He stirred when she called his name, and then raised his head sleepily.

"Sorry," Marian said without coming into the room. "Thought you might like to know—it's six and I've got a shakerful of martinis cooling in the fridge."

He put his head down again and stared at the ceiling.

"Ben? Did you hear?"

He said, "Yeah," and that was all.

Marian didn't come beyond the doorway. "I might even join the two of you tonight. Would you mind? Ben?"

He slid his legs off the couch and sat up, rubbing his forehead with both hands. "Six?" he said.

"Six. Have you been sleeping all this time?"

"A little," he said.

"Aunt Elizabeth hasn't come down yet. How'd you like to call her? I'm right in the middle."

"I don't imagine I'd be very good company tonight."

"Well . . . why don't we try it anyway?" She felt the tension concentrate itself in her hands which she clasped behind her. "You're not going to let me drink alone, are you?"

"No, Marian," he said wearily, and there was something distant and chilling in the way he said her name. "I wouldn't think of it." He gave her a brief, ironic smile, and that was chilling too. "Anything to accommodate you."

She said, "Thank you," and looked away. The typewriter, she saw, was just where she had left it, still covered; the paper in a neat pile on the side of the desk, with the mimeographed syllabus on top; the reference books and the American Lit texts were stacked evenly. Nothing had been touched.

"I'll be on the terrace," Marian said. "There's caviar on ice, if you're interested—the good stuff, six whole ounces of it." She paused and then dropped the strained geniality. "If it's a new beginning, then we ought to do it up right." She had tried to put just enough of a plea into her voice.

Ben lowered his hands. The smile was back. "How many of those do we get, Marian—new beginnings?"

"Just as many as we need, darling," Marian said.

"Oh," Ben said, but she had already gone.

He did go up to Aunt Elizabeth's room eventually. She had expressed it exactly, he reminded himself: "I don't know how Marian feels about anything anymore. Except this house." At least that wasn't something he was imagining. But even if her feelings mirrored his—the house was becoming more and more of an obsession—what was he supposed to do? Pull them all out for Marian's sake; pretend that the only reason for going back to the apartment was to save Marian from her own weakness, and that he was acting decisively and self-lessly? It would be almost simple if he could honestly say that were the only threat he saw in the house. But what about the rest of it—the threat that was either wholly imaginary, or that actually (and incredibly) existed, independent of his own mind? How *could* it exist? How could he reasonably counter Marian's argument that it was a *house*, nothing more—and pretend to even a semblance of sanity?

Just thinking about it made the throbbing in his head drive itself deeper, and the film passed over his eyes again, rippling the panels in the door to Aunt Elizabeth's room. He waited for the pain to pass, counting the seconds and using the numbers like talismans—up to six this time, longer than usual, and seven, and—seven. It stopped. He closed his eyes and took a deep breath, steadying himself against the doorjamb. When he opened them again, the film had dissolved and the edge of the pain blunted itself to that slow throbbing.

He waited and then knocked, several times, until he thought he heard Aunt Elizabeth's voice.

She was in bed when he entered the room, her back to

the door, exactly the way he had left her. He called, "Aunt Elizabeth," and she turned toward him just slightly, saying, "Benjie . . ." with a weariness in her voice that made him forget the pain.

"Did I wake you?" Ben said.

"No." She tried to turn a bit more, and then let her head fall back against the pillow. "I've just been dozing."

He moved nearer the bed. "You're all right, aren't you?" Her face looked very small and white and her body seemed lost in the vastness of the bed.

"Yes, of course," she said. "I'm just so tired I can't move."

"I shouldn't have disturbed you."

"I'm glad you did," she said without moving. "I can't sleep my life away."

"Another forty winks?" He came closer. How terribly old she looked to him, her legs and arms so thin, all veins and bones.

"No," she said, and raised her hand an inch above the bed. "I've got to get up. Just give me a minute or so to put myself together."

He watched her close her eyes and swallow hard. "Aunt Elizabeth?" he said, trying not to sound too alarmed, "Are you sure you're all right?"

"Of course I am, Benjie. What time is it?"

"Around six."

"And how—" she paused to swallow again "—how's my martini doing?"

"It's in the works."

"That's the best medicine I can think of at the moment. Wait for me on the terrace, will you?" She looked in his direction, a little to the right of where he was standing.

"Aunt Elizabeth? I'm . . . a little worried."

"About me?" He nodded and she repeated, "Me?"

Ben said, "Yes."

Her voice became a bit steadier. "I won't have that, Benjie. Now you go downstairs and bring those martinis out to the terrace. I'll be down in a jiffy." He waited. "Did you hear me, Benjie?"

"I heard you."

She looked up at the ceiling again. "Worst thing you can do to an old lady—" again, a swallow and a pause for breath "—is encourage her self-indulgence. Out with you."

"How many times must I tell you? You're not an old lady."

"Oh, Benjie," Aunt Elizabeth said, "I think it's about time we put that idea to rest."

She asked him to close the door after him ("Now, please. I won't be looked at in this frightful state"). Reluctantly, Ben left the room.

Aunt Elizabeth waited, and then once again tried to lift her head from the pillow, biting her lower lip to ease the strain which she could feel travelling down the length of her spine. It was even more severe this time, wrenching enough to make her moan and drop back against the pillow.

"Dear God . . ." The effort left her too exhausted to speak the words. She repeated them to herself: "Dear God . . ."

To find herself so completely drained of strength that she couldn't even rise to a sitting position—how was it possible? She had gotten out of bed that morning (with some difficulty, more than the day before, but she had gotten out); had walked back to the bed just a few hours ago, with only a little assistance from Ben. If the weariness and the dizzy spells had been common the past few days, they had certainly not been this debilitating. What was wrong with her?

Dwelling on it, she told herself; thinking herself into a state of paralysis. It was panic that was crippling her, nothing physical. *Will*, she reminded herself. She drew a deep breath.

It was frightening—to feel so helpless, so suddenly. Surely Ben had noticed, which, on top of everything else, she found humiliating.

Again? Again. Empty the mind first.

The fogginess that surrounded the bed was distracting her, feeding the panic. She closed her eyes, concentrating on the simple mechanics of propping herself up on the bed.

She began to slide her hands over the bedspread to position her elbows; the material, a smooth black and gold satin, abraded her skin. She raised her head again, very slowly this time. She could feel the trembling in the back of her neck and in her hands especially. Her elbows moved away from her sides, and the pain spread out, sharpest where her elbows pressed down into the mattress. She held her breath and tried to draw all her energy into her left arm, as she had done when Ben had come into the room. The elbow moved a quarter of an inch, then another, and with the movement came a wave of nausea to intensify the pain, and the frightening realization that it would snap under her weight; if she wasn't careful . . . so slowly careful . . . her arm would crumble under her.

Her arm. "Dear God," she thought again, "help me."

She shouldn't have sent him away, however humiliating the admission would have been. If she could call him . . . Once more, one more attempt and she would.

She swallowed hard and rolled her body just a little to the left, fighting the nausea and closing her eyes against the spinning of the room. A little more then; and if she could just not cry out . . . gather her strength against the pain . . . for only another quarter inch.

The pain welled viciously and shot itself into her arm from every part of her body. And though she tried to scream to release the horror of what was happening to her, the cry lodged itself in her throat for the moment or two she remained conscious and then slipped out as a thin stream of air, barely a sigh.

Marian brought the caviar out to the terrace on one of the gold trays she had found. The condiment bowls were silver.

"I tried to improvise," she said archly, "but nothing in gold worked. We'll just have to make do, I suppose." She gave a brave smile.

She had changed into a full, blue hostess gown with, appropriately, gold piping and blue-and-gold slippers.

Ben was leaning against the balustrade, looking at the

shoreline across the bay. When he turned to face her, she set the tray down on the glass table, and then spun around with her arms raised to display the gown. He had never seen it before.

"Like it?" she asked.

Ben nodded. "Looks kind of strange," he said. "I've gotten so used to you in jeans and a shirt."

"The change will do us both good." She smoothed down her hair. "I did whatever I could with—" She rolled her eyes up, hopelessly. "Promise—this week something drastic." She had made no attempt to cover the gray spreading at her temples. She touched it. "I should've remembered: my Aunt Marge, rest her soul—went totally gray almost overnight when she was about twenty-five. But totally. You think that's what's happening to me?"

"Looks that way," Ben said.

"I hate it, myself. Does it really bother you?"

"I've gotten used to that too."

"It's infuriating. You don't have a bit of it."

"It's all inside," Ben said. "Where's Davey?"

"Where else? In front of the tube. I made him a Shirley Temple. Shall I bring ours out?" She glanced at the terrace door as an afterthought. "Where's Aunt Elizabeth by the way?"

"Upstairs. I'm worried about her, Marian."

"Oh, she'll be fine," Marian said. "I'll apologize as soon as she comes down. Aunt Elizabeth isn't the type to hold a grudge. I was upset; she must realize that."

"It's not that," Ben said. "Something's wrong with her."

"What do you mean, wrong?"

"Physically. She won't admit it of course."

"Then don't press it, darling. If it's wrong enough, she'll tell us." He wasn't listening. He was looking at the tray of caviar; looking, as a matter of fact, everywhere but directly at her. That was something *she* was getting used to. She wanted to tell him: just once be distracted from something else by her; for five minutes let nothing, real or unreal, be wrong with any of them; let it be as pleasant and free of suspicion as it was in those first few days. But she had said as much several times to no avail. "I don't know about you," she said, "but I am *d*ying for a martini. You know how long it's been since I've had one?"

All he had heard was the question mark, and when Ben shook his head, seriously, Marian threw up two imaginary hands and pushed the tray in his direction. "Go ahead," she said, "dig in." She went into the house for their drinks.

Aunt Elizabeth still hadn't come down when Marian returned with the pitcher of martinis and three chilled glasses —two "ups" and an ice-filled "down" with extra vermouth.

"David opted for the sewing room," she explained. "Roger Ramjet's on the tube. I must say, some of those cartoons are damn funny." Ben was pacing a bit. The caviar, she noticed, still hadn't been touched. Marian held up the pitcher to catch his eye. "Shall I pour?"

Ben stopped. "I'd better go up and check her," he said.

Marian said, "Ben," with less patience.

"She was coming right down."

"Then she'll be down." She began to pour. "Can't you and I have one quiet, uncomplicated minute together? Like in the old days?" She brought his drink to him and made him take it. "To the old days," she said, touching her glass to his, "wherever they've gone. They seem to have gotten lost in all the confusion, haven't they? If it's my fault, I'm sorry." He was looking at his glass. Exasperated, she said, "Look at me? Please?" He did and she said, "Thank you," softening it with a smile. "You never told me—do I or don't I get another chance?"

"Chance for what, Marian?"

She shrugged. "To try to get things back into normal perspective. 'Things' being, I suppose, our life."

He was silent a moment. "What do you think?"

"I don't know. What I think might be just wishful."

The pause was longer. She watched for even a slight change of expression. There was none; he simply tapped her glass with his.

"Is that as loud as it comes?" she said.

Ben lifted his glass higher. "That's good crystal," he said: "You ought to know that."

She sipped her drink, watching him over the rim of the glass. And the idea of his leaving her, or even withdrawing temporarily from the house, must have been inconceivable to her to begin with, since she felt neither surprise nor relief at his reaction to the question, which turned out to be the quiet admission that, "I'm not ending anything, Marian."

She moved away from him and walked slowly beside the balustrade. The hedges were growing fuller beside the terrace; peonies were beginning to flower, and masses of rhododendron. She paused above a rosebush filled with salmon-colored buds. They would open in a day or so, and the yellow roses next to them, and of course the reds with all their different shadings. Their fragrance would fill the sitting room.

She looked beyond them, over the sweep of lawn. "Don't you love this time especially?" she said to Ben who was silent behind her. "The color gets so intense." She turned and walked back toward him and there was something commanding in the ease and grace of her movement. "It's looming bigger and bigger though, isn't it? The city, the return to reality." She was beside him. "If for no other reason but that . . . bear with me? Let me—revel in it just a while longer?"

"I told you, Marian," Ben said, "I have no intention of wrecking your summer."

"It ought to be a little less grudging than that." She ran her finger up his chest, then followed the line of his chin and lips. "There's no such thing as my summer. It's ours." She smiled a little ruefully. "'How I Spent Our Summer Vacation': how many words would you like, Mr. Rolfe?" There *was* no gray, she noticed, not a single strand; and except for the lines in his forehead and that pinched look between his eyebrows, his face was smooth and strong; the crushes his female students developed were reasonable enough. She let her eyes linger, relearning his face. "I love you, you know," she said.

"And I love you, Marian," he said simply.

"Despite—?"

"—nothing. It's a fact of my life: I love you."

The words and the soft helplessness she saw in his eyes silenced her. She could feel a jumble of contradictory emotions rising inside herself, and the frustration of trying to hear one voice above all the others—that and the simple physical closeness of Ben—made her eyes tear. And if she had given in to the impulse the moment it flashed through her mind, if it had lingered just a fraction of a second longer, then she would have said it to him: If you love me, *then for God's sake help me.*

It passed, however, and the image of the sitting room banked with roses flashed into her mind, and the hum and the way the maze in the door caught the light. She wiped her eyes with the back of her hand, and when she felt a little less vulnerable and sentimental, she laughed apologetically and said instead, "Now how about some of that caviar?"

He left Marian spooning caviar onto wedges of toast, and went back up to Aunt Elizabeth's room. He opened the door a crack without knocking, and called, "Aunt Elizabeth?" There was no reply. He opened it wider and saw her lying on her side in bed. "Hey," he said, "you stood me up." She was lying absolutely still. He moved more anxiously into the room, keeping his eyes on her back. She might not have heard. "We had a date—" he started to say, and then stopped beside the bed. He hesitated—she was so still and, what he could see of her right arm and legs, so white—and then leaned over and touched her shoulder.

She moaned, deep in her throat, and even that came as some relief. He touched her again and whispered her name. This time the sound was deeper, more pained. Her face was turned away from him, pressed into the pillow; she began to draw short, racking breaths, and when Ben rushed to the other side of the bed to face her, he saw that her left arm was twisted hideously under her. Her mouth was open, her upper lip pulled out of shape against the pillow. Grotesquely, the upper plate she wore had come loose in her mouth.

Ben dropped to his knees beside her and gently smoothed the hair back from her face.

"*Aunt Elizabeth.*"

Her breathing became quicker, more agonized. The side of her face was cold, almost bluish. He lifted his hand. If he could at least turn her onto her back, off the arm, or somehow cover that pathetic humiliation which, stupidly enough, he found especially unnerving. He touched the top of her head lightly to trace the pain, and then her feet and her legs, the moans growing as he touched closer to the arm crushed under her.

The realization jolted him: she's going to die. And if he tried to turn her over or move her in any way she'd probably go right in front of his eyes. She was going to die.

He brought his face closer, his lips almost touching her ear. His chest pressed against the side of the bed. Aunt Elizabeth trembled, and her cry made him pull back in alarm.

"Aunt Elizabeth!" he whispered, pleading. He watched her face for some hint of recognition. There was nothing; only that steady, terrible sound in her throat. He waited, scarcely breathing himself, until watching her, and his own helplessness, became unbearable. He rose to his feet slowly, looking down at her in disbelief; as he did, her face blurred, almost mercifully, and then the room. Ben covered his eyes and then pressed his fingers against the shocks of pain. He stumbled away from the bed, and when he found himself against the opened door, the pain had intensified and the film over his eyes grown more opaque. *Oh, Christ, please*, he thought, *let it pass. Let it pass.* He started the numbers to distract himself, and it was eleven this time before the hall outside came into focus and he could move unsteadily toward the staircase.

"The doctor I took Davey to—where's his number?" He was calling out to Marian from the open terrace door.

The urgency in his voice startled her. "What's wrong?" She had been sitting, looking over the rear lawn. She stood up.

"Where's that doctor's number?" Ben repeated.

"On the hall table, next to the phone. Why?"

She heard him say, "Aunt Elizabeth" as he disappeared from the doorway.

Marian came into the hall. Ben was flipping through the pages. "What's wrong with her?" Marian said.

"I don't know." He pulled a page free and threw the others back onto the table. "Christ, I don't know."

"What do you mean, you don't know?"

"Just what I said." He lifted the receiver and started to dial. "She's unconscious, she's—" He broke off and slammed his fingers down on the cradle. "Christ, I can't even think straight." He redialled the number.

Marian looked toward the stairs. "I'll go on up," she said.

Ben said, "God*damn!*" and lowered the receiver. Marian could hear the busy signal at the other end of the line. She stopped at the foot of the staircase and watched him pace, three or four steps in either direction. "Is there a hospital, anything you know of?"

Marian shook her head. "If it's busy, he's there at least."

"She's going to need more than a hick doctor." He started to dial again, and Marian went up the stairs quickly.

She stood at the foot of the bed, watching Aunt Elizabeth in the fading light. She tried calling her name, and when there was no response, only that pitiful gasping for air, Marian moved back from the bed, toward the lamp beside the chaise. She hesitated and then turned it on and stared at Aunt Elizabeth's face half-buried in the pillow. She lowered herself to the edge of the chaise and sat with her hands clasped tightly in her lap. And it was terrible, she knew, and brutally unfeeling, but she couldn't bring herself nearer the figure on the bed, who wasn't Aunt Elizabeth, who couldn't possibly be Aunt Elizabeth.

She turned her face to the door. Where was Ben, what was he doing down there?

If Aunt Elizabeth was dying—and God, how could she possibly look like that and survive?—Marian had watched death before; her grandparents, two of them, had died with her right beside them. Why should the possibility of Aunt Elizabeth dying in front of her fill her with such absolute dread?

She tried not to look at the bed.

Think of something comforting. Think of beyond the door and up the hall: the refuge of the sitting room, so close.

Ben came into the room and Marian sprang to her feet. "Did you get him?"

He said, "No," without looking at her, and went directly to the bed.

"The line can't stay busy all night. I'll go down and try again."

Ben knelt beside Aunt Elizabeth. "You do that, Marian," he said quietly.

She had started to walk toward the door. She stopped abruptly. "What do you mean?"

He touched Aunt Elizabeth's hair. "They're all busy," he said, "every number I tried. Even the goddamned operator is busy." He looked across the room at her and smiled that chilling smile again. "The phone's out, in a word. Surprise?"

It took her a moment to absorb what he was saying. She shook her head. "I don't know what you're talking about."

"There's no—!" He caught himself and lowered his voice. They had been talking in sick-room whispers. "There's no way to get through. To anybody."

Marian tried to think when was the last time that they had used the phone. The doctor, for David. And before that? She couldn't remember.

"If we can't get through," she said, "then we'll *take* her to someone."

"Who?"

"The first shingle we find, or a hospital, or somebody!"

"She can't be moved."

"How do you know that?"

"I tried." He sat back on his heels and stared at Aunt Elizabeth's face. The quick catches of breath were becoming more agonized.

"Then what do we do—watch her die?"

"I don't *know* what to do, Marian. I'm trying to think of something."

She had to get out of that room. It had become suffocating, and the sounds coming from Aunt Elizabeth were frighteningly ominous.

If she could calm herself and think reasonably, if she could go into the sitting room for just a few minutes.

"I'll try to reach him again," she said in the silence. "If I can't reach him, I'll take the car and go out and *find* someone. Or you can take the car. There's got to be some way."

Ben continued to stare at Aunt Elizabeth. The car. It hadn't occurred to him before, but if the phone was out, conveniently, then what help would the car be? It wouldn't be made that simple for them, would it? Let her try it. Just let her try it.

"Ben?" She was waiting.

Ben looked up at her. "You still don't get it, do you, Marian? It's still all in my mind." He touched the pillow. "This, like everything else."

Marian remained still, almost defiantly. They were at opposite ends of the room, with the awful fact of Aunt Elizabeth between them. And whatever spring had fed the tenderness she felt for Ben just a while ago, out on the terrace, had dried inside her. There was suddenly nothing. Whether she would feel the same way in another minute or so, or not, right now Ben and Aunt Elizabeth and everything else existed only to keep her away from the comfort of the sitting room.

It was getting darker, and if she waited for Ben to think his tortuous way to a solution, Aunt Elizabeth would die in Mrs. Allardyce's house.

"Stay with her," Marian said, and walked out of the room.

"I'll stay with her," Ben said. He touched Aunt Elizabeth's forehead very lightly. "Of course I will." He brought his hand down to her lips and tried to think of something else, like Aunt Elizabeth finally behind the wheel, doing eighty on a stretch of open road.

Marian went directly downstairs for the number, and on

the third try reached the doctor who remembered her with no particular interest. He asked for the symptoms which Marian described vaguely, and interrupted her to ask Aunt Elizabeth's age. She could almost see his head shaking at the other end of the line. He would, magnanimously, stop by as soon as he could, though at that age . . . She gave him directions (he had never been to the house, knew it only vaguely) and the phone number.

She went back up to the room and announced, "He's coming. Dr. Ross." She waited for Ben's reaction.

He hadn't moved from Aunt Elizabeth's side. He gave Marian an incredulous look. "You got him?"

"I got him." She couldn't resist adding, "The operator as well." He still looked incredulous. "Ross's line *was* busy for a while. The operator's might've been as well, I suppose."

"All the lines were busy, Marian," Ben insisted. "I didn't make it up."

"I'm sure you didn't. The important thing is he'll be here."

"When?"

"As soon as he can." She was standing just inside the room, and however childish it was, there was some satisfaction in Ben's puzzled expression. "I think it might be a good idea to keep David downstairs tonight. I can set up one of the servants' rooms. Is there anything you want me to do before the doctor comes?"

Ben shook his head and rose to his feet.

"There must be some way to make her a little comfortable," Marian said.

Ben carried the Windsor chair to the side of the bed. "I'm afraid to move her."

She watched him sit, facing Aunt Elizabeth. She had made her point, she supposed, and to mention the phone again would have been needlessly cruel. But it wasn't conspiring against them after all, she wanted to assure him, no more than the house was. And as for Aunt Elizabeth—well, hopefully the doctor would exorcise that suspicion as well. And leave room for the next wave of phantoms.

All she said, however, was, "I'll be downstairs if you need me."

Marian closed the door in case David should happen to come upstairs while she was still in the sitting room.

The lamp was on, the drapes drawn shut. Mrs. Allardyce's dinner tray was on the table beside the wingchair. It was untouched.

Marian moved around the room, slower and slower, as the knot began to loosen inside her. She lingered over the photographs and the flower-filled urns and vases; the gold candlesticks and the silver candelabra, and the two bronze holders she had found in the basement, huge and vaguely liturgical. She touched the tables and the porcelain figurines, the damask walls and the crystal, and she could feel the hum coursing through everything she touched, vibrantly. Especially the door. She traced the carvings with her hands raised and her eyes closed, and it was like touching something or someone loved profoundly, and then feeling the touch returned.

The gown rippled with the movement of her hands.

She moved away from the door, lifted a small cylinder of gold-tipped matches from the table, and lighted the candles in the bronze holders, and all the other candles in the room. She turned off the lamp and stood spellbound by the serenity and the dazzling beauty of the room.

The wingchair and the silver tray glowed in front of her, and before she realized what she was doing, she had sat down and brought the tray closer to herself. She unfolded the napkin and reached for the silver knife and fork. The presence directing her hands and imposing itself on her will was almost palpable, and she felt no desire to resist or question the force. She cut into the meat, and in a moment all she was aware of was the hum and the incredible fragrance of roses rising all around her.

The sounds crept into his sleep, more insistently: the rattling gasp for air and then the pained exhalation, hoarse and mortal. Ben opened his eyes.

She was in the same position on the bed, but her skin, shrivelled and tissue-thin, had the pallor of death. There were two dark hollows where her eyes had been, and the flesh was stretched transparent over the bridge of her nose. She had become incredibly old, mummified almost, and the more Ben stared at her, the more she seemed to age; her jaw slackened and her lips tightened inside her mouth.

He was asleep still, he had to be. Or he was hallucinating. He closed his eyes and tried to shake the image out of his brain. The sounds enveloped him.

The pain had intensified and there was something almost reassuring in the throbbing inside his head. It was the pain he trusted, not what he thought he was seeing, and the pain meant that, however real it seemed (even a bumper pressing against his leg), it was an hallucination. And if he waited long enough (*count*) and tried not to panic, he could will it out of existence—the transformation he was imagining would disappear and he'd see that in reality there had been no change in Aunt Elizabeth at all. It was all illusory, a projection of the pain.

He closed his eyes tighter and began to tick off the numbers.

Marian placed the silver on the empty plate and lay the napkin on the tray. She moved the small table to one side and then sat back in the wingchair, gripping the arms.

The fragrance had grown even stronger in the room, waves of it—gardenia as well as rose, and peony and honeysuckle and something like lilac, and other fragrances she didn't recognize. She raised her head and looked around the room, trying to trace the source. It was not only in the room, it was beyond it, she was sure. She rose from the chair and moved toward the sitting room door, and then past it, into the hall. The fragrance was there as well, and at the top of the stairs, and all through the house, drifting through the rooms from somewhere. She crossed the entrance hall and went into the living room.

When he heard the car approaching the house, he opened his eyes, and real or not, nothing had changed. He looked away from Aunt Elizabeth, toward the windows. It was dark. How long had he been asleep in the chair since Marian had told him about the doctor? The car was stopping near the front steps, to the left of the windows, and just as he was about to rise and look down at the drive, he realized from the sound outside that it wasn't the doctor. He stiffened in the chair and listened to the motor idling in the vast silence outside. Aunt Elizabeth's struggle for breath was more desperate. He thought he saw her stir, just perceptibly. The pain hammered at him, and then it projected another sound, one he hadn't heard before. It was somewhere in the house, dimmer at first than the throbbing of the motor. He tried to make it out. It was near the foot of the stairs—something sliding, being dragged over the wooden floor. And then it was on the stairs, coming up. A sliding, then a thud—a heavy bumping sound. And again. Slide, bump, slide, bump—the sounds coming faster and closer. He saw it again—the stirring on the bed: Aunt Elizabeth's right hand trembled and her head moved slightly, as though she were hearing the same sounds. The moaning was constant, deeper—a strength-less, animal-like keening that had to be the edge of death.

Ben's hands tightened white on the chair. He leaned forward and saw her twist herself onto her back. The sound was near the top of the stairs. Slide. Bump. He sat paralyzed, watching Aunt Elizabeth's eyes open to the sound, to the metallic rattling now, at the end of the corridor. Something was being wheeled toward the door very quickly. Aunt Elizabeth suddenly sat up in the bed, her tongue swelling between her lips. She turned her face to the door.

It was a dream, he wasn't seeing any of this, wasn't hearing those sounds. Not the choking or the chambered rattling directly outside the door, or the great blow against it that made the door fly open. He wouldn't give in to it, wouldn't look, not even when it was wheeled beside the bed, and the polished lid pulled open brutally by the chauffeur who moved toward Aunt Elizabeth then as she stared lifeless at the white satin lining. *He wouldn't look.*

The greenhouse. Marian moved through the living room, flicking on lamps as she approached the alcove and the glass door opposite the wall of shadowy photographs. The fragrance was stronger. She breathed it in, waiting with her hand on the knob and trying to see into the darkness beyond the door. The anticipation was making her hand sweat against the knob; she turned it slowly and pulled the door open. The warmth and sweetness spilled over her, and it was a moment before she could fumble for the row of switches just inside the greenhouse, and finally make the whole glory of the room burst on her.

The long shelves and tables were filled with color, sprays of it, with rows of billowing plants, an infinite variety of them, growing thick and vividly green. What had been stiff and lifeless now hung from the clay pots and brass planters, laden with blossoms. There were orchids, great climbing masses of them, and huge exotic blooms, and ferns with lacy sprawling fronds, and odd shaped leaves and petals riddled with the most intense colors. As far as she could see, up to the glass ceiling and all the way to the other end of the greenhouse, there was life, miraculous new life, with everything unnaturally large and bright.

She walked slowly down the narrow passages, pulling the folds of her gown closer. Filling herself with the wonder of it all. And if there was a certain uneasiness creeping in, very subtly at first, well, that was understandable in the face of such an awesome mystery. She stopped to touch the pattern of a leaf, to breathe in the fragrance, bending as if in homage to the sheer perfection of the flowers, of the life the house was offering her.

It was alive, all around her it was alive, and how else had it come alive but through her? And wasn't that the uneasiness she was feeling—the growing awareness of her power in the house, the enormity of the mystery enveloping her life, which, but for the sanctuary of the sitting room, would be unthinkable?

But there was something more immediate feeding the uneasiness—an emanation from somewhere else in the house that filled the greenhouse with a sickly, over-ripe sweetness.

Marian stopped suddenly. She was standing exactly where Aunt Elizabeth had been standing that morning.

She said the name aloud: "Aunt Elizabeth . . ." and felt something coil inside her. The sweetness became intolerable. She brushed past the overhanging foliage, flicked off the lights and closed the door behind her, fixing her eyes on the opposite end of the living room and then the head of the stairs and then the door to Aunt Elizabeth's room. She pushed it open and stood frozen in the doorway.

Aunt Elizabeth's head was thrown back against the pillow, her mouth pulled open hideously, her eyes staring back at the headboard. Ben was in the chair beside the bed, slumped forward, his arms clutching his stomach.

Marian approached the bed and stared for a long time at Aunt Elizabeth before her hand touched Ben's shoulder. Ben raised his face to her slowly.

"Oh, God," Marian whispered. "Oh, God."

Ben continued to stare up at her, blank and silent, even when she brought her hand to her mouth and turned her back to the bed.

A while later, the phone rang. It was the doctor who told Marian, "I'll be damned if I can find any Seventeen Shore Road, as *long* as I've lived here. Where in God's name are you?"

(10)

When Marian came back into the room, Ben had covered Aunt Elizabeth's body with a blanket. She told him about the doctor, and he replied, tonelessly, "It doesn't really matter anymore, does it?" He moved away from the bed, his face still blank with shock, and stood with his back to her, looking out the window. She came behind him.

"I'm so sorry, darling," she said quietly. When she tried to put her arms around him, he moved away from her, going to the bureau which was piled neatly with Aunt Elizabeth's effects—toiletries, the huge sunglasses, a few paperbacks, a lace handkerchief. Her paint box and the two canvases were against the wall, the straw sunhat on a chair next to them.

Marian watched him pace silently; every once in a while he would look at the small shrouded figure on the bed.

"We can't do anything until he gets here," Marian said. "Then who do you want to call?"

"I'll take care of it," he said, and it was like a casual wave of his hand, dismissing her.

He stopped pacing and leaned his elbow against a large armoire with spiring finials. He was facing the wall and massaging the back of his neck. Her presence was obviously as much of an intrusion as his had been in the sitting room.

"We'll have to tell David," she said.

Ben lowered his elbow and looked across at her. "Where is he?"

"Downstairs."

Ben thought a moment. "I'll tell him," he said, and before Marian could reply he had walked out of the room.

As stunned, as numb with fatigue as he seemed, he handled everything with a strength and determination that surprised her—the doctor, the call to the undertaker, and especially David's wide-eyed, inarticulate grief which found the release of tears only later, when Marian came into the sewing room.

Ben avoided her through it all, pointedly enough for her not to force herself on him, and shock and grief, she knew, were only partly responsible for the distance. It was unspoken this time but it was clear enough: the house, despite the testimony of the doctor, despite all reason, was responsible for Aunt Elizabeth's death, and Marian was acting in complicity with the house. He believed it, there was no question in Marian's mind that he actually believed it.

She had not willed Aunt Elizabeth's death, never for one moment; and whatever premonition, brief and frightening, she herself had had in the greenhouse, however beyond her understanding the mystery of the house was at this point, no amount of silence and suspicion would convince her that she had. The idea was unspeakable.

They would wait until morning to leave, he told her later, and her only reply was a cold, "Whatever you say." (Absolutely *unspeakable*.) He spent the night closed in the study, with David on the couch and himself, as far as she could tell, propped up in a chair. The shutting of the door was like a blow against her, which no amount of grief or confusion of mind could excuse as far as Marian was concerned.

She went back to the greenhouse and paced the aisles for a long while, until the turmoil inside her—the feeling that she was being forced, against her will, into an impossible position, one absolutely incapable of resolution—until it drove her up to the refuge, the sweet light and comfort of the sitting room, where there was, so quickly and so simply, peace and resolution.

The next morning she announced to Ben that she was not going back with him for Aunt Elizabeth's funeral.

She had come into their bedroom where Ben was packing a small suitcase. He stopped between the open drawer in his bureau and the bed. "Not coming back." He repeated it slowly, as if there were an anagram hidden in the words. The lines in his forehead and between his eyes deepened.

Marian shook her head and let him see how difficult the

decision had been. "I can't." She raised her hands helplessly.

Ben was silent for a few moments. He threw several balls of dark socks into the suitcase, moving away from her. "I suppose you've thought about it," he said.

"All night."

There was another pause; he walked back to the drawer and slid it shut slowly. "Okay," he said; "any way you want it."

"I don't *want* it, Ben," Marian said, and her voice became more sincere and apologetic. "There's nothing else I can do."

"I understand, Marian," Ben said. He lowered the lid of the suitcase and played with the latches.

Marian came to the edge of the bed and sat beside the suitcase, covering his hand with hers. "How can I leave her, Ben? You know how she depends on me for everything."

He pulled his hand away, and softened the gesture with a tight smile. "I said I understand, Marian. Don't agonize over it."

"I *am*. I know what Aunt Elizabeth meant to you. I'd give anything to be able to come back."

"Simple question of priorities." He snapped the latches shut and lifted the suitcase to the floor. "By all means stay." He went to the closet and pulled out a blue tie and a blue-and-black check sport jacket. "David comes with me of course."

"David?"

He closed the closet door. "David," he said firmly. "Can you pack a bag for him?"

She hadn't planned on his taking David, hadn't even considered David in making her decision; and the locked-out feeling of the night before came back to her, more intense, deeper than mere hurt or resentment, though there was that too. She rose from the bed and had to clear her throat before she could ask, "How long do you expect to be gone?"

Ben shrugged. "I have no idea."

It was becoming harder for her to speak. "That's no kind of answer, Ben," she said.

"I'm being honest. There'll be things to do after the funeral."

"I know, but—three days? Four? A week?"

"I'll let you know, okay?"

"When?"

"As soon as I know myself."

But you *will* be back? she wanted to say. But of course they'd be back, how could they not come back? He must have seen the question in her face, because he looked at her very deeply, and it was either pain or weariness, or just that simple fact of his life once again, that seemed to creep into his voice and warm it a little. "When this is over, Marian, we'll talk."

"Yes," Marian said, and maybe after a small separation she would feel comfortable enough with him to speak, to have it out finally one way or another.

"One more time," he said, and the warmth had gone out of his voice with the ultimatum.

She nodded slowly and waited for something inside herself to be called up again, either through love or through fear. There was neither, only a vaguely unsettling resignation. She tried telling herself that there was nothing important enough to keep her alone in the house, nothing worth the pain of separation. From David. From Ben. Who had been her whole life. Who *were* her life.

None of it worked, none of it was strong enough to make her say to Ben, "All right, I'll leave the house. I'll come with you." If it was a question of choice this one time, the new life or the old, then the choice had to be the house and Mrs. Allardyce. That was her chief responsibility (Ben and even David could do without her for a few days), and that, she'd admit to herself eventually, would be the really wrenching separation. This one time.

She told Ben again how truly sorry she was, how she would give anything to be able to call back her words to Aunt Elizabeth on the day of her death, how truly she had loved her, and would mourn her.

"I'll pray for her soul," Marian said.

Ben's eyes clouded. He nodded and turned away from her.

She saw him raise his hand to his head and then feel his way almost blindly to the edge of the bed.

"Ben?" she called. "Are you all right?"

He leaned forward. "Pack David's bag," he said. His hands covered his face, his fingers bent and bloodless against his forehead.

She hesitated until he said, "I'm all right." It was pain, not grief in his voice. He lowered his hands then, and went into the bathroom without looking at her.

She called his name again and there was no reply, only the sound of water running.

Marian went into David's room, and while she was piling his clothes into the suitcase, she started to weep quietly. She was still weeping when she saw them to the car. Ben's face was pale and there were beads of sweat like blisters along his hairline. He was all right, he insisted again, and his kiss, when Marian brought her face down to the open window, was brief and mechanical. The car pulled away and she strained to see David look back at her through the rear window, which made her weep for a long time after they had passed out of sight, beyond the green and rolling sweep of lawn.

Whatever her resolution, the loneliness of those first few hours without them would be unbearable, she had thought. She was wrong. Halfway around the house, distracting her-self with the new growth in the flowerbeds, her eyes were dry, and while she would miss them of course, right now she felt secure and completely at peace in the vast, quiet shade of the house and the trees. Even the realization (and had it ever occurred to Ben?) that she was without a car and was, effectively, sealed off from the outside world, heightened her sense of freedom.

There were suddenly no encumbrances, nothing to distract her from the house. And, curiously, no guilt at all in the feeling —as though the spirit of the sitting room had been released and was hovering guardian-like over her as she walked the grounds.

She had come under the rounded bay in the west wing. She looked up at the curtained windows and felt Mrs. Allardyce very close, even closer than in the sitting room. And if ever, surely she would show herself to Marian now, with the two of them alone together in the house. And maybe reveal even a part of the mystery. The pool, the clocks, the greenhouse, the grounds; the force in the sitting room that at times made Marian feel like an extension of her.

Last night came back to her. The dinner tray. Had it happened or had she only dreamed it? She couldn't remember.

The breakfast tray, when she went up to the sitting room, was untouched; and so, later, was the lunch tray. Each time Marian carried the food back down to the kitchen and eventually ate it herself. Had she done the same the previous evening, or actually sat in Mrs. Allardyce's wingchair and used her silver, her linen, her tray? In her place? She still couldn't remember with any certainty.

Around four, just as she finished clearing out Aunt Elizabeth's room, Ben called her from the apartment. He brought up the car immediately. "I just wasn't thinking this morning. You might've guessed as much."

"I've got everything I need here," Marian said.

"I don't like you being that isolated. What if there's an emergency?"

"There won't be any. Stop worrying."

She asked him about the funeral which would be on Thursday. There were frequent pauses on his end of the line, which Marian did nothing to fill in; when he spoke it was all slow and toneless and wearying.

"You haven't changed your mind, have you?" he asked her.

"About coming in? Honey, I told you—it's impossible. Now please don't make me feel any worse about it."

"That's not my intention," Ben said. "It's just that . . . it might be a little easier if you were here." There was another pause. She could hear the courtyard noises in the background. "Christ, Marian—" Ben started to say. He stopped and she could hear his breath catch. She ran her finger along the edge of the hall commode. "How the hell did we wind up like this?"

Please—not now, she wanted to say to him; give it a little rest. Instead, she said, "Don't worry about us, darling."

"I do."

She changed the subject to the apartment, and his voice became a little less mournful. "It's just the way you left it."

"Hot?"

"Cool."

"Noisy?"

"Listen." He held the phone closer to the window.

Marian put a roll of her eyes into the laugh. "Hello to the Supervisor. And a big kiss to my baby."

"I'll call you tomorrow, okay?" Ben said.

"I'll be here."

They both waited. "Miss you," she said to end it. "'Bye."

Ben said, "'Bye."

The house was no different, no more intimidating at night, not even with all its long shadowy stretches, and basements and sub-basements, and the sporadic sounds of wind and wood creaking. She moved easily through the rooms—regally even, in the blue-and-gold gown she had put on again for the evening.

A little after nine she turned off all the lights on the lower floor and went back up to the sitting room which was banked even more with flowers cut that afternoon from the greenhouse and the flowerbeds. The dinner tray was where she had left it at six.

Marian lifted the matches from the table and relighted all the candles, working her way toward the hieroglyphs in the door. She stood in front of them for a while, and then cleared her throat and knocked gently, feeling the pulse of the room against her knuckles.

"Mrs. Allardyce?" She waited, and then announced: "They've gone." She brought her face closer to the door, listening. "They won't be back for a while, I suspect." Another pause. "There's just me now . . . just the two of us . . ."

Her voice had lowered to a reverent whisper which would hardly be audible beyond the thickness of the door. The side of her head touched the carvings, and her right hand.

"I've been doing what I can," Marian continued. "I don't know what else to do. I don't honestly know what's expected of me, Mrs. Allardyce. It would be so much easier if you could somehow tell me . . . just a little more." She moved her head away from the door and slid her fingers down the sculpted surface. "It's so difficult, so frustrating to have this door between us all the time." Her hand fell to her side. There was only the hum intensifying the stubborn silence beyond the door. "In any event," Marian said, "they've gone."

She raised her arms and brushed the gray back against her temples. Ben, David—abstracted to an anonymous "they." How many times had she just said it without thinking? She walked slowly across the room and lost the thought, watching the candlelight glow in the faces on the table. And then, near the edge, framed in lace-like silver and dimming the mass of faces surrounding her, she saw Aunt Elizabeth staring up at her.

It took a moment for the numbing shock to pass, and then Marian's hands jerked up to her mouth to stifle the cry. She squeezed her eyes shut, the palms of her hands came together, forefingers pressed tight against her lips, and all she could think was *no* and *no* and *no*. The room became suffocating all of a sudden, and the hum seemed to be boring into her. She opened her eyes again and caught herself against the edge of the table. It trembled, and a metallic rattle wove its way over the surface.

She looked at the picture again, and again, closer, and each time a chill passed through her. It was a small color photograph of Aunt Elizabeth in the bright silk print she had worn the day they arrived at the house. She was looking up blankly, her eyes a washed-out blue; her hands were crossed placidly in her lap. There was something about the pose and the face

—the line of the mouth especially—that looked tampered with and unfamiliar, as though a strange hand had tried to recreate her features.

The shock passed slowly. Marian breathed in a long draft of air, and gradually the hum faded into the background again and became a gentle, soothing presence that steadied her hand as she reached out to touch the picture.

"Aunt Elizabeth," she said mournfully, "Aunt Elizabeth."

She looked from the picture to the carved door across the room.

"It's—true?" she called faintly. "It's true?" And for the first time her voice rose strong enough to penetrate the door. "Oh, God—*is it true?*"

She tried staying in the sitting room that night, tried, as she had done so many times, to find reassurance, a quieting of her fears, a bolstering of her faith, in the sanctuary of the room. But this time it was different; it wasn't a vague premonition she was bringing to the room. The face among all those other frightening faces was confirmation enough; and so, when she thought back, was the transformation of the pool, the ticking of the clocks. The light—the elevation of her understanding she had been asking for beside the carved door had come down on her with devastating power: there was a malevolence in the house and she was being used as its agent.

Well, she'd end it; she'd have them come back—the Allardyces. Somehow.

She walked out of the sitting room and went downstairs for the list of names. There had to be some means of reaching them—a number or an address she and Ben had overlooked. She studied the pages carefully and there was nothing; and nothing in any of the antique desks scattered throughout the house, or Roz's bedroom, or Brother's.

She'd leave then without reaching them. What responsibility to the house and Mrs. Allardyce could she have in view of such a monstrous deception?

She went up to her own bedroom and sat in her own wing-chair.

A picture. A small silver-framed photograph which she might so easily have overlooked.

To have seen it, to have been allowed to see it. To have a small part of the mystery of the house put in front of her eyes so clearly. To be made a part of it.

She'd *still* leave.

Leave the greenhouse and the lawns and the sitting room she'd banked with flowers. Leave the Kirmans and Aubussons, the Chippendales and Sheratons, and all the crystal and gold and silver she'd unearthed and polished. Leave the bombé chests and consoles and commodes and fauteuils and clocks and chandeliers that had become an indispensable part of the landscape of her life. And the space and the peace, and everything she'd always wanted, everything that but for her would be moldering in closets and basements and under layers of dust. Leave the mystery and the approbation of a force beyond her understanding. Leave what had become the deepest and truest reflection of what she actually was.

For the old life, the abrasive and frustrating third-rate existence.

Because of a small photograph of an old woman who was dead.

Marian got up from the wingchair and went out into the hall, and then wandered slowly through all the rooms of the house for a long time. And then over the grounds in the moonlight, to the pool and down to the bay, and over the dewy, terraced lawn in front of the house. She turned back and looked at the full, overwhelming sweep of the house glowing like white marble in the light.

Then she went back upstairs, this time into the sitting room where she intended to stay just briefly. The small table beside the wingchair had been moved and the plate on the dinner tray was empty. And it might have been her imagination, but there was a small click in the area of the carved door just as Marian came into the room. She went to the door, tried it—it was locked—and listened; and again it might have been her imagination, but under the hum there was the sound of floorboards creaking and light footsteps moving away from the door into the recesses of the bedroom.

The depth of her reaction surprised her: the confirmation of an actual presence beyond the door wiped the picture out of her mind, and the Allardyces, and the clocks and the pool. It left her shaking and filled with a kind of exaltation that was exhausting and revivifying at the same time.

She went to the wingchair and sat, watching the door until what was left of the tension and anguish drained out of her slowly. Then she leaned back against the gold brocade and slept. Deep and dreamless.

Friday, four days after they had left the house, Ben came back with David. Marian was in the greenhouse when she heard David calling her. She looked up at the sound which came nearer, into the living room, and let the flowers she had just cut spill out of the cut-glass vase onto the table. He was coming into the alcove when she pulled the greenhouse door shut behind her, and cried out, "Davey!" She bent and threw her arms around him. "What a surprise, what a beautiful surprise!" She hugged him closer, and then held him at arm's length. "You look like you've grown a whole foot in a couple of days. God, how I've missed you!"

David was staring at her hair. "Your hair's all gray," he said. "How come?"

Marian let him go and raised her hands to the sides of her head. There were only streaks of blonde now, thinner each day. After a moment she laughed. "Mommie's getting older," she said, and hugged him again. "Most of it's from missing you so much."

She saw Ben come into the hall with the suitcases. He stared at her hair too when she walked up to him and put her arms around him.

"Welcome back," she said and kissed him, and the tension between them was back immediately. She tilted her head away from him when he tried to touch her hair. "Don't make me more self-conscious about it," she said.

"Aunt Marge or not," Ben said, "it's going to take some getting used to. It's happened pretty fast."

"If it bothers you I'll do something about it when I get a chance." She looked at David who was still fascinated by her hair. "Did you eat lunch?" she asked them both.

"I had a Big Mac," David said.

"But no Yankee Doodles, I bet. There are some in the fridge."

Ben held out the small suitcase. "How about taking this up to your room first?"

Marian waited for David to leave. "How did he take it?" she asked Ben.

"All right, I guess." He moved away from Marian and looked at the walls and the chandelier and the staircase. "He hasn't talked about her at all."

"That's normal, I suppose," Marian said.

Ben shrugged. "I suppose." He looked even more tired than she remembered. The lines in his forehead had deepened and there were others, thinner, around his eyes and mouth.

"I wasn't expecting you," Marian said.

Ben stopped in front of the brass Regency clock which read two-ten. "I tried calling you; yesterday a couple of times, and again this morning."

Two of the times she had heard the phone. "I might've been outside, or upstairs," she said. "Incredible, isn't it—one phone in a house this size?"

"I didn't know what to think," Ben said. "You might've given me a call."

"I would have, darling, eventually." She smiled. "Why don't I put some coffee on?" She started to go toward the kitchen.

"Marian?" He waited for her to look at him. "Would it have been better if we hadn't come back? Honestly."

She gave him a long, uncomprehending look. "You've got to be kidding," she said.

"The fact is, I'm not."

The clock ticked quietly in the pause, and overhead the chandelier gleamed.

"Coffee on the terrace, okay?" Marian said.

What he had said stayed with her, and as much as she tried to deny it to herself, or qualify it (maybe if they hadn't come back so suddenly, or had given her a little more time to assimilate the mystery of the house), it was true: it *would* have been better if they hadn't come back. For four days the house had managed to fill her life completely, more richly and intensely than anything ever had in the past. More even—and she had come to terms with the admission painfully and very slowly, in the solace of the sitting room—than Ben and David had. The question of a choice was still inconceivable; as inconceivable as the idea of ever having to give up the house. But wouldn't—*wouldn't*—it have to come to that eventually?

Their sudden presence (their intrusion really) and their imposition of a life she was rising above on her new life brought back what the sitting room had dispelled her first night alone in the house: the tension, the tightening knot inside her. And it was only later in the day (Ben sitting on the terrace with a book open in his lap, David adding new track to his "Hot Wheels" set), that she realized what was making the knot tighter and the tension intolerable. She left the kitchen and went quickly up to the sitting room, where face by face she searched through the pictures on the table. And there was some little relief at least in finding that the only familiar face was the face of Aunt Elizabeth. And *that* she had already learned to come to terms with.

The pain hadn't stopped when Ben had left the house; it had continued with its incessant throbbing throughout the four days he had been away, some days less intense but still a constant presence. The blurring of his vision as well, more frequently and for longer periods of time. The fear that it might happen on the Expressway, with David in the car, had kept him in the right lane all the way from the house and all the way back. The anxiety had only intensified the pain and brought with it a feeling of nausea that passed and then recurred periodically under the strain of the four days in town.

The hallucinations, however, had stopped, and it was that fact especially that made him hold on to the idea that it was the house that was working noxiously on his mind. Just as it had worked on Aunt Elizabeth, and was now working, in an even more sinister way, on Marian.

How could three weeks—less even—wipe out nine years? There was nothing left in her that he could recognize, no point of contact. Even watching her with David, the few times she came out of the house that day, there was something strained and false, and the shows of affection seemed to be performed from memory, without any genuine feeling. If there was any feeling at all, it was reserved for the house—for the gold-rimmed china she had set out on the dining room table which was hung with web-like lace, and the three gold goblets, like chalices, and the centerpiece—a crystal bowl filled with fresh flowers and flanked by two silver candelabra —and all the other pieces that glittered in the light from the chandelier.

She had called him in from the terrace, and David from the TV in the sewing room. David still hadn't appeared; Ben stood behind his chair and watched Marian strike a match and light the candles. He thought of Aunt Elizabeth who, as far as Marian was concerned, had never even existed at all. She blew out the match and smiled across the table at him. Then she went to the wall switch and turned down the chandelier.

"Lovely, isn't it?" she said.

Ben let his eyes wander over the table while Marian called David again. He nodded slightly. "Life . . . sure as hell goes on, doesn't it?" he said.

Marian pulled her chair out and sat down. "And why shouldn't it?"

David came in. "We're eating *here?*" he said.

"In honor of your return," Marian said.

He started to sit, then excused himself and went into the kitchen. Ben was still standing.

"You're going to sit down, aren't you?" Marian said.

Ben's hands tightened on the back of the chair. "Frankly, Marian," he said, "I don't have that much of an appetite tonight." Marian looked up at him, between the candelabra, and then began to slice into an orange gelatin mold, silently. "Aunt Elizabeth is dead," Ben said, as if to remind her. "Doesn't that mean anything to you?"

"It means a great deal to me," Marian said, and then called, "David!" impatiently.

"I don't think anything means a great deal to you, Marian," Ben said, "except this goddamn house."

She scooped a slice of the mold onto a plate. David was coming back into the room with an opened bottle of Coke. He looked from Ben to Marian and slipped into his chair quietly, placing the bottle in front of him on the table.

Marian avoided Ben's stare; her eyes shifted to the moist bottle. "I don't think we really need that on the table, sweetheart, not on that pretty lace. Why don't you pour it and take the bottle back to the kitchen?"

David looked over his place setting. "There's no glass," he said.

"That's even better than a glass," she said, indicating the goblet. "It's gold."

"I think I'd rather have a glass," David said.

Ben kept looking down at Marian. His voice was raised slightly: "You heard your mother, Dave. You're messing up her table."

Marian closed her eyes; her shoulders tensed. "Are you going to *sit?*" The silver serving spoon hit against the plate.

"I told you—" Ben said, "I don't have much of an appetite."

He shoved his chair closer to the table and walked out of the room, through the kitchen and out onto the rear terrace. He leaned against the balustrade and stared down into the flowerbed which was filled with fresh green shoots between the rosebushes and the flowering shrubs. The sun had lowered to just above the trees beyond the west wing of the house, intensifying the colors and the shadows on the terrace. He stared harder into the flowerbed, at the spidery cracks in the soil, spreading out from the new shoots. There was a slow, whispery sound somewhere above him, and then another, and then Marian's voice behind him.

"Forget about me," she said, "—I just don't think that was a very smart thing to do in front of David."

Again, he heard the sound above him, like something sliding. He turned and looked up at the roof of the house; the tiles he could see on the gables and the central portion of the house were a stained and faded black, warped, with many of them cracked or missing completely. Like the gray shingles beneath them. The sound stopped.

Marian was standing near the open terrace door, all white and gold, with a long-sleeved silk blouse and a gold brocade skirt that swept over the scrubbed flagstone as she walked toward him.

"Any idea, Ben," she said, "exactly how we resolve it? It's intolerable this way, isn't it?" She leaned against the balustrade, beside him, looking at the house.

"That's just what it is, Marian," he said quietly, "—intolerable." He looked over the vast spread of the house. "And nothing's going to change as long as we've got *this* in our life." He looked at her. "Except you." Her eyes lingered on the red-draped windows in the west wing. "Take it out of our life, Marian."

"And give it up . . ."

"Give it up. Now."

"You can't ask me to do that."

"I'm *telling* you, Marian. You've got a choice."

"It's an impossible choice!"

"Impossible? Your family or a *house*?"

"You don't know what you're asking me to give up, you have no idea!"

"All right then, tell me. Tell me exactly *what* I'm asking you to give up. Come on, Marian, what's the hidden part, what is it you've been in on all the time?"

"*Nothing!*" She turned away from him quickly, her skirt rustling against the stone balusters. The sound seemed to echo and come at him from the roof of the house. He looked up and as he did one of the dull black rooftiles slipped loose and fell over the eaves of the gable. Ben's hand went up in reflex. The tile fell slowly, and he saw it dissolve silently on the flagstone. He looked up at the roof again, and where the tile had been was an unwarped, rich black rectangle, conspicuous among all the faded tiles in the roof.

"She depends on me!" Marian was saying. "There's no one but me to take care of her. You can't expect me to give up that kind of responsibility."

He was silent, long enough to make her look back at him, and then up at the roof, following his stare. The movement beside him called him back, and he said, vaguely at first, and then more controlled, "I didn't come back here to stay, Marian; that's not why I brought David back either. If you're willing to sacrifice your family to a house, to an old woman . . . I suppose there's nothing I can do about that. But, Christ! —we've got to mean a little more to you than that. Or am I wrong?"

He heard it again, another sliding sound, and Marian's voice rising above it, pleading now, "I *can't!* There's no way I can give it up. Not now—"

"*When?*"

"I don't know! In a while maybe, but, God, Ben—not now!"

Again. She had to have heard it; it couldn't be that clear to him and not actually exist. The dark black area of the roof had spread a little, another tile falling and dissolving no more than ten feet away. Why wasn't she seeing it as well? Or was she, and only pretending not to?

Marian was looking directly at him, deliberately it seemed, with a concentration that seemed to be blocking out everything else; very close but not once touching him, despite the intensity that had come into her voice.

"It has to be now," he started to say, but the words came out weak and distracted, and what he was asking her, what he was trying to tell her was too important for him to be distracted by anything else, especially something that might be happening only in his mind. And so he asked her suddenly, "You see it, don't you?" and pointed up at the roof.

She kept her eyes on his face, even more intently, never once looking in the direction of his pointing finger. Another tile slid off the roof and dissolved dreamlike in front of him.

"You *do* see it," he insisted.

"See what, Ben?" she said, and there was weary sympathy in her voice. Still, she refused to look, or to hear.

He searched her face for even the slightest indication that she had seen it, had heard the sound, but there was nothing. He lowered his hand slowly and turned his back to the house, staring blankly at the bay. "All right," he said, "it's selfish . . . it's unreasonable, it's insane, it's whatever you want it to be; but I'm asking you to give it up anyway."

"What is it I'm supposed to see, Ben?" Marian persisted.

He shook his head helplessly. "It doesn't matter." He waited. The sound had stopped again.

"In that case," Marian said, "dinner's still on the table."

Ben grabbed her arm and stopped her, his voice trembling now. "I'll ask you just once more. Come back home with us."

It was a plea, flat and abject. And why couldn't he see it? How much clearer could she make it? She *was* home.

She clenched her hands tighter and tighter at her sides, until the pressure drove the words out of her with a finality he would have to accept: "I CAN'T! I CAN'T! GOD! DON'T YOU SEE THAT YET? I CAN'T!"

He thought he heard her sob in the long silence, just once, very quietly. And then touch him, letting her fingers pass lightly over his shoulder. He felt her move away from him, and when he turned he was alone on the terrace. Above him, the fresh black tiles absorbed the last of the sun.

He didn't see her again that night; and while he did go

back into the dining room where the candles had burned halfway down and the food remained cold and untouched on the
table, and then up to their bedroom which was empty when
he turned on the light, he wasn't consciously looking for her.
He'd pushed it to a choice and Marian had chosen—finally,
unequivocally. And while the implications of the choice were
shattering—what in Christ's name would they *do*? After the
packing up and the flight back to the apartment, *what then*?
—To stay in a house whose malevolence was destroying them
(and why, *why* couldn't she see that?) would be the clearest
evidence of his own insanity.

Madness, terror, cowardice, whatever—they'd leave in the
morning, he and David, and if he saw her before they left
. . . Well, *of course* he'd see her; she'd come into the bedroom
eventually, from the sitting room where he knew she had
locked herself, and maybe being alone in there and having
time to realize exactly what kind of choice she had made and
what it would mean to all of them . . .

He moved the chair from beside the bed, closer to the open
door, where he could watch David sleeping in the dim light
across the hall. And waited, and felt the throbbing inside his
head accelerate and drum above the soft chiming of the clocks
throughout the house. It was after three when a stillness that
was almost palpable descended on the room and the house.
He had been dozing, and it woke him with a start. He looked
across the hall at David who was sleeping with the covers
thrown off him. Ben rose from the chair and then fell back into
it as the film, more opaque than it had ever been, came over his
eyes—not merely a blurring, but a shadowless white; and with
it a deep feeling of nausea. He sat without moving, feeling his
hands sweat against the fabric of the chair, and a tightening in
his groin that made him gag and then suck at the still air in the
room.

The feeling was still there when the clocks chimed four
times. Then he heard rain, very softly. And even softer at
first, the sliding sound again that he had heard on the terrace.
Again, and then again, louder—above him, outside the win-

dows. And then down the hall and below him and all around him, the sounds rising and becoming chambered. And even when he covered his ears with his hands, he could still hear the tiles slide with grating sharpness.

The clocks chimed again, barely audible under the sounds that continued to shake the house. Ben pushed himself out of the chair and felt his way to the door. There were vague outlines now in the whiteness, and then David in bed, clearer, as Ben approached him and leaned over him.

"David!" He shook him and David stirred and moved away from his hand. He called, "David!" again, and as he did he felt his eyes clearing. But the sounds continued, stronger. David was fast asleep. A first dim light was penetrating the darkness outside his windows.

Ben went out into the hall and looked first at the double doors still closed at the end of the corridor, and then at the top of the staircase where the metal inclinator jutted out from the wall. He headed for the stairs, and then down, into the living room, where the sounds followed him with no lessening of intensity.

He crossed the room, faint and gray in the rainy dawn, and went to the clouded French door which he rubbed and tried to see beyond. He pulled it open and the fine, mist-like rain covered his face and arms with a gentle coolness. The sounds were on the terrace as well. He backed across the flagstone, toward the stone balustrade, looking up at the side of the house.

The tiles were falling from the roof with that same dream-like motion, dissolving in the air and silently on the terrace. The gray shingles below them as well, slipping from the sides of the house, cascading down, as if the house were throwing off its old skin and revealing an immaculate whiteness underneath that glistened in the rain. Wherever he looked they were falling—tiles and clapboards and weathered cornices. He moved down the length of the terrace with his back to the balustrade, feeling his way with his hands, unable to pull his eyes away from the frightening apparition of the house.

There was a sudden break in the balustrade and he felt himself falling backwards, down the three steps descending to the lawn and the wide flowerbeds following the line of the terrace. He grabbed at the last baluster and broke his fall, landing on his knees and his right hand in the soft wet earth that was pushing up a thick bed of green—spear-like shoots that seemed to be growing around him as he pulled himself to his feet.

The clapboards showered down, faster, louder. Ben moved below the terrace, still looking up, following the balustrade until it curved and stopped against the glass of the greenhouse built out under the west wing of the house. He lowered his eyes to it and then moved closer to the glass and stared inside. And then rushed into the house and pulled open the greenhouse door. And stared again.

And instantly found himself upstairs again, lifting David out of the bed.

Marian heard the sounds very dimly beyond the closed doors to the sitting room. She was half-awake in the wingchair. She opened her eyes and listened. It had been Ben's voice raised indistinctly down the corridor. She rose and went to the inner door, unlocked it, and went out into the small corridor. There was another sound then, more distant. David?

She opened the door and came down the five steps. David's room was empty when she reached it, the covers hanging off the bed. The light was on in the bedroom opposite, hers and Ben's. She heard something downstairs—the front door closing. She rushed to David's window and looked down.

They had reached the bottom of the steps. Ben was pulling David who had his blue terrycloth robe wrapped around him. David stumbled and Ben lifted him, carrying him along the gravel drive toward the garage.

Marian called, "David!" feebly through the half-closed window. She tried to raise it; it was stuck, and she hammered the heels of her hands against the frame. It wouldn't move. She lowered her face to the opening and shouted, "Ben!" several times, and then saw them disappear, without turning, beyond the frame of the window. And felt something that had been dying inside herself spring back to life—instinctively, without her willing it; despite what she had said, despite the choice she had been forced into making on the terrace. The *fact* of it—the jolting fact of it now . . .

She hurried out of the room, and when she reached the bottom of the long white flight of stairs outside, she saw the car pull away from the garage and disappear in the colorless gray that was misting the field.

It was the rain against the windshield blurring his vision, and the slow streaking arc of the wipers, and David's frightened voice protesting sleepily beside him that was distracting him, and making the car swerve over the gravel. The thick green of the woods appeared ahead of them, and again David cried, "Where are we going?"

"It's going to be all right," Ben said, and when he lifted one hand from the wheel to touch him reassuringly, the car swerved sharply and David had to throw his hand against the dashboard to protect himself.

And then again he asked for Marian. Why wasn't she with them, where were they going without her?

The car slowed in front of the dark green tunnel of the woods, even darker and thicker in the mist shrouding the narrow gravel road.

"Sit back in the seat," Ben said to David, and leaned closer to the fogging windshield.

He drove a few feet in, passing over the vines that in a day had raised fresh green shoots. Ben's hands tightened on the wheel; he accelerated slowly, pushing into the dense growth choking the road and forming a solid wall of green a few feet ahead of him. His foot pressed down on the gas pedal; the car lurched forward and then stopped, the rear wheels spinning over the gravel. He backed up a bit, and then came forward again faster. Branches screeched against the sides and roof of the car. He stopped, and David saw him wet his lips with his tongue and then strain to see ahead and left and right. He shifted into Park and told David, "Wait," pushing his door open against the foliage.

David shivered and sank lower in the seat, pulling the blue robe closed over his chest.

Ben squeezed himself along the side of the car, his hands raised to protect his face. He moved forward, trying to see beyond the solid green ahead. A vine noosed suddenly around his foot; he stumbled and as he caught himself against the hood of the car, a twig struck against his face with a force that made him reel and press his way back into the car. He sat with his face buried in his hands, his fingers rubbing against his forehead and eyes.

"I wanna go back," David said, watching him, seeing the mud caked on his pants and hands, and the streaks of dirt across his face now.

Ben raised his face and shifted the car into reverse, backing fast down the rise of gravel; and then forward, faster, smashing into the bushes with a snapping of wood and a metallic scraping. Faster. Breaking through. He was hugging the wheel. A branch slapped against the windshield, and against David's sealed window, making him jump and cry out. The car accelerated, the twigs and leaves striking against it with growing fury. Ben was pushing forward blindly. A branch caught under the wiper on his side and snapped it. There was sound on all sides of the car, and green lashing at the windows. The leaves glued themselves to the windshield and the rear window and all the side windows. And if he could just break through to the road, just press down blindly on the pedal and break through. David heard the sounds he was making, the incoherent pleading, and he began to cry. The car sped forward suddenly and then came to a wrenching halt, throwing David off the seat. Ben's head hit the windshield, and it was only a second later, it seemed, that Marian was opening the door on his side and trying to push him away from the wheel; repeating his name and shaking him back to consciousness, saying, "Let me in." And then turning to David who was whimpering in the back

seat, and saying, soothingly, "It's all right, sweetheart, everything is going to be all right now."

Ben looked at her distantly, waiting for her face to come
into focus. He let himself be pushed to the passenger side.
The leaves had been wiped from the windows. Marian, her
hair gray and streaming, and the white and gold she was wearing soaked through, turned on the ignition and began to back
the car slowly down the drive, the leaves merely whispering
against the top and sides. The road ahead, when he could
see, had, incredibly, cleared, and the wiper on the driver's side
swept slowly over the glass.

Marian was watching the rearview mirror, carefully backing over the twenty or so feet the car had penetrated into the
drive. The field spread behind them, and beyond it, out of
view, the house. They had almost backed out of the woods
when Marian found herself pressing harder on the brake
pedal and then stopping the car. She stared ahead through the
rain-streaked window at the drive twisting beyond the trees
and climbing up to the dirt road past the woods and the two
stone pillars marking the gate.

The road. It was as close, as simple as a movement of her
foot a few inches to the right. Just press down on the gas
pedal . . .

She kept the car idling a few seconds, and then let her foot
up on the brake slowly, as the thought passed, as suddenly as
it had come to her. The car rolled backwards out of the drive.

She braked again, one last time, and then resolutely looked
away from the narrow opening in the foliage. She turned the
car, and began to drive back to the house.

Ben continued to stare at her and then said, very slowly,
"You're accepting it . . . all of it. You know . . . and you're
accepting it . . . Aren't you . . . ? Aren't you . . . ?"

Marian's face remained impassive, while the house rose
out of the mist and loomed ahead of them, white. Whiter.
Blinding. Dissolving the mist and the glass in front of him
and the sweep of the wiper, and the sound of David behind
him. He closed his eyes against it, and when he opened them

again, he was sitting in the back seat, and the padding around
him was thick and rich and a deep gray, and in front of him,
driving, was the chauffeur. Ben tried not to see him, tried to
look beyond him at the whiteness rising again, coming at him
like a great annihilating force, like a blow against his brain.

   White. White nothingness. White.

(11)

For the first time in over a week she had gone to sleep beside
him, in the double bed in their room, with a guilt or a sympathy or a fear strong enough to overcome the magnetic pull
of the sitting room. She had led him up to the room herself
after she had brought him and David back to the house, had
even undressed him and, later in the day, carried the lunch
and dinner trays up to him, just as she still did, ritualistically,
for Mrs. Allardyce. And spooned the food into his mouth.

   Something, somewhere between the drive and the house,
or in the house, had happened to him, so traumatic that it had
effectively anaesthetized his mind, reducing him to a state of
shock that was as deep and paralyzing as a coma. He couldn't
see, as far as Marian could make out, or could only see dimly,
and couldn't hear, or wouldn't, and wouldn't speak as well.
At least not to her.

   If it was shock, then it might well pass eventually, she had
reassured herself. But some part of her—the part that found
comfort in the sitting room, and that did indeed, as Ben had
said in the car, accept it, all of it, as much of it as she could
understand (and when would the understanding be complete?)—knew instinctively that it was something deeper than
shock; instinctively enough to make her search through the
faces on the sitting room table before she had come into bed
with him that night.

   It was before seven the following morning when the sound
of a car coming down the drive, and then the slamming of
its door in front of the house jarred her awake. She had been

sleeping on her right side, facing the open bedroom door and the sound below David's windows. She propped herself up, listened for a moment, and then turned to look at Ben beside her. And gasped when she saw him sitting motionless in the chair next to the bed, staring at her, continuing to stare at the empty bed when she rose and came beside him, lowering herself and searching for some sign of recognition in the open blankness of his eyes.

They've come back, flashed into her mind, and if she hadn't been looking at Ben at that moment, if his absolute helplessness hadn't summoned up what was left of her old self, would the feeling of relief have been so overwhelming and so liberating? *They've come back*.

She crossed to David's room, and there it was below the windows, parked directly in front of the steps—the Allardyces' huge old Packard.

"Oh, God, they've come back!" she said aloud, and went back for her robe and slippers, repeating it to Ben, and then leaving him and rushing halfway down the stairs before she saw Walker standing in the middle of the entrance hall and smiling up at her.

"Mornin', Mrs.," he said, and tipped his sweat-stained baseball cap.

Marian looked beyond him expectantly, at the door he had left open. "Where are they, Walker?" she asked. "The others."

"What others?" He replaced his cap, and tested the rug with his scuffed shoes.

"The Allardyces. Roz and Brother." She came down the rest of the stairs.

Walker looked up at the walls and the ceiling, inspecting. "Why, away of course," he said casually.

"*Where* away?"

"Just . . . away. Like always." He smiled and said, "Excuse me," walking away from her into the living room. She followed him. "Sorry for the interruption," he called over his shoulder; "thought I'd be in and out before any of you was up." He was surveying the room, passing his hands over the tables and lampshades and figurines, and nodding approvingly to himself.

"You mean they haven't come back with you?" Marian insisted.

"How could they?" He walked to the end of the room and disappeared into the alcove leading to the greenhouse. When he came back in he looked genuinely impressed. "Nice job," he said, "darn nice job."

"Walker, listen to me," Marian said without hearing him, "—they've got to come back. Will you tell them that for me? Please?"

"What for?" Walker said. "Place is yours, ain't it? From whenever to . . . whenever." He walked past her, back into the hall, and then down the corridor, peering into the dining room and the library and the kitchen and the servants' rooms, with Marian close behind him.

"I've changed my mind," Marian said suddenly, "I don't— it's too much, it's more than I can handle."

"Don't look that way to me, Mrs.," Walker said.

"Whatever it looks like—you've all got to come back."

"Afraid that's not for me to decide. Or you, for that matter, Mrs."

"But you'll tell them anyway, won't you?" Marian pleaded.

Walker shrugged. "I'll tell 'em."

They were back in the hall. Walker pulled out a round gold pocket watch and checked it against the Regency clock on the console. "To the minute!" he said, snapping it shut. " 'Scuse me again." He climbed up the stairs, leaving Marian alone in the hall.

She brought her hands together, prayer-like, and pressed them to her lips, bowing her head thoughtfully and pacing until Walker came puffing back down the stairs, carrying a small Pan Am flight bag which he was zipping shut.

"Why did you come back?" Marian asked him.

He raised the bag. "Pick up a few things. His nibs's pills mostly." He started to walk across the hall.

Marian called out to stop him. "Are they far, Walker—Roz and Brother?"

"Not so far."

"If it was an emergency, they could get back, right away?"

"There's no emergency that I can see."

Marian walked up to him, beside the front door.

"Walker . . ." she said, "Aunt Elizabeth is dead."

"The ole gal?"

Marian nodded.

"Sorry to hear that," Walker said. He paused. "And the others?"

"I don't know!" Marian said helplessly; her voice rose and broke on the words. Walker looked toward the staircase, cautioning. "Ben—"

"Your husband."

Marian nodded again. "I don't know what's happened to him; all of a sudden. His mind—it's—"

"Rested," Walker said peacefully.

"No!"

"Just rested, that's all. We all need a little rest once in a while, Mrs.; mind as well as body." His voice had softened strikingly.

"I don't know what to do!" Marian pleaded.

"Just what you been doin', Mrs.," Walker said. He started to go out the door.

"*Walker!*" It filled the hall, part command, part plea. Marian stood where she was, in the middle of the hall, and waited for Walker to take a few steps back into the house. "I don't want it anymore." She shook her head to emphasize the words. "Not this."

"You don't want . . . what?" Walker asked.

Marian took a deep breath, and for the first time she gave it a voice—the suspicion that had grown to certitude: "I won't sacrifice everything. I won't see them hurt. I can't, Walker. Not for *anything!*"

"No, Mrs.," he said, "not for anything. But what about for

everything?" He waited for her to absorb the question, and then added, *"For her?"*

Marian hesitated, and he could almost hear the voices warring inside her. "Not even for her," she said weakly.

"For the gold and the silver?" he reminded her, and it was his voice but it was Roz and Brother speaking as well, and the voice she had heard inside herself so often. "For her house and everything she has in it? Whatever's hers is yours, Mrs., if you want it. You ought to know that by now . . ." He moved closer to her. "How much of a sacrifice is it—for all of this?" He looked up at the chandelier, the ceiling, the staircase, and Marian's eyes followed his. "Think of it, think of all the others who managed to do it, to burn everything but her out of themselves. Our mother." He paused. "What you see here is all her. Accept it, Mrs., and you accept her too." Marian was silent. "Besides," Walker added with head-shaking sympathy, "I'm afraid you got nothing to say about it at this point."

"But I don't *understand!"* Marian said helplessly.

"There's a lot we don't understand and accept anyhow," Walker said, touching her arm very lightly. "Be patient, Mrs." The touch became less than a reassuring pat.

"Tell them to come back, Walker," Marian repeated.

"How can I, when it's all begun?"

"It can stop, can't it?"

"You want it to stop, Mrs.? Down inside yourself, the deepest part, you really want it to stop? You want to give up all of this?"

"Yes." She said it inaudibly.

"When *you* begun it?" Walker continued. "You, Mrs. You're the one's been polishin' the wood and the silver. You been bringin' up her tray three times a day. You're the one's been fillin' her room with flowers. You're the one she depends on . . . for everything." He brought his face very close to hers. "And when you see her, Mrs.—it's all goin' to be worth it. In your heart you know that, don't you?"

"I *haven't* seen her!" Marian cried.

He hushed her, his hand on her again. "You will. You will."

"Is that why you came back? To tell me that?"

Walker's hand tightened on her arm. "Accept it, Mrs. All the way now. Bring her back to us. Our mother."

She repeated the words after him soundlessly, several times, like a silent prayer: "Our mother." He was gone when she raised her eyes. She saw him crossing the porch and disappearing down the front steps.

"Walker!" Marian ran after him and stopped on the porch. Walker looked up at her.

"Please . . . ?" she said one final time.

He was on the bottom step; he raised his foot to the step above and leaned forward, making the wood creak.

"Step's a little loose down here," he said. "See to it, will you?"

He got into the car, turned clumsily, and drove off without looking back at Marian. She watched it until it had passed completely out of sight.

Then she went upstairs, past Ben and David, without looking into their rooms, and sat for a long time in the gold brocade wingchair. Until she had worked up the strength and the resolution to approach the door and press her hands against the carved surface.

"Help me," she whispered, "to accept it. Give me the strength. And whatever's weak . . . whatever affection in me is still keeping this door between us . . ." She waited, scarcely breathing, and then the words came out in a burst of passion: *"Burn it! Burn it out of me! Burn it out, all of it!"* Her fists hammered against the door. *"Burn it out, burn it, burn it . . ."*

As often as she went up to the sitting room, which was constantly, she would let her eyes travel slowly over the multitude of faces on the table, until she had memorized the shape and position of each of the silver-framed pictures. There was, blessedly, no change—not on the day of Walker's visit or the day after or the day after that. And if there had been, if suddenly another frame, or two, had materialized, then what would she have done? Gathered them up, Ben and David, as

Ben himself had tried to do, and spirit them away from the house? Or accept it, the way Walker had said? Submit herself to the incomprehensible will of the house and accept it with a resignation that had to be more than she could command.

Despite Walker's assurance and despite the intensity of her plea in front of the door, it hadn't been burned out of her; there was still an affection as strong as her longing to be part of the mystery of the house that was binding her to them. Bringing her, on several occasions, into David's room in the middle of the night where she would sit and watch him sleep for hours, protectively. And making her seize hopefully on the merest flicker of recognition she thought she saw in Ben's expressionless face; the slightest movement, however illusory, that might indicate a remission of the paralyzing shock that had locked him, unreachably, inside himself.

And while she watched, while the priorities alternated hourly, seemingly beyond any ultimate resolution, the house continued to flourish: the rooftiles and clapboards and flagstone gleamed, the cracks in the long stone balustrade healed themselves, there was new color in the rugs and drapes and fabrics, and a deepening richness in the wood and stone. And without incident, with nothing to alarm her.

Except Ben, if she cared to dwell on it. And David's reaction to Ben, to the silent, staring presence in the bedroom opposite his, or on the terrace; or, on one occasion, under the beach umbrella beside the pool where Marian had seated him and watched closely for a change in his expression which never came; not even there.

It had been a testing, Marian became convinced, like a biblical trial in the desert: would she have been willing to give everything up—for the house, for Mrs. Allardyce; for the force or the abstraction behind them which she had seen in the deepest part of herself? The continuing approbation of the house was evidence enough that she would have. And, thank God, it had never had to reach the final testing point.

She searched through the photographs less frequently as the week wore on, and stopped coming into David's room during the night, and sleeping beside Ben in their bedroom. Her nights she began to spend in the wingchair in the sitting room once again, and a good part of her days as well.

During the week her hair went completely white.

She had brought him over the rise of lawn once again and made him sit under the faded beach umbrella beside the pool, and watched him a while, and then, when there was nothing, watched David splashing in the low water, the pool incident of two weeks ago wiped completely out of his mind. When the umbrella's shade passed beyond Ben, Marian moved from the edge of the pool and adjusted the angle of the pole to protect him from the fierce mid-day sun. His lips were dry and there were beads of sweat on his brow and upper lip, which she dampened with a wet towel. And then, calling David out of the pool and ordering him to rest in the shade until she had come back with their lunch, Marian went back to the house.

David dried himself and then sat on the concrete floor, at Ben's feet in the circle of shade. And looked up at him without speaking, without even trying to reach him anymore. Except to touch him surreptitiously every once in a while— his foot or the hand resting limply on his knee. And that didn't work either, and for the rest of his life his father would stare beyond him as though he didn't even exist, however close to him he tried to come. Even when he stood up, as David did now, right in front of him, leaning forward on the arms of the chair and staring directly into Ben's eyes.

He tried to think of something to say to him, and all that came to him beside the pool was the fact that, whatever his father used to think about him, he really *could* swim, without the tube, without anything at all. And if he wanted, he was ready to show him, and wouldn't that be a surprise big enough to cure him of his sickness?

He announced it to Ben, and still there was no reaction, even when he kept repeating, "Do you want to see? Well, do you or don't you?" And beside the frustration, there was a little bit of anger creeping into his voice. He shook Ben's arm. "C'mon! *Do you?*" And whether he wanted to or not, he'd show him; he'd do it right in front of him, while he was looking straight into the pool.

Marian would bring the tray up to Mrs. Allardyce later, after she had shepherded them both back to the house. She lifted the cups of cold consommé and the pitcher of grape juice onto the second tray, red plastic, and carried it to the kitchen door. She twisted the knob, not far enough for the door to open. She raised her knee to support the tray and twisted it again and pulled in. The door wouldn't move. She muttered, "Dammit," put the tray on a counter, and tried again. It was locked. Her fingers went to the inside latch; she turned it right and then left, her fingers whitening with the effort. Still, it wouldn't open! It couldn't have locked itself—

She hurried to the window, panic growing in her, and strained to see beyond the rise of lawn, down to the pool which was hidden from view. And then it hit her, even without seeing. Her hands jerked up to her face, and almost voiceless, she said, "No! Oh, God! *No!*" She ran to the front door and that was locked too, and she screamed it out now, filling the house: "NO!"

He had swum all the way to the middle of the pool where he stopped, winded, and began to tread water clumsily, turning to face Ben who seemed to be looking directly at him.

"What'd I tell you—?" he tried to say, but his mouth filled with water. He gagged and tried to raise his chin, but the water slapped against it, higher and higher, as if an unseen hand stirred it and sent it over him in faster and rougher waves. He breathed it in and choked on the burning in his lungs, and flailed wildly and more desperately, crying out to Ben who blurred distantly in David's eyes. The water rose over his head, the rolling waves beating him lower and lower.

Ben's hands began to tremble on his knees, fighting against the heaviness that weighed them down. His eyes were fixed on the center of the pool which might have been a shadow passing through the whiteness in his mind, and a cry penetrating dimly from far away. His hands rose strengthless to the arms of the chair, under the umbrella that was now blazing with color, and as he tried to push himself forward, his mouth opened on a great, soundless moan. The chair shook under his weight. He lifted himself and moved an inch beyond the perimeter of shade, and then another, before he fell forward.

The moan unshaped itself, and two thin lines of blood started to run from his eyes, absorbed by the sun-baked pavement, which pressed, smooth and polished, against his face.

They were all locked, every one of them. She came into the living room, blind with terror, and whatever was in her stumbling path, however precious, she threw it aside until she reached the doors to the terrace; and they were locked, and all the other doors from the room as well. She turned and searched the room for something to smash through the doors, and as she did, she saw the walls brightening with color, as though the paint were being poured down them, and the panels and rosettes and cornices carving themselves vividly into the ceiling, and everything in the room taking on a splendor that was dazzling. And she knew immediately what it was that had already happened at the pool, and hurled herself against the locked glass doors until they shattered. And went back down to the pool where she saw what was behind the continuing approbation of the house.

The stairs were almost too much for her. She stopped several times and rested her face wearily against her hand on the bannister, and then pulled herself up again. When she reached the upstairs hall she hesitated, as though she were suddenly unsure of her direction. Then she saw the double doors ahead of her, and stared at them for a long time. She started to move toward them, but stopped at the door of the room that had been Ben's and hers. And hesitated again. She went into the room, into the bathroom where she pulled off her wet clothes and wiped her hair dry. Not thinking of anything at all, too drained and dead inside ever to think of anything again. Whatever she was doing, she was doing automatically.

She chose the long blue-and-gold gown and dressed herself, and pulled a comb through her white hair. Then she went down the hall, looking neither left nor right, and entered the sitting room.

The pictures were there, of course, at the very edge of the table. Ben and David, each of them with that same blank and lifeless stare, their eyes fixed on a point that would always be somewhere beyond Marian. Ben. And David. She touched them. And if there were any tears, any emotion at all, left in her, she would have asked, "Why aren't I there with them? Why have I been saved?"

Saved . . .

She sat in the wingchair, her hands opening and closing against its arms. She heard the hum and stared into the door, silently, feeling something deeper than she had ever felt before build slowly inside herself. Deeper than anger or hate or betrayal or loss—total, unrecoverable loss.

There's nothing more, she said to herself; and then she said it again, aloud, still staring at the door.

"There's nothing more. Nothing. It's all in order now, all the way it should be."

She waited, and then rose and walked toward the door.

"And there's nothing, nothing at all left."

She stopped and her eyes travelled again over the maze in the door. She raised her hand and touched it, and the hand tightened into a fist which struck against it, just once.

"Is this how it ends?" she asked. "With this still between us? After I've given you everything?"

The fist loosened, and almost beyond her control began to move over the surface of the door with a slow, caressing motion.

"Mrs. Allardyce?" she called softly. "Mrs. Allardyce?" She rested her face against the door. "There are times when you've been so close to me . . . and I've seen you so clearly in everything that's in your house . . . Why should this door still be between us now . . . when I've given you everything?" She waited for the strength to well up and power her voice and her hand, and when it did she pounded the door. "There's nothing more to give!" she cried. "Nothing. Nothing. Nothing. Nothing. *Nothing* . . ."

She heard the *click*, and felt the door move against her hand, just slightly. The suddenness of it, under her cries, stunned her. She stood absolutely still, and then a smile, part astonishment, part triumph, began to transform her face. Her hand went down to the gold knob and pulled the door towards her. The hum grew, deeper and more resonant as the door opened wider, pushing out against her, even after she had pulled her hand away.

It was massive, incredibly thick behind the carved facing, like the door of a great vault. The smile froze on Marian's face as it continued to open, beyond her control, with the hum growing even louder, shaking her, shaking the room with its power, and a thin light issuing, becoming stronger. She threw herself against it, trying to stop the movement of the door, to cut off the overwhelming force of the hum and the terrible blaze of light whitening everything. The door pushed against her, opening wider, and she felt herself screaming at it, screaming at the vastness, the magnitude of the power being released on her. And then felt nothing, and heard nothing, and saw, in the heart of the whiteness, a point, a shadow, which she knew was the source of the light, rushing toward her. Closer. Closer. The features swirling and gathering themselves out of the shadows. Hideously old, leaning forward in a great chair, with her eyes blazing out at Marian. Closer, more penetrating, burning everything out of her—grief and affection and memory—burning it out finally, until there was nothing. She raised her hand to touch the figure, and it was a gesture of acceptance. The eyes blazing in front of her faded then, and the figure dissolved, leaving the chair empty. For Marian. Who closed her eyes and began to move forward slowly, hearing the voices chambered in the vast silence.

"Our mother . . ."

"Our darling . . ."
"Restored to us . . ."
"In all her dearness . . ."
Marian stood in front of the chair.
"Her glory . . ."
"Her beauty . . ."
"Her youth . . ."
She turned.
"Always with us . . ."
"Always . . ."
"Always . . ."
And sat.
"Always . . ."

She clutched the arms of the chair and felt the force of the hum not outside herself but in her, issuing forth and driving itself into the house and grounds, all the way down to the smallest bit of crystal, the tenderest green shoot. And somewhere beyond the chair there was the sound of a great door closing, on a vault, or a tomb.

They materialized as if by instinct almost immediately, the Allardyces and Walker. And went, with silent reverence, through all the rooms of their mother's house, which had never looked so rich and shining and perfect.

"Not since last time anyway," Brother said in his wheelchair.

They travelled over the grounds, as much of them as they could cover in a single day. The trees and shrubs were full, the grass the deepest green, and the house shone white and immaculate on the hill.

"Ah . . ." Roz said.

And whatever there was to mar the serenity of the scene, Walker was ordered to attend to.

The house was photographed from the angle of the wide field in front of it, to capture the moment of perfection, and eventually the picture was brought into the alcove between the living room and the greenhouse. Walker raised it to the wall filled with similar photographs, and then stopped and looked over his shoulder at Roz and Brother.

"There's no more room on the wall," he said.

"Well, make room," Roz said, handing him the hammer and a picture hook. "What do we pay you for anyway?"

He stood on his toes and lifted the picture higher, beginning a new row on top of all the others.

"How's that?" he asked.

"Fine," said Brother.

Walker hung the picture in a position of prominence while Roz looked on approvingly, and Brother rose from his wheelchair to celebrate the moment.

MORE CLASSIC HORROR FROM VALANCOURT

THE AMULET
Michael McDowell
Introduction by Poppy Z. Brite

THE MONK
M. G. Lewis
Introduction by Stephen King

THE ENTITY
Frank De Felitta
Introduction by Gemma Files

NIGHTSHADE AND DAMNATIONS
Gerald Kersh
Introduction by Harlan Ellison

RATMAN'S NOTEBOOKS
Stephen Gilbert
Introduction by Kim Newman

THE MONSTER CLUB
R. Chetwynd-Hayes
Introduction by Stephen Jones

THE ELEMENTALS
Michael McDowell
Introduction by Michael Rowe

THE DELICATE DEPENDENCY
Michael Talbot
Foreword by Jillian Venters

THE CORMORANT
Stephen Gregory
Introduction by the author

FOR A COMPLETE LIST OF TITLES AND ORDERING INFORMATION,
PLEASE VISIT US AT VALANCOURTBOOKS.COM